Amanda James has writte asked her parents for a typ imagined her words woul dream of becoming a writ 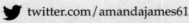 .... she had her first short story published.

Originally from Sheffield, Amanda now lives in Cornwall and is inspired every day by the wild and beautiful coastline. She can usually be found playing on the beach with her family, or walking the cliff paths planning her next book.

twitter.com/amandajames61
facebook.com/MandyJamesAuthorPage

THE GARDEN BY THE SEA

AMANDA JAMES

One More Chapter
a division of HarperCollins*Publishers* Ltd
1 London Bridge Street
London SE1 9GF
www.harpercollins.co.uk
HarperCollins*Publishers*
1st Floor, Watermarque Building, Ringsend Road
Dublin 4, Ireland

This paperback edition 2022
1
First published in Great Britain in ebook format
by HarperCollins*Publishers* 2022

A catalogue record of this book is available from the British Library

ISBN: 978-0-00-850501-1

Printed and bound in the UK using 100% Renewable Electricity
by CPI Group (UK) Ltd

For my family, with love.

Tamsin Rowe had been up in the loft, sitting on the packing crate for far too long. What had started as a mission to find her mother's sewing kit had turned into a two-hour stroll down memory lane. Big bundles of her past were up here, and quite a few were undone and scattered around her feet, like presents on Christmas morning. Right now, she was back in her wedding day, twenty years ago. With the wedding album across her knees, she ran a finger along the edge of the bride's veil and wondered where that slip of a girl had gone. In the elegant high-necked gown, confetti in her hair, with her new husband smiling down at her, love shining from his eyes, she'd thought she was the luckiest woman alive. And she had been. But Tamsin would be forty-four next birthday, and although she couldn't wish for a better man to share her life with, there was something missing for both of them. No, not something. Someone.

Still, no use yearning for things that weren't meant to be. Tamsin placed the wedding album back in its white box and tied the pink ribbon around it. She was just about to take the sewing kit and go, when she noticed the corner of an old carved wooden box sticking out from under some old curtains she'd been meaning to throw away. Pulling it free, she smiled. This was the old 'magical' Tintagel seed-box that had been passed down from her great-grandmother and her mother before that, and on down the line. Tamsin's own mother had told her some nonsense about it being magical, and having soil inside from the garden of the legendary King Arthur. Tamsin should have chucked it years ago, but her mum believed the old tales. It had a lovely carving of a tree on it too.

Ten minutes later, she was still there with the box on her lap thinking about her parents, the hopes and dreams of her youth, and wondering what the future had in store. *No use getting maudlin, Tamsin. You have to make the most of what you have, and what you have is so much more than many people.* To cheer herself up, she decided that she'd make a lovely dinner for Derek when he got home and wear that dress he loved so much. The yellow one with the big red poppies. It wasn't new, but he said it made her look like a summer's day. Tamsin had much to be happy about and the thought of being in Derek's arms lifted her spirits.

About to shove the box back where she'd found it, she hesitated and remembered her mum's words. Tamsin held it to her chest and said to the wooden rafters above, 'Dear Magic Box, please grant me my heart's desire. Bless me and Derek with the child we've always wanted.' In the loft space, her voice sounded small, feeble and more than a bit desperate. Feeling slightly daft, she sighed and put the box back. Wishes were for kids on starry nights, not silly middle-aged women who should know better. Still, she thought, as she extinguished the light and climbed down the loft ladder. Sometimes miracles do happen.

Chapter One

Present day

If you have a garden and a library, you have everything you need
– Cicero

Benches are often taken for granted or, worse, ignored, their importance not even crossing the minds of those sitting upon them. Lowena shifts position on hers, feeling the old wood creak under her, and decides they are invaluable. She also considers the hundreds of people over the years who have sat where she's sitting, gazing out across the Atlantic in all its moods, watching the gulls wheel above, broadcasting their plaintive cries across an ever-changing sky. A bench with a view like this is conducive to contemplation. The hopes, dreams and fears of those bench-sitters, emotions both happy and sad, will have found a temporary home here, as their owners sought a place to rest.

Maybe this bench is a keeper of secrets whispered to the wind, or mumbled into damp tissues. A silent confidant of deep desires, heart-felt wishes and regrets. Lowena has a few of those, though thankfully not that many for a woman who's almost forty. At this time of day and this time of year, sitting on a coastal bench in north Cornwall, Lowena thinks she is one of the luckiest people in the world. A fresh salt breeze tousling her shoulder-length curls, gentle waves rolling to a damp beach, tinged pink by the fingers of a languid sunset, and a hearty casserole waiting at home in the slow cooker. Simple pleasures.

A glance at her watch and a chill seeping through her warm parka tell Lowena its's time to go. She's not done badly though, sitting here for nearly an hour on an early spring evening. It was just what she needed after working in the library all day. She loves her job, but it's a bit short on fresh air. On the walk back to the car park, she realises it's April tomorrow, and her mum's favourite month. She remembers every year Tamsin Rowe always saying the same thing: *March is too much like winter, and May is too much like summer, but April, April is the epitome of spring.* It won't be long before her mum will be out in her little patch of garden, weeding and organising new planting for her borders and pots, buying tomato plants and seed potatoes to layer under rich compost in the trusty old barrel she's had since she was a new bride.

Lowena wonders where her mum gets the energy at

eighty-five. Since her dad passed away three years ago, her mum has thrown herself into her garden and her various clubs and recently has even started beach cleaning. Lowena's reached the conclusion that her mum's keeping every minute occupied is probably a barrier against loneliness, and preventing memories of almost sixty happy years with her husband swamping her days. After dinner, Lowena will ring and see how she is. They haven't spoken for a couple of days and last time they did, her mum said she felt like doing a spot of painting in the kitchen. Skirting boards and possibly the window sills. Lowena wondered if she was taking on too much, but didn't say so. It would have made her mum more likely to do it. She sighs. Although her mum is fit as a fiddle, there's a fine line at eighty-five between being fiercely independent and plain reckless.

As twilight is consumed by night, Lowena puts her key in the door of her Truro home and is greeted by two things: the wonderful aroma of casserole, and the pitiful meow of her black and white cat, Conrad. 'Oh, come on, Conrad. Stop putting it on. I'm only an hour or so later than usual.' Conrad, unimpressed, circles her legs and then sits looking pointedly at the food cupboard. Lowena crouches down and gives him a tickle behind his ears. 'I just fancied a run out to Treyarnon Bay after work as it was such a sunny afternoon. You have biscuits in your dish, anyway.' Conrad walks to the food cupboard and glares up at her. 'Yes, okay. Don't get your whiskers in a twist.' As she spoons food into his dish, Lowena imagines that all over the UK, other cat owners are having a one-sided conversation like this. Conrad threads himself around her legs some more, and then as soon as dish hits floor, attacks the food as if he's not eaten for days. 'You're a pain in the bum, aren't you?' She strokes his head. 'But I adore you.'

As Lowena pushes her own plate away half an hour later, the phone rings. *Must be Mum*, she thinks, as her mum is the only one who uses the landline nowadays. She says mobile phones sound too distant, as if the person talking is down a well, or up a mountain, and what's the point of them anyway? Why does everyone need to be in constant contact? When she was a girl nobody had a phone. And we were no worse off for it. Smiling at this, Lowena picks up the phone and makes herself comfy on the sofa. 'Hi, Mum.'

Silence.

'Mum?'

A rasping breath and a cough.

Lowena leaps up. 'Mum! What's happened? Mum!'

'I… I've had a f-fall…'

'Oh my God! Where? Are you hurt?'

'…Yes, I've been on the floor… a good while… Enna?'

The line goes dead and Lowena's stomach rolls as she imagines her poor mum lying on the cold kitchen floor. Has she fallen while painting? Broken something? Why the hell didn't Lowena warn her against tackling such a job? She'll never forgive herself if… Stifling a sob, she calls an ambulance and flies out of the house.

6

Lowena watches her mother sleeping. She's been watching her sleep for the last two hours, her nose and mouth covered with an oxygen mask, a drip by the bed, and various tubes creeping around her body like synthetic vines. Her mum's face is as white as the starched white pillows propping her up, her slender frame tucked in under crisp sheets secured by hospital corners, a white cast on her left arm. Only the remnants of her once dark-brown curls mixed with waves of silver-grey save her from totally disappearing. A nurse said the doctor would be popping in to speak to Lowena around midnight. Just a few more minutes to wait. Nobody is very sure what happened to her mum, just that she fell, has a broken wrist and fractured hip, and is very poorly. She's on an antibiotic drip and the doctor will be able to tell Lowena more.

The feel of her mum's hand in hers is a comfort. Even though it's as light and dry as an autumn leaf, it's warm, and the blue raised vein under Lowena's fingers throbs with a steady pulse. She raises the back of her mum's hand to her mouth and brushes her lips across it.

'Don't worry. You'll soon be home and back to normal, Mum,' she says. Then she sighs. Ignoring how frail her mum has become is something Lowena has become practised at over the past few months. It's her defence against reality. But her mind only allows ignorance for a while. Sometimes upon waking, in the small hours, worry burrows a path into Lowena's consciousness and asks difficult questions about the future. She's mostly successful in giving partial answers and dismissing unwelcome thoughts, but right now under the harsh striplight, curtained off from the rest of the ward and the world, these questions won't be silenced.

'Lowena Rowe?'

Lowena looks up at a young male doctor who's just stepped through the curtain. 'Yes?'

'My name's Doctor Lawson,' he says with a smile, and they shake hands. Despite his youth, his gentle brown eyes are underscored by dark circles and his smile struggles to sustain its shape, as if it has run out of energy. Lowena wonders how long he's been on shift. 'I expect you have a few questions, so I'll quickly give you an update on your mum's condition.'

'Thank you,' Lowena says, unsurprised to hear a tremble in her voice.

He pulls up a plastic chair and sits opposite. 'Okay. We think your mum fell from a step ladder that was propped against the sink. I understand she'd been painting the kitchen windowsill above it?'

'I think so, yes. There was a paint pot and brushes in the sink. When I arrived at her house earlier, the paramedics said she'd obviously climbed back onto the ladder to get down, and her foot slipped, or the ladder toppled.'

Dr Lawson pulls a sympathetic face. 'Yes. Older people can sometimes forget they're not as nimble as they once were, I'm afraid. We think your mum, as well as breaking her wrist and fracturing her hip, might have bumped her head and become unconscious, disoriented. She may have been on the floor as long as two days, because she's very dehydrated and weak.'

Lowena's hand flies to her mouth. Dear God. Poor

Mum! On her own, in pain, frightened, but unable to move. Blinking tears away she says, 'Two days... Oh, no. I had no idea. We keep in touch regularly and Dot, her friend and neighbour, goes round every day.' Lowena shakes her head. 'But I'd forgotten she's gone to stay with her daughter in Devon for a week.'

'Hey, it's not your fault, Lowena.' He passes her a box of tissues. 'You can't be held responsible for your mum's actions twenty-four seven.'

Blowing her nose, she says, 'Mum must have been in so much pain dragging herself from the kitchen to the phone in the living room.'

Dr Lawson nods. 'Hmm. But the main thing is that she did it eventually, and now she's with us and receiving the best care. She's being rehydrated, and she's on painkillers and antibiotics as she has a chest infection.' He looks at Lowena's mum. 'She is very poorly. But she's not ready for intensive care just yet. Hopefully it won't develop into pneumonia. The next twenty-four hours will be crucial.'

His words send a chill through the length of her. Crucial? What exactly does he mean? 'Are you saying her condition could worsen and...' The rest of the sentence is left unsaid, though it's loud in the silence.

'Let's not get ahead of ourselves.' Dr Lawson stands and puts a hand on her shoulder. 'Mrs Rowe is a determined woman, as many of her generation are, and as we've seen from her painting exploits.' A corner of his mouth lifts. 'But as I said, she is very poorly. We'll just have to see how things go, okay?'

Lowena nods as numbness wraps itself around her chest.

'Do you have any more questions?'

'No... I don't think so. Thank you, doctor.'

'I'll be off then. And so should you be. Get some rest and come back tomorrow. You need your sleep. We'll phone if there's a change.'

Once more alone with her mum, Lowena fights back tears. She knows her mum can't see her crying, but she needs to keep strong for her. Losing her now, so quickly, so unexpectedly, cannot happen. Taking her mum's hand between both of hers, she tells her how much she loves her and sends a silent plea to whoever might be listening. 'Not yet. Please. Not yet.'

Lowena's been home ten minutes when she realises, she left her mobile on the bedside cabinet in the hospital. *Shit!* There's no way it can wait until tomorrow, in case the hospital tries to phone during the night. The landline is out of action because she left the handset on the sofa after she called the ambulance, and it's out of charge. Lowena's bedside clock says 1.30am. Wearily, she pulls her coat back on and heads out.

When she arrives back at The Royal Cornwall Hospital, the ward station is unmanned, but Lowena can hear low voices coming from behind a curtain just inside the door. Now what? Should she wait for the nurse to come back out? No telling how long she'll be though. Lowena's sure it will be okay to pop through without asking permission first. She just wants to grab her phone and go. Hurrying along to her mum's bedside, she stops and looks around. The curtains of her mum's bay are pulled back and the bed's been made. Lowena is sure this was the bed. Can't have been... But the next bed has the sleeping form of a much younger woman. This woman was in the next bed to her mum's earlier. She spins round when she feels a hand on her shoulder.

'Miss Rowe?'

It's the nurse whom she spoke to earlier in the evening. 'Yeah. I forgot my phone... I'm just looking for my mum. Have you moved her to intensive care?'

'No. Can I have a word privately?' The compassion in her voice and the eyes full of sorrow strike Lowena dumb, and she allows the nurse to take her arm and lead her out of the ward. Doom-laden thoughts crowd to the front of her mind and she tries to erect a barrier against them, but her gut instinct allows them through. Lowena's offered a seat on a plastic chair in the office and the nurse says, 'I'm afraid your mum passed away not long after you left. We tried to phone, but obviously your phone rang here in the ward.'

Lowena shakes her head as the bottom drops out of her world. This can't be happening. Can. Not. 'No. Doctor Lawson said she didn't have pneumonia... She wasn't ready for intensive care... and...' A lump swells in her throat, strangling further speech.

'I'm afraid she went into cardiac arrest. Your mother had suffered trauma and shock. She was very weak. Her system couldn't cope... Plus the chest infection and her injuries...' The nurse gives a sad smile. 'I'm so sorry.'

Lowena crumbles mentally and physically. She wraps her arms around her middle, slumps forward in her chair and lets the tears come. The nurse rubs her back and makes soothing noises, while all the time running through Lowena's mind is, *Mum... oh, my lovely mum. I never got to say goodbye.*

Chapter Two

It's like looking in a mirror. Well, except Lowena's mum looks a good bit younger than her in this wedding photo. But then she would, at only twenty-four. She has the same soft green eyes, straight nose and full mouth, quick to smile. The hair, though curly, is much darker than Lowena's chestnut mane, but other than that, they could be twins. Lowena sits on her parents' bed, places the wedding album on her lap and traces the shape of her mum's face with the tip of her finger. Sunlight slants in through the bedroom window, falling across the photo of the bride and groom, bringing it to life. Her mum, in a high-necked beaded wedding gown, confetti in her hair, looks adoringly up at Lowena's dad. He's smiling down at her, looking like a film star with his Brylcreemed blond quiff, shiny shoes and charcoal suit.

Lowena swallows a lump of emotion as she remembers her parents showing her this album when she was little.

'Your dad could charm all the ducks from the pond in his youth,' her mum said.

'But I didn't want them. I went for the most beautiful swan instead,' her dad had replied. They were so in love then, and all the way through their fifty-eight-year marriage. Lowena could never remember a cross word between them. Or between her and them. Lowena's childhood had been filled with laughter and happiness, her teens too. Even though her mum and dad had been in their forties when they had Lowena, they'd got along more like friends than parents and child. She hopes that they are together now, wherever they may be.

Six weeks have passed, but Lowena thinks she'll never get used to the empty feeling that slips into her chest a few seconds after waking each morning. Her parents' faces blur as her eyes well, and she dabs at the corners with a tissue. Tissues are never far from her hands these days. Taking a deep breath, she has a word with herself. *Come on, Lo,* as her dad sometimes called her, *time to get on with the job.*

The job, right now, is spending the weekend sorting everything out in her parents' house before it goes on the market next week. It's proving to be a huge task, more so as she keeps stopping to reminisce over photos, ornaments and even her mum's old earthenware mixing bowl Lowena remembers from her childhood. Her mum used to let her run a spoon around the left-over cake-mix for a sneaky taste. She stares into space, remembering the baking days they shared together, and then notices the time. Not much done so far. Thank goodness Anna, her lovely and very efficient friend from work, is coming over to help organise things. She won't allow all this endless wallowing. She can be a bit bossy and domineering though, but Lowena knows she has the best intentions. As if Lowena's thoughts have summoned her, there's a knock on the door.

'You finished, then?' is Anna's opener. She hw2as a roll of black bags in her hand and a grin on her face.

'Ha! Chance would be a fine thing. This is my second day and I don't seem to have got very far.'

'I bet you've been agonising over every nick-nack, photo and item of clothing, haven't you?' Anna asks, as she bustles inside.

Lowena follows. 'As if.'

'Hmm.' Anna puts the black bags on the kitchen table next to a pile of crockery and glassware and runs her fingers through her short auburn hair as she eyes the crockery. Then she pulls open a few drawers and cupboards before coming back to the table and folding her arms. Anna sighs and narrows her sharp blue eyes at Lowena. 'How much have you *actually* put aside for charity or the dump?'

'That pile over there is for charity.' She points to the countertop. 'The one near the back door is for the dump.'

Anna laughs. 'Pile? You mean the measly five or six items in each?'

Lowena holds her hands up. 'Okay. You got me.' She tries a smile but it wobbles.

Anna loses the humour. 'Hey, it's going to be fine. Totally understandable that you're taking your time. I remember my mum being the same when my gran died. Me too. We spent more time blubbing than packing things away. But this is why I'm here. I told you the other day that

15

I'd be ruthless, but fair.' She does a cheeky wink and puts a hand on Lowena's arm. 'Come on. Let's make a start.'

Three hours later they stop for tea and cake. The kitchen and dining room are tidy and organised, and the living room is well on its way. 'I couldn't have done this without you, Anna. Thank you.' Lowena puffs a damp curl from her forehead and chases a few crumbs around her plate with a fingertip.

'That's what friends are for. And we'll have finished the upstairs by the end of the day.'

'Hope so. A man with a van's coming for the sideboard, sofa and chairs in the living room. A clearance company for the bed and wardrobes. There's not that much to sort out upstairs after. Mum's clothes will be the h-hardest.'

Anna takes a sip of tea. 'Bound to be.'

Lowena swallows a mouthful of cake and a lump of emotion. 'Clothes are so personal, aren't they? I can see Mum in most of them… can even smell her perfume on some, the scent of the washing powder she's used since forever.' Memories of her mum at various points in her past roll in Lowena's mind like a film reel. Her mum on the beach helping her build a sandcastle. Her mum in the garden teaching her the names of flowers. Her mum in recent times, laughing at something Lowena had said as they had afternoon tea. All those precious moments she'll keep safe in her heart. But oh, how her heart aches for one last afternoon tea, or a walk on the beach.

Anna's voice brings her back to the task at hand. 'There's no reason you can't keep a few. Maybe she has a few nice retro pieces you could make use of?'

Lowena brightens. 'That's a good idea. I think I saw an old 60s summer dress in the wardrobe the other day when I was looking through. Yellow with big red poppies on it. I'd never even seen her in it.'

Anna points a bit of cake at her then pops it in her mouth. 'There you go, then.'

'Mum was a bit of a clothes horse in the 60s, I think, judging by the photos. Matching dresses, handbags, shoes, the lot.' Lowena grabs a pack of photos from the table drawer and pushes them across to Anna.

'Wow yeah!' Anna shuffles through them. 'She had a real Jackie Onassis thing going on with those shades. Gorgeous woman. Looks just like you.'

Lowena flushes. 'Hardly gorgeous. I'm not bad, I suppose, in a good light. Past my prime now though, as they say.'

'You are not! You're only a few months older than me, aren't you?'

'Forty in December.'

'Well, there you are. I'm thirty-nine next week, and deffo not past my prime, darling!' Anna does a sexy pout and fluffs her elfin haircut.

Lowena bursts out laughing and it feels good. It's been a long time since she's had the inclination. 'You're a great tonic, Anna. Mum would have loved you.'

Carrying on the dramatics, Anna tilts her head to the side, lifts one eyebrow and replies, 'Everyone does, sweet cheeks.' They sip their tea in comfortable silence for a few moments and then Anna asks, 'So how old was your mum when she had you? Can't have been too young.' She frowns.

'Just struck me, if she was in her thirties or so in this 1960s picture.' She flicks a red nail at the photo in her hand.

'No, she wasn't young. She was almost forty-four. Mum and Dad had been married for twenty-odd years when she fell pregnant with me. Mum always said I was her miracle baby, just as they'd given up hoping. They thought a child of their own was never going to be.'

'That's wonderful. You must have brought them so much joy.'

'I think so.' Lowena looks around the kitchen and then through the garden full of the beautiful array of flowers her mum planted last year. Lowena's heart squeezes. She never did get a chance to plant the potatoes in the old barrel... or the tomatoes this year. 'We all got on so well, despite the big age gap.' She swallows. 'This old house was always full of laughter.'

Anna nods and pats Lowena's hand. 'And it will be again, when another family comes to look after it.' She gives Lowena an intense look. 'You know, this house is just bricks and mortar. You'll be taking the memories of your parents with you. Always. And you'll have lots to remember your mum by. She's the one who gave you your love of books, wasn't she?'

'Yes. She worked in a library part-time too. Dad was a plumber and more practically minded. But Mum and I would sit for hours discussing books and wonderful new worlds and the lives and loves we discovered between their pages.'

'Perfect,' Anna says, standing and picking up their mugs and plates. 'And now back to work.'

About to tear off a black bag from the roll, Lowena's hands tremble and out of nowhere comes: 'I feel so guilty, Anna. If I had warned Mum not to do the sodding painting, she might still be here with us. Why didn't I? Too busy? Too full of my own life? Why didn't I offer to do it for her? Why!' Fresh tears pour hot and furious down Lowena's cheeks.

'Hey, hey. Where's this come from?' Anna takes the roll of black bags from Lowena's hands and holds them between her own. 'It wasn't your fault. You always said she was stubborn, wouldn't listen to advice. She was a strong, independent woman and not about to admit she couldn't do the stuff she used to.'

Lowena has told herself exactly this for weeks, but it helps to hear it from someone else. But in her mind the guilt's still muttering under its breath. 'Yeah, she was... but I could have at least tried to do something—'

'It wasn't your fault. Are you listening? Was. Not.' Anna's eyes hold Lowena's in a steady gaze.

Guilt stops muttering as Lowena takes a big breath. 'Okay. Thanks, my friend.' She picks up the black bags. 'Now let's get on with it. All your chattering is holding me up...' Lowena dodges a play punch in the arm and hurries upstairs laughing.

———————————

Two hours later it's almost done. Just a few little things left in the under-stairs cupboard and that's it. 'Right,' Anna sighs, shrugging her denim jacket on. 'I'll get going before my husband sends out a search party.'

'Thanks, Anna. I don't know what I'd have done without you today.' Lowena gives her friend a quick hug. 'Apologise to John for me, for stealing you on a Sunday.'

Anna wrinkles her nose. 'I'll do no such thing – besides, it got me out of cooking Sunday dinner. He's doing it for once.'

'Lovely. How's Sophie getting on at uni?'

'Loving it, and working hard. Not sure her lazy, good-for-nothing brother will be as keen when it's his turn next year.'

'Harry's always been the laid-back one, hasn't he?'

'Yeah, like his dad.' Anna laughs and walks down the hallway to the front door, tossing over her shoulder, 'Wouldn't have any of them any other way though. Love the bones of 'em.'

Lowena stands at the door to wave her friend off. 'See you tomorrow at work. Thanks again.'

From the path, Anna nods and then looks up at the roof. 'Just had a thought. Have you cleared the loft?'

Lowena's mouth drops open. 'Bloody hell! I forgot all about it.' Then a quick succession of hazy memories floats through her mind offering tentative relief. 'Hang on. I'm almost sure that we cleared most of it after Dad died.' Having said that, Lowena's not certain as that was another emotional time. 'He used to stick all his junk up there. Awful hoarder. There are only a few things now… I think.'

Anna rolls her eyes. 'Come on. Let's go and see.'

The contents of the musty darkness blink into existence

under the ancient loft-light dangling from a rafter. Lowena puts her head through the hatch and after scanning the area for a few moments her heart lifts and she shouts down the steps to Anna waiting on the landing below. 'I was right, thank goodness! There's just Dad's old fishing basket that Mum couldn't bear to part with because of the happy times he had out on the river, some tatty garden furniture that Mum said would come in handy but never did, and some old toys of mine.'

'Yay, that's a relief! Do you need me to help?'

Lowena scrambles from the ladder all the way into the loft and tests the weight of the old wicker basket. 'Just with the fishing basket, please. The other stuff is small enough for me to manage on my own.'

'Okay, chuck it down!'

'Er, it's a bit heavy for that!' A giggle in her throat at the mental image of Anna flat out on the landing with a basket on top of her, Lowena drags the basket to the loft-hatch and manoeuvres it through to Anna, who's halfway up the ladder.

'Okay, got it.' She groans. 'Blimey, it weighs a ton.' She sets the basket down in the spare room and then shouts back up. 'I'll get off now, okay?'

'Yes, see you tomorrow, and thank you!'

Lowena picks up an old folding garden chair by the damp cold metal arm and shakes her head as she unfolds it. The stripy blue and white plastic material is ripped and frayed and rust grows along the frame like a fast-growing cancer. The material of the whole set is probably rotten through, so it's the tip pile for them, unfortunately. Next are two cardboard boxes full of old dolls, cuddly toys and Lego. Why her mum insisted on keeping these, Lowena doesn't know. Unless she hoped for a grandchild one day? An unexpected wave of sadness rushes over her. One of her few regrets was missing out on the chance to be a mother. Lowena thinks she'd have been good at it. There was a time when she thought she would be, a good few years ago, but it wasn't to be. And getting maudlin isn't going to help her complete this last task. With that in mind, Lowena lugs everything down to the landing and goes back up to the loft for the last check around.

About to leave, her eye is taken by a small grey shape right at the back of the loft. In the dim light, Lowena's unsure if it's actually an object or a shadow of the loft, so she picks her way carefully around the joists to have a closer look. Yes, it's definitely a bundle of something wedged against the bottom of a rafter. Under what turns out to be an old curtain, covered in dust and cobwebs, is an old but rather lovely ornately carved wooden box with a tree at its centre, the twigs of its branches reaching out to the far corners like delicate fingers. Something at the back of her consciousness wakes up and paints a picture of small hands holding this box. Her hands. Lowena frowns and searches for more, and then she remembers.

When she was about ten, she and her mum had been up in the loft – she has no idea why. Probably looking for a toy or something. Lowena had found this box and asked her mum what it was. Her mum had smiled and told her a very strange tale. Apparently, the box had been passed down through the family for generations. It was originally a 'magical' seed-box, which was thought to contain seeds and soil from Tintagel, the mysterious seat of the legendary King Arthur. It was said that whoever had the box would be blessed with a beautiful garden, bountiful crops and love of their fellow man. Lowena's mother had said it was probably all nonsense, of course, but she hadn't the heart to get rid of it. And then she had winked and added, 'Besides, I made a wish on it once. I wished for a lovely little child, and not long after, I found I was carrying you. The best little seed in the whole garden!'

This memory sends a flood of warmth to Lowena's heart, and she smiles as she caresses the outline of the carved tree. The old legend was correct in her mum's case. She'd been blessed with a beautiful garden and bountiful crops, and she'd always done her best for her fellow man. If her mum could help someone, she would. Lowena disengages the 'S' clasp and opens the lid. Inside is some uninspiring dust-dry soil, just as she remembered, so she shuts the lid again, in case she coughs or sneezes and disperses it all over the loft. What to do with it? Maybe she could use it as a jewellery box and tip the earth out? Her mum couldn't bear to part with it and neither can she. It's too beautiful, for one thing. Maybe she'll just keep it safe like her mum did. Or better still, take it home and sprinkle the soil on the few patio pots she possesses.

On the drive home she glances at the passengers on the seat next to her. A box of toys, a box of soil and, in the back, a fishing basket, a few items of clothing, the earthenware mixing bowl and some ornaments, each of them a symbol of a happy memory from Lowena's youth. A silent promise to her mum is made that she'll use all of them in some way. Perhaps she'll even wear the yellow cotton dress with the red poppies to her friend's engagement party next week. That's settled then.

Far from settled is the answer to a question that Anna asked earlier today, however. What will Lowena do with the proceeds of the house once it's sold? Will she invest it somehow, or just stick it in the bank? This is something Lowena has asked herself over the last few weeks too, but without resolution. As she pulls up outside her house, there's a seed of an idea brewing in the fertile soil of her imagination. The root and branch of this idea is a big step for someone who could be considered set in their ways. And don't 'they' say not to make any big decisions for at least a year after a bereavement? Lowena gets out of the car and collects her passengers. She thinks a year might be a bit long... but six months should do it.

Chapter Three

It turns out to be nearly nine months, but today Lowena's seen the one. The one that makes her heart skip a beat and her spirits soar. *The one* is a cottage by the sea, with a rambling jungle of a garden, and it has her name on it. Well, not quite, but it will very soon – to do that, she has to pop into the estate agent's in Padstow. As Lowena gets out of her car at the harbour carpark, a playful breeze tugs at her curls and leaves a sharp salt-tang kiss from the sea on her lips. Lowena tilts her face to the sun, smiles and takes a few deep breaths as she looks out over the River Camel and a few little boats bobbing up and down on the gentle swell in the harbour.

She can hardly believe it's nearly spring again, but there are signs everywhere. The birds having raucous conversations in the hedgerows, new green shoots unfurling on the trees, and that feeling in the air that something wonderful and new is waiting just around the corner. In Lowena's case, it's a move from Truro, the only place she's ever lived, to a new house and a new job as head librarian in the gorgeous little coastal village of St Merryn. She shakes her head in wonder as she sets off to the estate agent's. Everything's happened at once.

The day Anna had helped Lowena clear her mum's house, she'd told her that Ben Mawgan, a friend of Anna's husband, had inherited a substantial amount of money, and was talking about making an old barn into a community space in St Merryn, though he wasn't totally sure what he'd turn it into. As she'd arrived back at her house that evening, Lowena had a fabulous idea. And before she could talk herself out of it, she'd jumped in with both feet – very unlike her. In her mind, there was no question. It had to be a library. Libraries were closing all over the place, and they were such a huge loss to the community. It would be her mission to get one opened, and then she'd run it too.

Ben had turned out to be a lovely guy, and attractive with it – not that she was interested, of course – and amazingly he'd thought the library idea was fantastic. Together they'd come up with a plan to get the library up and running – part-time to start with and then they'd see how it went. Lowena helped boost Ben's contributions by throwing herself into crowdfunding and raising money in the wider community. Ben had insisted it wasn't necessary and he'd cover it, but Lowena said it would help centre the library in people's minds. If they'd raised money for it, then it would actually be *their* community library. They agreed that Lowena would pay herself a small wage from the ongoing funding. She'd been working there for three weeks and couldn't believe how popular it was already.

The second part of her idea was the move. Firstly, for practical reasons. The journey to Truro and back every day, particularly in the tourist season, would be a nightmare. Secondly, and most importantly for Lowena, because St Merryn was very near her favourite spot – 'her' bench with a view, as she thinks of it, overlooking Treyarnon Bay. In order to be at the front of the queue for a great place, she sold her house in Truro and lived in a holiday cottage in St Merryn so she'd be more attractive to sellers. No chain and cash ready. But at no point did Lowena think she'd be lucky enough to find a place to buy *actually* right on the bay.

Today she did. And despite the cottage's run-down and old-fashioned décor, it's totally perfect; or will be once she's put her stamp on it. The garden might take a little longer, to say the least. Lowena smiles as she runs the images of the waist-high grass, jungle of weeds and tangled hedges in her mind. With any luck, she's inherited her mum's green fingers.

Felicity, the estate agent who showed Lowena round the cottage earlier, looks up from her computer and her carefully drawn thick, dark eyebrows shoot up into her hairline as Lowena walks in. 'Oh. Hello again, Ms Rowe. I wasn't expecting you.'

'Yeah. Well, I've had a little think and I want to buy the cottage. No time like the present.'

'Hmm.' Felicity scratches her head with her pen and frowns. 'Kittiwake Cottage?'

What's that supposed to mean? This isn't the reaction she'd expected. 'Yup, Kittiwake. That's the only one you showed me round.'

Felicity puts her head on one side and screws her face up. 'Thing is, we've had two offers in the last half-hour. The seller's considering them right now. As I mentioned, it's only been up two days, and despite the work that needs doing, it's proving to be very popular, because of the view.'

Lowena's heart thuds to the floor. Felicity must have said those words at least four times during the viewing, but she'd thought it was just a selling ploy. She can't bear to lose it now. Her heart is living there already, and her head's planning the decoration. 'Are the other buyers proceedable? In chains, or what?' The note of desperation in Lowena's tone makes her cringe, but this cottage is so important to her.

'Both proceedable. One is in a chain, the other isn't, so—'

'I'll offer full asking price. I'm a cash buyer.'

Felicity's eyebrows do a wiggle this time and she twists her mouth. 'Right… I'm not at liberty to spell it out, but the other offers are good too.'

A whoosh of breath escapes Lowena and she leans forward, places both hands on the back of a chair and says, 'I'll offer the asking price and another ten thousand on top.' Then panic at what she's just said sparks like a live wire in her chest. Can she afford this? Yes. Yes is the answer. Yes, she can. And she'll put another ten forward if need be. She'll live on dry bread and wear rags if she can make Kittiwake Cottage her home.

Felicity's all smiles now. 'If you're sure. I'll give the owner a call now. Would you like a coffee while you wait?' She gestures to a coffee pot on the table next to the chair Lowena is leaning on.

I'd prefer a stiff gin, to be honest. 'Yes, thank you.' She sits down and smiles as her coffee's poured and notices her hand isn't as steady as it could be as she raises it to her lips. Maybe it has something to do with the fact that Felicity's sitting in front of her, calling the owner of Kittiwake Cottage. She tells her that Lowena is in an excellent position as she's chain-free and a cash buyer. Then she drops in the extra ten thousand bombshell. Lowena imagines the owner doing a happy dance at the end of the line.

'Of course, Mrs Kelsey, take all the time you need,' Felicity says down the phone as she nods and smiles across at Lowena. Lowena nearly chokes on her coffee. Eh? What's to think about? She doesn't want Mrs Kelsey to take all the time she needs; she wants to know right now. 'Yes, that's right, we close at five-thirty. Bye.'

'Five-thirty? I can't last until then.' Lowena gives a little laugh, though she's far from amused.

Felicity looks at her watch. 'Only two and a half hours.' Lowena thinks she tries for a sympathetic smile, but it comes across as patronising. 'Mrs Kelsey has to wait until her husband gets home to discuss it all, that's why she can't answer straightaway.'

'Can't she phone him?'

'I'm not sure. Maybe she wants to talk to him face to face.'

'But I'm offering more than they are asking. Substantially more...' Lowena swallows a barrage of indignant words getting themselves ready to come tumbling out.

'I'm sure it will all be fine. These things are never fast.'

This time the patronising smile doesn't even try to be sympathetic. 'Besides, I have to let the other clients know about your offer. It's only fair.'

'Oh… right,' Lowena says in a small voice, as the vision of her wonderful dream home is beginning to slide down the cliff into the jaws of a nightmare.

Outside in the harbour carpark, Lowena leans against the boot of her car and sucks in gulps of fresh sea air. In the sky over the estuary, sunbeams play hide and seek with the clouds, and a gust of wind reminds her it's still only March. Lowena pulls the zip up on her coat and decides she needs to talk to Anna. Anna knew she was looking at a house today, but not what's happened since. Most importantly, Anna will have a voice of reason to calm the whirlwind of anxiety inside Lowena's head.

Back in the warmth of her rented cottage, Lowena feeds poor starving Conrad his third meal of the day, and puts the kettle on. Then she checks her voicemails, in case she's somehow missed a call from Felicity on the short drive from Padstow, grabs the chocolate digestives, her mug of tea and makes herself comfy on the sofa.

'Anna, it's me.'

'Hello, me. How did the house viewing go?'

'I'm not sure. That's why I'm ringing you. My stomach is tying itself in knots – I'm *so* nervous.' Lowena tells her the latest.

'Another ten grand? Bloody hell! You don't do things by halves, do you?'

'I know. But I've fallen completely in love with it.'

'Which one is it again? I've got my laptop right here; I'll look it up.' Lowena tells her. There's a tapping of keys and then an exhalation on the end of the line. 'Wow... It needs a bit of TLC.'

Lowena's stomach twists. This is not the voice of reason and calm from Anna that Lowena had envisaged. 'Yes, but look at the view from the garden.'

A snort. 'Garden? Jungle more like.'

Lowena huffs. 'Great. So, you don't like it?'

'Er... I think it could be really fab... Just needs a lot of work for that kind of money.'

'I'm not afraid of hard work.' Lowena's reply is stiff as she slumps against the cushions and closes her eyes. Has she made a mistake?

'Hey, I'm sure it will be okay. I doubt the others will up their bid.'

Because it's a money-pit and nobody in their right mind would consider spending over the odds? 'Let's hope you're right.'

'Oh, hang on! Shut the front door! I didn't see the last pic of the view. It's STUNNING! You can see right over the ocean and bay! Wow! I'd pay twenty grand over the asking for that view...'

Lowena opens her eyes and sits up so fast a few drops of hot tea splash on her jeans. 'Really?'

'Er, yeah. It is un-bloody-believable, Lowena.'

Lowena's heart soars. 'It is, isn't it!' Then it plummets again. 'But what if I lose it? What if the others go higher?'

'I'm sure it will all be fine.' Anna clears her throat. 'But could you go higher?'

'I could... but I'd struggle, now I'm part-time and I've taken a cut in salary.'

'Lowena, let's not give up yet. You've got another hour until the estate agent's closes...'

'I know. I wish I didn't want this so much. But everything seems to be coming together right now. Being next to the ocean, the job that I adore...'

'Yeah, except you don't work with me anymore, and you miss me more than you can say. Don't forget that bit.'

'Yeah, there's that.' Lowena giggles. 'And now the dream house. Will my dream come true though?'

'It will. Fingers crossed. And ring me the minute there's news, good or bad. Okay?'

'Okay.'

After they end the call, Lowena wanders into the kitchen and stands staring into space. Her eyes drop to a little red light on the washing machine and she realises the washing is still waiting to be taken out from this morning. Also, the dishwasher needs to be put on and the kitchen floor is filthy. And what to have for dinner later? She ought to see what's in the fridge or freezer and sort something out. A bit of cooking and mindless housework is exactly what she needs to stop her literally counting the sixty minutes in the next hour.

As she works, her thoughts drift to her mum, as they often do. She wonders what she would have made of the move, and the eyewatering amount of money the old cottage is priced at. Her mum would probably have said it wasn't worth it. But she also would have said that if you are set on achieving something, then do everything you can in your power to make it happen. Lowena owes her strength and sense of purpose to her mum. A direction, a goal, something to strive for, is what's been instilled into her since she was little. That, and to always help somebody if you can. At first Lowena rebelled against always having to do the next thing, then the next – and going the extra mile for others, when all she wanted to do was slob out in front of the TV. But as she's got older, this philosophy has become like some of the much-coveted hand-me-down clothes she's grown into. Even though her mum's gone, her legacy will always live within her daughter, and Lowena will always be very thankful for that.

Chores complete, Lowena sits looking at the minutes on her clock tick down. 17.23. Why the hell hasn't Felicity called? Three more minutes and she will ring her instead. Lowena can't go a whole weekend without an answer. 17.24. Unable to take the suspense any longer, she throws the phone into a recently arranged pile of colourful cushions on the sofa. Then it rings.

Chapter Four

I n the post office queue, Janet Harris leans in, cups her hand to one side of her mouth and whispers in her friend Milly's ear. 'See her at the front getting that parcel weighed?' Milly nods. 'She's moved into the old Penrose place at the end of my road.'

'Penrose?' Milly furrows her brow.

'Yeah. Lily Penrose's place.'

Milly gives her head a quick shake along with her newly set grey curls. 'Didn't know her.'

Janet pulls her neck in, then she stops as she remembers it accentuates her double-chin. 'Yeah, you do. She married Don Penrose. He was in our class at school. You always thought he had a soft spot for you, but turns out it was Lily he had his eye on.'

'Oh, you mean *Lilian* Penrose. I always knew her as that. But she and Don never lived at the end of your road.'

Janet sighs and smooths her salt-and-pepper bob. 'You're losing your marbles, Milly. They lived there fifty-

35

odd years. Then he died and she died two years after.' She drops her voice to a whisper again. 'Her daughter's just flogged the house to *that* woman.' She jabs a finger towards the front of the queue for emphasis.

Milly draws herself up to her full height of five-foot nothing and harrumphs. 'I am not losing my marbles. They didn't live at the end. They lived *towards* the end of the road but round a bit to the right. Their house looks over the beach. Jan and Graham live right at the end.'

Janet treats Milly to an eye roll and another heavy sigh. Sometimes Milly can be so infuriating. 'Oh, for goodness' sake. I didn't know I had to be so precise in my descriptions.' She cups her hand and whispers again, 'Anyway, her name is Lowena and she's on her own.' Janet widens her eyes as a signal, in the hope that her friend would get what she meant. 'On her own at her age – must be forty if she's a day. No wedding ring. And who can afford to buy a house for that price on their own?'

Milly shrugs and looks bored. 'No idea. Somebody who's well off.'

Dear, oh dear. Had Milly no curiosity? 'But where's she got her money from? She's got no husband.'

'How do *you* know? Just because she has no ring on doesn't mean to say she's unmarried. Or like you, might have had one, and divorced.'

'No. I don't think so.'

'But you don't actually know, do you?' Milly narrows her eyes. 'Anyway, how do you know she's called Lowena?'

'Shh, keep it down, she'll hear us,' Janet hisses. 'She told me. I was going up my path the other day and she was walking past. Introduced herself and said she'd moved in down the road. She works at the new library in St Merryn.'

'Really? I didn't know there was one.'

'Yes. Only been open a few weeks. I might go and have a look soon.'

'You don't like reading.'

'I do if I find the right book.'

'You're just going for a nosy.'

Janet sniffs in lieu of a response. 'Why don't you come with me?'

'Might do.' Milly opens her mouth to say something else, but Janet gives her arm a sharp elbow as Lowena comes towards them. 'Ow!'

'Hello, Lowena. Busy in here today,' Janet says, with a smile.

Lowena's soft green eyes light up in a smile. 'Oh, hello... Janet, isn't it?'

Janet nods and inclines her head towards Milly. 'Yes. And this is my best friend, Milly. We've been friends seventy years, since we were four.'

'We were five, so sixty-nine years.'

Janet tuts and flashes her eyes at her friend. 'Milly likes to be precise.'

'Hello, Lowena. How—' Milly begins.

'Lowena's just moved in at the end of my road... well, *and* round to the right a bit. How are you finding it? Don was ill for quite a few years before he died, but he wouldn't let anyone tend the garden for him. Loved his garden he did. Wouldn't let anyone go near it.'

'You just said that.' Milly rolled her eyes.

Janet glares at her, and then smiles at Lowena. 'So it will take you ages to get it shipshape.'

'I've not even attempted it yet. But I'm sure it will give me hours of pleasure.'

'Give you backache more like. You want to get a man in to do it,' Janet says, and folds her arms. Here's the perfect opportunity to find out more about her mysterious neighbour. 'Have you got a husband?'

Lowena's cheeks puff into pink rounds as she laughs. 'You don't beat about the bush. No. No I haven't... and I've never had one either, in case you're wondering.'

Janet thinks there's a knowing look in Lowena's eyes. Perhaps she overheard her and Milly gossiping. Bloody Milly never could whisper properly. 'Oh, that's a shame, 'cos you need a man to do that garden. You won't be able to do it on your own.'

'I know a professional gardener,' Milly offers. 'He's my nephew and very reasonable.'

'Thank you. I'll bear that in mind. Now, I really must get on as I'm running late. Lovely to have met you, Milly, and I'm sure I'll see you both soon.' Lowena gives a little wave to them both and hurries out.

Janet and Milly shuffle up the queue a few paces. 'So what do you make of her, then?' Janet asks, wrinkling her nose. Something was definitely off with that Lowena one.

'I think she seems nice.'

Milly thinks everyone is nice. That's her problem, too trusting. Janet decides to share one of her suppositions with her. 'Mm. I reckon she might be one of those lesbians.'

38

Milly whirls round agape. 'Eh? Just because she hasn't got a husband?'

'Not just that. It's what she was wearing too – very bohemian. Multicoloured baggy cotton dungarees and a bandana thing wrapped round all that hair. Works in a library too. Dead giveaway.' Janet prides herself on being able to read people.

'You an expert on lesbians, then?' Milly frowns at her and shuffles along the queue again. 'Stop jumping to conclusions, Janet, it'll get you into hot water.'

Janet says nothing. Milly has no idea what she's on about. But Janet will find out all there is to know about her new neighbour, that's for damn sure. There's something about Lowena that doesn't add up. A single woman, with all that money. Maybe she's into something shady. Hmm. She owes it to their Neighbourhood Watch to find out, so a visit to that new library with or without Milly is on the cards. And sooner, rather than later.

Lowena's hardly stopped to draw breath over the past few weeks. It's as if she's living in a whirlwind and she's surprised to find she loves it. There's been decorating to plan, new furniture to buy, the garden to ponder on, the bench with a view, which is a stone's throw away, on which to do the pondering, and all the jobs in the library to get on top of. Lowena reflects on her good fortune umpteen times a day. How lucky is she? Conrad adores the new place too, particularly the garden. He disappears on adventures for hours and comes home with his fur covered in little sticky grass seeds and makes interesting patterns across the stripped-pine floors with his muddy feet. Still, she can't be cross with him as he's settled into his new home as quickly as she has. The house is everything she dreamed it would be, and working at the library is the cherry on top.

And without really trying, she's making new friends in the locality. A few people are starting to become regulars at the library, and the musical Rhyme Time sessions for toddlers and their parents that she organised are going from strength to strength. She's even started to find out the names of some of the neighbours. After her meeting in the post office this morning, she thinks Janet is something of an acquired taste, but Lowena reckons her heart's in the right place.

As this is one of her days off, Lowena thinks she'll make a start on the garden. Contrary to Janet and Milly's opinion, she needs neither a man nor a professional gardener. It might be a lot for one person to tackle, but Lowena will enjoy doing it. It doesn't matter how long it takes. She's in no rush. Okay, she's only ever had a few pots on a patio in the past, mainly because she's had a postage stamp of a garden. But now she's got plenty to go at, she's determined to make her mark. She chuckles to herself as she remembers the conversation with Janet. Maybe she's channelling old Don. He wouldn't let anyone go near his beloved garden either.

Lowena makes a tuna sandwich with the fresh wholemeal bread she got from the baker's opposite the post office. Truscott's has been a bakery for three generations, according to Kevin Truscott, the latest in the line. And it's no wonder they've lasted so long, she thinks as she swallows the first mouthful of the crusty light sandwich. Just heavenly. The scent from the custard slice she bought for later this afternoon means it might not actually last that long either. As Lowena eats, she considers the kitchen again. The old country-style pine cupboards have seen better days. The hinges are wonky on some, and stiff and creaky on others, as if they've grown weary, or in noisy protest at opening and closing so often. But would a completely modern look fit in with the old cottage? What she is sure of is that the rust-orange paint on the walls needs to be replaced. Though not tiny, it's not a huge space, and a white or pale lemon would give it a lift.

Siding her plate, Lowena runs a fingernail over the chipped paint behind the sink and the dull aluminium taps. Perhaps replace those with shiny new ones and the sink with a white Belfast, and some easy-to-clean colourful tiles as a splashback? She taps her fingers against her top lip and looks round the whole room. That old built-in oven needs replacing too, with an eye-level grill and microwave. Then her mum's voice pipes up in her head: *And you have a never-ending pot of money, do you, Mrs Moneybags?*

'No, Mum,' she says out loud with a smile. 'I will do it bit by bit.' Turning back to the sink, she looks through the window at the tangle of weeds threading themselves through what Lowena thinks was once a rose arbour at the end of a bumpy and broken path. 'Okay. Time to tackle you lot.'

An hour later there's a twinge in her back, a salt moustache on her top lip – not from the sea over the hedge – and a furnace in her cheeks, and despite her gardening gloves, her hands and arms look like she's had a fight with a sabre-toothed tiger. Lowena sits on a large upturned patio tub to examine a painful ankle. The tell-tale white bumps of nettle rash wind around from ankle to calf like an unwelcome tattoo. How the hell did nettles get inside her wellington boot? The answer is revealed as she tips her welly upside down and a few squashed nettle leaves plop out. Must have happened when she forked the cut-down heap into the wheelbarrow. Marvellous.

Lowena hops over to where the nettles used to be. Where's a bunch of dock leaves when you need them? Spying a few under the hedge, Lowena grabs them and limps over to the small gap in the hedge she's made with an old pair of secateurs. Suddenly weary, she decides to sit on the upturned pot, tend to her wounds and peer at the ocean through the brambles for a bit. Once seated, she shoves a hand in the small of her sore back, crosses her ankle over her knee and rubs the dock leaf on the offending rash. Almost immediately, the pain eases and Lowena's struck by the power of nature. Most people know about the treating of nettle rash with dock leaves, but there's a wealth of plant and herbal lore that the majority of humans, herself included, know nothing of. There are books on it in the library, and she makes a mental note to read one or two in the near future.

Even though she's tired and sore, Lowena can't fail to feel the benefits of being out in this wonderful space. The pleasant spring sunshine on her back, the smell of the ocean mixed with wet soil and chopped nettle on the air, the ache of muscles she's not used for a very long time – all of it makes her feel alive. Grounded in the moment. The little halo-shaped gap in the hedge affords a sweeping view of Treyarnon beach and, if she sticks her head right through, 'her' bench and clifftop. As Lowena pulls her head back a sabre-toothed bramble takes the opportunity to gouge a line across her cheek. Ouch! Okay. That's it, and that's all!

Lowena jumps up and stumbles down the wiggly old path to a dilapidated shed where she's stored the old potato barrel of her mum's, a lawnmower, pots, compost and some of her mum and dad's old gardening tools. There's a tasty-looking pair of shears that her dad always kept in tip-top condition, sharpened and oiled. Lowena thinks they should be still okay, though she only saw a glimpse of them bundled into an old black sack when she shoved them in the shed a few weeks ago. If they don't work, she'll buy some new ones. There's no way the sabre-toothed bramble, will get the better of her!

The chill of the dingy shed wraps itself around Lowena's shoulders like a hug from a serial killer, as she steps from the sunlit garden. Rubbing her arms, and carefully avoiding an intricate and, by the looks of it, very large spider's web strung between a couple of boxes and the lawnmower, she peers into the dark corner where she stowed the shears. Yep. There in the black bag next to the strimmer.

Lowena slips them free of the plastic, and an unexpected

pang of emotion clouds her eyes. Dashing away a tear, she smiles as she handles the well-oiled shears, lovingly cared for by her dad. The blades open and close with a satisfying *shush* and Lowena tests them on the lid of a cardboard box. They slice through as though the lid's made of silk. Dear Dad. He always took the utmost care with everything. Her and her mum especially.

About to step outside again, Lowena's eye is taken by the magic Tintagel box, balanced on a bag of compost. On a whim, she sets the shears down and picks it up, tracing the delicately carved tree with her fingertips as she had almost ten months before. She chuckles to herself. Maybe it's time to test its magic. Opening it carefully, Lowena's surprised to see the edge of what looks like paper sticking up through the dust-dry soil. Surely that wasn't there before? Though logically it must have been; she's just dislodged the soil, that's all. Or on the move here it will have got jiggled about.

Lowena kneels down and places the box in front of her on the damp wooden floor. As she gently moves the soil away with her forefinger, a yellowing square of faded paper is revealed. Its edges have been folded over two or three times to form a packet, and as she carefully lifts it to the light, something shifts inside it. Something shifts inside her too as excitement moves her shaking fingers to tease the folds open. *Seeds!* Thirty or so. But what kind? Lowena shakes her head. It doesn't matter what they are, because they won't grow now. They must have been tucked away in here for…? Lowena doesn't know, but she's guessing at least forty-odd years. Maybe more if they hadn't been put there by her mum. But what did her mum say? *Whoever had the box would be blessed with a beautiful garden, bountiful crops and love of their fellow man.*

In a sunny and sheltered corner of her garden, Lowena clears a weed-free spot and kneels down with the box. Her heart is lifted by the smell of wet, rich soil turned over with her new red trowel, and the mystery of who placed the wrapped seeds in the box all those years ago. She knows the chances of them growing are slim, but if they stay in the box, the chances are none. Lowena closes her eyes, thinks of her parents and her future and makes a wish before sprinkling the seeds evenly over the prepared ground. Then she adds a small handful of the dust-dry soil, before covering them with a layer of damp earth. The remaining soil from the box she sprinkles into the salt wind. She smiles. *Come on, old box, work your magic.*

Chapter Five

Lowena is in The Library Barn listing the jobs for that day. Firstly, she must process the crates of stock that have arrived. There are new books or items that customers have reserved, which need assigning and shelving by surname. The other items that have been reserved are DVDs, audiobooks on CD, music CDs and one Ordnance Survey map. Secondly, there's stock rotation work. Lowena has to find and relocate stock to other libraries in Cornwall, and crate the stock going out. She will have her reciprocal delivery at the end of the month. Then, tomorrow morning, she's expecting to chat to a local artist, Hayley, who's coming to do a talk on art next month. She wants to see the space in the library in order to plan where to put her paintings and set up. So, plenty to be going on with.

Halfway through the morning, Lowena gets a call from Ben asking if he can pop in to see how she's getting on. She says it will be a pleasure as she's not seen him for a few weeks, and she's been wondering when he'd pop in to see how she's been using his old hay barn. Lowena sits at her desk and hugs herself as she gazes around the library. It's hardly an old barn now. It's one of the most gorgeous buildings she's ever been in. Reminiscent of the skeleton of an ancient whale, the exposed rafters are set in arches running the length of the roof. As the sun warms up the day, there's the scent of solid pine, good wood oil and Scandinavian forests in the air. Well, how she imagines them to smell, never having been in a Scandinavian forest.

Ben's due in five minutes, so Lowena runs water into the kettle in the little kitchen tucked away in a back corner. It's coming up to lunchtime, so once he's here, she'll lock the door and put the *Closed* sign up. The last borrower left a little while ago and she's looking forward to a cuppa and a catch-up with Ben. He has an easy way about him and is such a nice, caring man. She knows all about his working life, but nothing about his personal background. But then some people like to keep their private life private. In passing, Anna told her he'd lost his wife, but that was about it. An ex-teacher, his day-to-day is now concerned with community projects, some of which involve disaffected youth. The inheritance that allowed him to donate the barn had similarly freed him from the classroom. He feels that working in the wider community is his calling.

As she's wondering whether to ask if he'd like a ham sandwich, Lowena hears him call her name. Popping her head round the door of the kitchen, she waves as he walks towards her. Lowena notices the easy way about him extends to his posture and long stride. Though he's over six foot tall and broad-shouldered, he's as graceful as a dancer.

Ben waves back, a smile lighting up his hazel-green eyes. Lowena feels an annoying flush in her cheeks, and scuttles into the kitchen to avoid Ben seeing it. This is the second time she's blushed in his presence. Okay, he's great looking. Stereotypically tall, dark (apart from the silver streaks above his ears) and handsome. But she's forty, not fifteen, for God's sake.

Still with her back to him, her head in the fridge, Lowena asks if Ben would like a sandwich.

'Oh. That would be great, if you don't mind. I'm starving.'

'Course I don't mind. I might even be able to run to a packet of crisps too. We'll have to share though.'

'Oh, wow!' He chuckles and pulls a chair out at the little two-seater table. 'What more could a man ask?'

In answer, Lowena's imagination presents a plethora of alternatives to crisps. Shocking and unexpected, mostly involving her kissing him. *For goodness' sake.*

Unsurprisingly, despite the coolness of the fridge, the flush won't go, so she hurries out to lock the library door and put up the *Closed* sign. On the way back to the kitchen Lowena takes a few deep breaths and tells herself to behave. It's been quite a while since she's had… what? A crush? She supposes that's what it is. Stupid at her age. What do they say to do if you want to stop nerves? Picture the person naked? Oh. Wait.

'Okay, all sorted.' She breezes past him and starts to butter the bread. 'Won't take a mo to do this.'

'It's really nice of you, Lowena. I skipped breakfast as I

had to shoot down to Camborne early to see one of my boys. He'd told his mate he was going to end it all.'

Lowena puts the bread down and turns to face him, the turn in the conversation banishing her high colour. 'Oh my God, Ben. What happened?'

He sighs and twists his mouth to the side. 'Luckily, I talked him round. He'd told his mate, so we think it was mostly a cry for help. He agreed to speak to a counsellor, so I took him over there and that's how we left it for now. Poor boy's had a rough time at home. Can't tell you about it, as it's confidential.' Lowena nods her understanding. 'Suffice to say, some youngsters have it hard. Really hard. Camborne is one of the poorest areas in Cornwall, in fact the country. I left teaching determined to help make a difference. I wonder if I do sometimes.' He frowns and scrubs a fist over his stubbly chin, the pain of caring etched into the lines under his eyes.

Lowena sighs and turns back to making the sandwiches. 'You're doing such a great job, Ben. Wish there were more like you, because so many youngsters deserve better from life.'

'They do. But there are quite a few exciting projects on the go right now. One is particularly popular, and it's getting them outside in the fresh air. They're helping the elderly with their gardens, and also learning how to plant vegetables in an allotment.'

Lowena brings the sandwiches over. 'That's wonderful. I'm taking on my own wilderness at the moment. And I'm thinking of growing a few veg too, but I know nothing really. My mum was the gardener, Dad too. Though I do have a few of their tools, and an old potato barrel Mum had for hundreds of years.'

Ben laughs at that. 'And do you enjoy it?'

Lowena takes a bite of her sandwich and thinks about her nettled ankle, scratched face and aching back. 'Despite the battle scars from the brambles.' She jabs her finger at her cheek. 'I love it.'

'I did wonder why your face was scratched,' Ben says, through a mouthful of bread. 'Assumed it was your cat.' His eyes sparkle with humour.

'Conrad would never lift a paw to me.' She laughs and takes a sip of tea. 'Do you have animals? I can't remember.'

'Not now. Used to have a dog, but he went downhill after my wife died. He left us not long after.' Ben takes another bite of his sandwich and looks over her shoulder with a faraway expression. 'Mind you, Harold was getting on a bit. Though my eldest, Beth, is convinced it was because he missed her mum so much. Harold was always loyal to Diana. Adored her.'

His account was fairly matter-of-fact, until the last two words. Unspoken emotion and a tangible ocean of melancholy shaped them. Now he's blinking and concentrating hard on stirring sugar into his tea. Poor guy. Lowena swallows the last of her sandwich and says, 'Sorry if I triggered upsetting memories, Ben. Must be difficult. I lost my parents, and that was bad enough, so no idea how you must have felt losing a life partner.'

Ben shakes his head and sighs. 'It's not your fault. And it's been five years almost... Just sometimes, it hits me, you know?' A frown furrows his dark brows and he fixes her with an intense stare.

Ben looks so vulnerable right now that she's lost for words. Without thinking she says, 'I do. It must have been so hard for you. Was your wife ill for a long time or…?' He clears his throat and Lowena wishes the ground would open. What was she thinking, asking him that? Picking at old wounds. She quickly adds, 'If you don't mind talking about it, that is?'

'No, of course not. She had breast cancer. Was ill for two years. Diana had a double mastectomy and chemo, but unfortunately it spread. She was thirty-nine.' Ben pushes his empty plate away. 'The children were fourteen and sixteen.'

Now what? Why the hell had she placed her foot on this tight-rope walk? 'I don't know what to say, Ben.' At least that was the truth.

He gives her what she thinks of as his half-moon smile. One side of his mouth turns up and causes a half-moon dimple shape in his cheek. Ben leans back in his chair and folds his arms. 'Nothing to say. It was a horrific few months after… but Beth and Jacob are both through the other side now. Beth's a trainee doctor and Jacob's at uni studying graphic design. And I'm so busy with the youth work, I hardly have time to think about anything else.'

'That's good, I guess. And I know the youngsters will appreciate you.'

'Talking of appreciation, that was a lovely lunch, Lowena. Thanks.'

'There's chocolate cake if you fancy some?'

'I do indeed.' He does the half-moon, and Lowena finds it hard to draw her eyes away.

As Lowena brings fresh plates and cuts the cake, they chat more about his work with the youngsters and his other community projects and then he asks how the library is going. Before she knows it, the hour's gone and it's time to open up again.

'It's been great chatting, Ben.' Lowena stands up and collects the dishes. 'But there might be readers waiting outside. Best get to it.'

He glances at his phone. 'Blimey, that went fast. I never got a chance to ask you about your life... your past. It's been all about me for the last hour.'

'Oh, I have a very boring past, Ben.' Lowena smiles and feels her colour coming up again under his steady gaze. He really is very gorgeous.

'Sure that's not true,' he says, following her to the door.

''Fraid it is.' Lowena unlocks the door and turns the *Closed* sign to *Open*.

'Hmm. Well, I'd like to be the judge of that.' Ben wanders over to the library shelves and runs his fingers along the titles, head cocked on one side as he reads them.

Lowena wonders what he means and is aware of the door opening behind her but doesn't turn to see who's come in with the fresh breeze. She follows Ben as he does a tour of the books and they stop by the self-help section. 'Are you looking for anything in particular?'

'No. Just having a look. You've really got this whole set-up working so well in such a short time. I'm impressed.'

'It wouldn't be possible without your donation of the barn. I adore working here.'

Ben smiles, stops looking at the books and looks at her instead. 'Listen, Lowena. Would you like to go out for a drink sometime? I'd like to hear your so called "boring" life story.'

This is so unexpected that Lowena opens her mouth but can't marshal some words into a coherent sentence. Plus she doesn't know if she'd like to at all. Lowena's few relationships haven't ended well in the past, so she'd decided to put all that nonsense behind her. And Ben is such a nice man, she'd enjoyed spending time with him today and she didn't want to ruin the friendship. 'I... er... I...'

Ben looks uncomfortable and steps back a few paces. 'Hey, I didn't mean to embarrass you. I didn't mean it as a date or anything. Just as friends, you know? But it's fine if you'd rather not.' He flashes a quick smile.

With a fire in her cheeks, she garbles, 'No, I rather would.' *What the hell?* 'Yes. I mean, that would be lovely. Thank you.'

His expression brightens and he nods. 'Great. I'll give you a call soon. See ya!' He raises a hand in farewell and steps backwards with a crunch onto a waste-paper basket, sending it flying. Behind the bookshelf Lowena thinks she hears a stifled giggle. But she has no time to investigate as, with matching fiery cheeks, Ben picks the basket up and points to the dent in the side. 'So sorry. I'll buy a new one.'

Lowena steps forward and takes it from him. 'No, don't worry. It's an old one of mine. I'll sort it.'

Ben mumbles something, raises a hand again and hurries out.

There are more noises from behind the shelves. Whispering and a 'shhh'. What on earth? Lowena hurries around the end of the bookshelves just in time to see Janet and Milly trying to tiptoe away at the far end of the next row. She coughs and they whirl round.

'Oh, hello,' Janet says with a Cheshire Cat fixed grin. Milly just looks embarrassed and sighs.

A wave of irritation sweeps through Lowena. *Cheeky buggers, earwigging on her conversation.* Politeness out the window, Lowena says, 'Hello, ladies. If I didn't know better, I'd think you'd just been eavesdropping.'

Janet loses the grin and drops all pretence. Lowena can practically see her hackles rising one by one. She links arms with Milly and marches her back up to Lowena. In their pastel-shade duffel coats and sturdy boots, they look like a couple of Paddington Bears. 'Not at all. We were looking at books – this *is* a library, you know. We couldn't help it if you were conducting your love life in front of us.'

'Love life?' Lowena snaps. 'A friend was asking me to go for a drink. Not that it's any of your business.'

'Hm. That's what he said. But I could tell by the body language between you that you're more than friends.'

'I assure you we are not!' Hang on, why is she justifying herself to the village gossips? Then another thought occurs. 'And how exactly could you see our body language through a row of books?'

Milly, guilt personified, glances at a small gap between the books on the shelf in front of them. Her button-brown eyes flit to Lowena's and away. 'I'm sorry, Lowena. There's no excuse. Janet saw that gap and I allowed her to snoop. I should have spoken out.'

Janet fixes Milly with her ice-blue gaze, harrumphs and pulls her neck in. 'Oh, for goodness' sake, Milly. It was hardly a secret – they weren't whispering or anything.'

Furious at Janet's lack of contrition, Lowena says, 'No. It wasn't a secret, but we didn't know we had an audience!'

Lowena receives another harrumph from Janet and an apology from Milly and they beat a hasty retreat. She realises she's been squeezing the flimsy waste-paper basket to her chest in her anger and it's now fit only for the bin.

For the next hour, Lowena is alone with her thoughts. Quite frankly she could do without their company because they are both conflicting and inconclusive. Most revolve around Ben. It will be a long time before the sting of humiliation leaves her. How could she imagine that Ben was asking her out on a date when he was only being friendly? He is outgoing and charismatic, always involved in one project or another. She is a bit of a homebody, not particularly outgoing or charismatic, and, as the mirror frequently tells her, past her best. Lowena guesses that he won't call as he promised. She wouldn't if she were him. And that will likely mean that their fledgeling friendship will plummet from the highest branches in a death dive now, too. *Well done, Lowena*. Exactly the opposite of what she'd hoped for.

Back in the little library kitchen, she quickly washes up

the sandwich plates and tries to banish more unwelcome thoughts without success. Damn that bloody Janet and Milly. Well, Janet really. Like a couple of school kids misbehaving, Milly's the one who's 'easily led'. The gossip about her and Ben would be all over Treyarnon Bay by teatime. The Neighbourhood Watch gang will have a field day. Sod them. Lowena needs to concentrate on her garden and her work. All her worries can be shoved into a deep pit and firmly covered over. Unfortunately, ten minutes later, her thoughts have grabbed a big rescue shovel and started digging quicker than a cartoon dog, so she's relieved when someone comes through the door.

It's an elderly man dressed in a checked flannel shirt and baggy green trousers that have seen better days. He raises a hand to her in acknowledgement and then removes his cap and clasps it to his chest. Smoothing his unruly mop of white hair, he gazes at the rows of books, takes a step forward, then turns the other way and sighs. Lowena can tell he feels a bit out of place and uncertain what to do next. 'Hello, can I help at all?' she asks, walking over.

Relief swims in his grey eyes. 'I think so. I'm looking to start one of these email letter things.' He twists his cap in his hands as if he's trying to wring it dry. 'A friend of mine told me that libraries can help with that sort of thing. Do you? Because I'd feel a right fool if you didn't.'

'We do indeed.' Lowena smiles and points to a corner of the library where three computers sit. 'Let's go and sit at one of those and I'll help you set everything up.'

The man makes himself comfortable but folds his arms.

'I must tell you that I'm not very good with computers. To be honest, I've never had a go on one.'

Lowena had guessed as much. 'Don't worry. Can I ask your name?'

'Mervyn.' He extends a hand. 'Mervyn Penleven.'

'Lowena Rowe.' She sits beside of him. 'Now, is it just emails that you want to set up?'

'Yes. I have family in Australia. My daughter, her husband and two grandchildren. Well, the grandchildren are grown up now. But one of them, Matthew, is coming here to study and he said we should try and keep into touch by email-letter. We have been writing to each other over the years and speak on the phone. But Matthew says it's easier to do email-letters.' Mervyn laughs. 'He's trying to drag me into the twenty-first century.

Lowena smiles. 'It's much quicker than snail mail, and you don't have to say email-letter. Just email.'

'That's what Matthew says.' He pulls a scrap of paper from his trouser pocket. 'This is his email-letter, I mean email address.'

'Okay. Let's get started, Mervyn.' Over the next while, Lowena learns that Mervyn is eighty, used to be a farmer and misses farming life. He'd hoped for a son but didn't get one. Lowena bites her lip at this. His daughter, Lorraine, wasn't interested in farming, and had made it clear in no uncertain terms that she wouldn't dream of taking over the farm when he got old. She didn't see eye to eye with her mother, got married and went to live in Australia. Mervyn's wife died ten years ago, so there's just him now. A sheep farmer, he's let the land go, but still lives in the old farmhouse. Though Mervyn tells her this in a matter-of-fact way, Lowena can detect the sense of loss and slight bitterness seeping in now and then.

'But at least you keep in touch with your daughter?' she asks hopefully.

Mervyn scrubs his knuckle over his bushy eyebrows. 'Oh yes, but not often. We talk on the phone. But I'm hard of hearing. Keep having to ask her to repeat things, which irritates her. Pretends it doesn't, but I can tell. They have come over here too. Last time was six years ago, as it's not cheap. Lorraine's always on at me to visit, but I won't fly all that way. Hate being up in the bloody air.' He does a wheezy laugh.

'So, you've not seen them all for six years?'

'No. But as I say, our Matthew's coming over soon to study at Exeter University. He's doing forensics – clever lad.'

Mervyn is surprisingly quick at picking up the basics of emailing and he's obviously proud as a dog with two tails when he's composed the short message to Matthew. 'There now,' he says, pressing send, a big smile brightening up his craggy features like sunlight on a cliff face. 'I've done it. I've been dragged into the twenty-first century, Lowena!'

'You certainly have, Mervyn.'

He furrows his brows and thrusts his face close to the screen. 'So, when will he answer?'

Lowena hides a smile. 'We have no way of knowing. It depends how busy he is, and the time difference will have a bearing on it. It's only about three in the morning there.'

'Course it is.' Mervyn stands and smiles at her. 'Thanks

very much for helping me, Lowena.' He folds the notepaper with his login details and newly set-up email address. 'I'll be back tomorrow to see if he's answered.'

'It might be as well to get an iPad, or a phone, Mervyn, if not a laptop? We aren't open every day, and it might be frustrating to come down here each time you need to see Matthew's reply.'

'Oh… I'm not sure I could cope with all that.' He sticks his cap back on. 'I'm a simple man and a bit long in the tooth to learn new tricks. I spend my time doing my garden and pottering around the town shops.'

'Nonsense! You picked up emailing very quickly once you'd got over the strangeness of it. I'll help you choose an iPad or a phone soon if you like?'

Mervyn raises his eyebrows. 'You would? That's very kind.'

'My pleasure. I love gardening too, but I'm a novice. Maybe you could give me some advice.'

'I'd be honoured.' The craggy face lights up again. 'In fact, that's another thing I came in for. I wanted a gardening book.'

Lowena directs him to the gardening section and leaves him to browse. Mervyn has lifted her mood and she feels like she's really made a difference to his life this afternoon. Instead of feeling a bit adrift, he'll be able to make quick connections with his grandson now, especially if he gets a mobile. Okay, he might have some backward ideas about gender, wishing he'd had a boy to carry on the farm, but Lowena thinks that's generational really. He's basically a kind-hearted man. Janet's not far off his age, yet a very different personality. She'd benefit from taking a leaf out of his book.

At the end of the day, thoughts of Ben and the embarrassing incident pop into her mind for a spot of endless torture. So she banishes them to the pit and covers them over. Then she leaves and locks up the library before they can escape and follow her home.

Chapter Six

Mornings like this lift Lowena's heart and soul. Her mind, body and spirit are transported heavenward, then to the far horizon, where the china-blue sky shares a cobalt kiss with the ocean. The ecstasy of being alive right here, right now, and in this place is sometimes overwhelming. Lowena swallows a ball of emotion and hugs herself as she gazes at the view from the end of her Cornish garden. A robin alights on the handle of her spade, cocks its head at her and then, perceiving her as no threat, flutters down to pull a fat worm from the freshly dug earth. After a few seconds it flies off, and Lowena realises she must be doing the same shortly. She got up early to plant potatoes before work, and apart from a spot of digging, has mostly gazed at the view. Perhaps it's because she's not entirely sure what she's doing.

Okay, how hard can it be? She picks up a bag of seed potatoes and tries to remember what the man in the garden centre said. For the barrel, she has to layer the potatoes, and for the ground, they have to be buried in rows 30cm apart and about 12cm deep. Then he'd lost her by talking about first earlies, second earlies and main crops. Lowena had nodded and smiled where she thought it appropriate, said things like *Oh yes, of course, we don't want them to get blight* as if she understood what blight was. And *I'll use the multipurpose compost for the barrel, thanks.* As he seemed to think this was best. Why hadn't she asked him to explain things more, instead of pretending she knew what the hell he was on about? Pride. And we all know what pride comes before, don't we? *Right. Get a wiggle on before you're late for work.*

Half-an-hour later, Lowena stretches her arms to the sky, clasps her hands and bends her torso to the right and left. This is tiring work, but she's discovered that getting her hands dirty and setting the little wrinkly tubers with their nubs of new life under the earth engender feelings of calm, hope and wellbeing that she'd never expected. Okay, she'd thought it might be a nice pastime, but the idea of eventually harvesting a crop of vegetables and flowers from this rambling jungle of a garden gives Lowena a real sense of achievement. Maybe it's because in busy modern lives, many people are separated from the land and its importance to our survival. Lowena feels she's making a reconnection to the earth and learning some of the skills her ancestors would have taken for granted. Her mum used to say how rewarding gardening was, but until now, Lowena hadn't really understand what she'd meant.

Conrad appears as she's putting the tools in the shed and she scoops him up and kisses his nose. He tries to twist

out of her grasp, but Lowena showers his head with kisses
before she sets him down. 'I know you don't like public
shows of affection, but sometimes I can't help myself,' she
tells him and sets off for the cottage to grab a quick shower.
Conrad races ahead and waits by his feeding bowl by the
back door, a hopeful look on his face. 'No second breakfast
for you, young man. And don't dig up my potatoes while
I'm gone either.' Conrad yawns but doesn't reply.

At the library, Lowena helps a man find some appropriate
books to help his son with homework, then she does the
weekly fire alarm check and orders some CDs for a young
mum who wants them for her disabled dad. Next, she puts
the kettle on, as Hayley Porter, the artist, is coming in to
discuss her upcoming talk. They've spoken briefly on the
phone, so Lowena's looking forward to finding out more
about her. The door opens promptly at eleven, and in comes
a tall, striking woman; late forties, Lowena guesses. She's
dressed in vibrant African-print dungarees, and has long
beaded plaits past her shoulders. Lowena's outfit of navy
work trousers and a beige top couldn't feel dowdier next to
this woman.

'Lowena, I presume?' The woman's stunning olive-green
eyes lock onto Lowena's and she smiles and offers her hand.

'Hayley. Great to meet you.' Lowena shakes her hand
and ushers her through to the kitchen. 'Would you like
some tea?'

'Oh yes, please. Hope I'm not interrupting your work.'

'No. We're normally quiet on a Thursday. I've put a sign on the front desk for people to ring the bell if I'm needed.'

Over tea and biscuits, they discuss Hayley's talk. 'The main thing I want to get across is that art is for everyone. You don't have to know about the great painters to know what you like. A lot of tosh is talked about all art forms, and some sections of the art world are very pretentious.' Hayley runs an orange-painted nail along her jawline and three chunky wooden bangles on her wrist clunk together. 'Art is a wonderful way of expressing yourself. That goes for creating it and buying it too.'

Lowena nods. 'I totally agree. You have a shop where you sell your work, don't you?'

'Yeah. In Treyarnon Bay at the top of the road to the sea. That's what the shop's called.'

What a surprise. 'Really? I've just moved to Treyarnon and I've seen The Road to the Sea, just never got round to going in yet!'

Hayley grins. 'Well, my door's always open. And we're neighbours as I live above the shop.'

'Excellent. I'll be over for a visit soon.' Lowena laughs. 'Is the shop doing okay?'

'It does better in summer when the tourists are here. But it should start to pick up in a month or so when we hit late April and May. Having said that, I've only been in Cornwall two years, so nothing's set in stone.'

'Where were you before?'

'London. I had a successful business, and was a partner in an art shop. We had a small gallery too. We sold mostly other people's work, so no time to do my own. And sadly, it was pretentious... In the end, I couldn't stomach it. I'd had enough of the rat race. The final straw was when I broke up with my partner. Edward and I were an item as well as business partners. Nearly twenty years together and one day I looked at him and wondered what had happened to the sweet guy who believed art could help change the world.' Hayley's eyes mist over as she stares at the wall over Lowena's shoulder. 'He'd become all about the money. Soulless.'

It occurs to Lowena that she was sitting in the same seat yesterday listening to the life-story of Ben. Maybe she had that 'confessional' kind of face. 'That's a shame. But you're happy here?'

Hayley's eyes flicker back to Lowena's. 'Oh yeah. I used to come here on holiday as a kid and fell in love with the ocean. I would like more friends though... I've found some locals a bit, shall we say, "distant"? But I'm used to it. Growing up in a white middle-class suburb of London with a black dad and white mum will do that.'

This didn't come as a total surprise to Lowena. Small-town mentalities were far from scarce, unlike brown and black faces in Cornwall. 'Hmm. Prejudice can rear its ugly head from time to time, I'm afraid.'

'Oh, don't get me wrong. It's not blatant.' Hayley furrows her brows. 'Well, not within my earshot, so far anyway. No, it's more when I'm out and about, there's a forced politeness and an arm's-length approach to me.'

'Well, hopefully your talk will change that a little, when locals get to know you more.'

'With any luck.' Hayley sits back and smiles. 'I'm

looking forward to it. And I meant it when I said my door's always open. It would be nice to have a neighbour over.'

'I'll definitely take you up on that. I haven't any friends here either, having just moved. And you must come to me. I have a view of the ocean from the bottom of my garden. Or should I say jungle? It's a work in progress but I'm absolutely loving it.'

Hayley smiles. 'I can see that. Your whole face lit up when you talked about it. And a view of the ocean. Wow, that must be stunning! Worth a painting, I expect.'

A tickle of excitement grows in Lowena's chest. 'You'd like to paint my garden?'

'Yeah. I can tell it's a very special place.'

Hayley's understanding of what the garden has come to mean to Lowena is uncanny, as she only realised it herself this morning. Lowena hopes she and Hayley will become good friends. 'Yeah, it's already very special to me. But it won't seem like that at the moment to you, because most of it's a tangle of weeds and brambles. I have set some potatoes and sprinkled a few seeds... oh, and cleared a big space in the hedge so I can see the view, but that's about it.'

'Sounds perfect to me. Nature in the wild, atmospheric and beautiful. We'll have to arrange a day for me to come over and have a look.' Hayley's enthusiasm is palpable. Then it comes to a quick halt and she puts her hands up. 'Hey, sorry. I shouldn't just invite myself over like that. I—'

'No, you should! It will be great to have you over. We'll arrange a time right now.'

After dinner Lowena is sitting down to watch TV with Conrad on her lap when her mobile goes off on the coffee table. Conrad refuses to move as she bends forward to grab the phone and digs his claws into her thigh to make sure he clings on. 'Ow, Conrad!'

'No, it's Anna. Since when has Conrad taken to calling you?'

Lowena laughs and settles back down against the cushions. 'I wouldn't be surprised if he did. Bloody animal wouldn't shift just now and clawed me.'

'Get a dog. They're much better behaved.'

Lowena pokes Conrad. 'Hear that, mister? Your days are numbered.' The cat closes his eyes and languidly stretches out his back legs.

'Just ringing to ask how your week went.'

'It went well, thanks.' Lowena's embarrassing moment with Ben at the library flashes through her mind but she decides not to share it. 'Today was particularly good. I met a local artist, Hayley, who's going to give a talk next week. She's also coming here to have a look at my garden. Says she might paint it.'

'What? Your rambling weed patch? It nearly swallowed me up last time I came.'

Lowena clucks her tongue. Anna was never very good at seeing hidden beauty. She can sometimes be a bit superficial in that respect, and is more impressed with designer this, that or the other. 'Yes. But then you don't have an artist's eye.'

'She has an artist's eye? What, in a box or something? Gruesome.' Anna laughs at her own joke.

'Hilarious. And then yesterday I helped an elderly gentleman called Mervyn set up an email account, so he can keep in contact with his grandson. He came in today to collect the message and was over the moon that he'd replied! After work I helped him choose a mobile phone, so he could keep track easily. It's a very basic one and Mervyn's already getting the hang of it. I wrote down step-by-step instructions for him, and he'll ring me if he gets stuck.'

'That's brilliant, Lowena. You're certainly bubbling over with enthusiasm. Though I hate to admit it, because I miss you at work, this move was for the best. I haven't heard you as happy for ages.'

Lowena thinks about this. 'You know, you're right. Before, I was in a bit of a rut. Now when I get up every day there's always the sense of adventure – the new, you know? And then there's my garden. I can't tell you how much I love it.'

'I can hear it in your voice. John and I will come over to see what changes you've made to it soon. It might be nice to have a barbecue when the weather warms up a bit too.'

Lowena's mind presents a picture of friends in her garden, floating about in summer clothes on a balmy evening, clinking glasses and chatting while the ocean rolls as a backdrop.

'Perfect.'

Ten minutes later, Lowena's back on the sofa with a glass of wine and some peanuts. Conrad's gone out, so she engages the foot rest, stretches her legs out and covers herself with her fluffy blue TV-watching blanket. Bliss. There's the fab new series everyone's raving about to watch on Netflix, and she's been looking forward to it. As she's about to press play, her mobile goes off under the blanket. Great. Who the hell can this be now? She hopes it's not Mervyn with email problems to sort out. Jabbing the screen, she sees... *Ben*. Lowena's heart flips. Is this the call asking her to go for that drink?

'Hi, Ben, how's tricks?' She hopes her voice sounds cheery, not 'rabbit-in-the-headlights'.

'Good, thanks. Listen, you know when we were talking yesterday about your garden and about the disaffected youngsters who grow things in the community allotment?'

'Yeah. I think it's a great experience for them. I—'

'So I was wondering if two of them might come and give you a hand sometime? They are good at clearing and weeding, which is what yours needs by the sound of it.'

Oh. This is unexpected. And his tone is all business-like, not soft and caring like yesterday. Also, she didn't want a couple of teenagers coming in and taking over her garden. Lowena's got some fledgeling ideas of how it's eventually going to look. But it would seem churlish not to accept the offer. 'Um... I think so. Just as long as they take direction from me. I don't want them just coming in and doing whatever they feel like.'

There's silence on the line for a beat too long. Then Ben replies stiffly, 'No, Lowena, they wouldn't do that. I thought you'd benefit from some hard graft from my lads, but there's no obligation if you'd rather not.'

Now she feels like a miserable old cow. This conversation is not going at all like she imagined it would when she saw his name flash up on screen. Her words tumble out fast and run into each other. 'I know there's not. I'd like them to come, it will be fun. And thank you.'

'Okay. I'll get back to you about the details soon. Bye, Lowena.'

'Bye, B—' Nice. He's already ended the call. Lowena kicks the blanket off and stomps to the kitchen for another glass of wine. Her stomach's all churny and Ben's made her feel like a naughty child. She obviously said the wrong thing, and now she's in the doghouse. And why didn't he ask her for that drink he'd mentioned when the two old witches Janet and Milly were eavesdropping? More importantly, she hadn't thought a drink was a good idea at the time, so why does she even bloody care?

Ben puts a packet of crisps between his teeth, picks up two pints from the bar and threads his way through the crowded pub looking for his friend. John waves to him from a corner table, straightens the beer mats and grabs the crisps from Ben's mouth. 'Hell's bells, it's busy in here tonight. Luckily I managed to nab this table as soon as it was free.'

Ben nods and sits down. 'It's Friday night in Truro out of season, not London. But then we are here late. Hope you didn't mind me yanking you from the bosom of your family at such short notice.' He takes a long pull on his pint and heaves a sigh as the cold liquid hits the spot. He needed that.

'I was glad to be rescued from watching Netflix with Anna. We sometimes have different ideas about what passes for entertainment.' John gives a wry smile and pushes a hand through his wavy dark-blond hair. 'And it's been too long since we had a catch-up. So how are things?'

'Generally, very good. My various projects are going well, the library too. How about the plumbing?'

'We're really busy. I was wondering if one of your boys might be interested in an apprenticeship? Pete and I are struggling to cover it all.' John smiles. 'Not complaining though.'

'That would be fantastic! There're at least five lads I know would snatch your hand off.' They talk about interviews and note down times that would suit both parties. Then the conversation dips and Ben struggles to get to the point of why he really called his old friend on the spur of the moment.

'You okay, mate? You've gone a bit quiet.'

'Yeah, just have something on my mind.' Ben's eyes flicker towards John's puzzled forehead and away. He'll feel better spilling his guts not looking at him. Addressing the squished-up crisp packet on the table, he asks, 'I wonder if I could pick your brains about Lowena?'

John sits back and folds his arms. 'Eh? Why's that then?'

Ben looks up from the crisp packet to the knowing smile on his friend's face. 'Erm, because I don't know that much about her.' That sounded about as feasible as the crisp packet suddenly growing legs and doing a dance on the table.

'Yeah, right.' John leans across, pokes him on the arm and says in a sing-song voice, 'Ben fancies Lowena.'

Ben feels a pink tide flood his cheeks and he takes another pull on his pint. 'What are we, John, ten?'

'You do though. You've gone red.'

This was a bad idea. 'Let's forget it, shall we. How are Anna and the kids?'

John pulls a contrite face. 'Hey, I'm only teasing. What do you want to know about the fair Lowena?'

Ben considers not telling him, then thinks, what the hell. 'Not sure, to be honest. I've always got on with her from the word go, but the other day I thought we really hit it off. I told her all about Diana and stuff... I felt close to her. We were having lunch in the library and Lowena was so easy to talk to. I could have sworn we had a vibe going, you know?' John nods his encouragement. 'So, a bit later I asked her out for a drink, and she reacted as if I'd just asked her to get naked.'

'What did she say?'

'Once I'd covered my tracks and said I'd meant just as friends, she said she'd go. But I think she was just being polite. Then I got flustered and stepped backwards onto her waste paper basket. Crushed the bloody thing.' Ben sighs and drains his glass.

John laughs. 'Sorry, mate. But you've got to admit, that was comical.'

'Yeah. It wasn't at the time though. I phoned her earlier this evening to see if she'd like a couple of the boys to help out in her garden, but she seemed a bit stand-offish about that too. I mainly rang to see how she was and suss out if she was just being polite about my offer of a drink. Anyway, I didn't bother in the end, as she was such a grump. I don't get it. So I wondered if you had any clues.'

'Hmm,' John says and drains his own glass. 'Same again?'

'Is that it? Hmm?'

'No. I'll have a think while I'm at the bar.'

John returns with the drinks a few minutes later. 'I reckon she's worried about changing your relationship. You said you got on well, so she might think the going for a drink bit would mess it up.'

'But I told her it would be as friends.'

'It wouldn't, though, would it? She could probably tell you liked her in that way.'

'What way?'

'Romantically.'

Ben shrugs. It would be nice to have a chance to find out if he did or didn't. 'Yes, I find her attractive, and a lovely person. But not sure we'd be right together. Hence the drink.'

John waggles his index finger at Ben. 'There you go, see. What if you weren't "right together"? Lowena would feel let down and maybe a bit hurt.'

'What, after only one date?'

'There you go again. You called it a date – shows you fancy her and she'd be able to tell.'

'Oh, for God's sake.' Ben sighs in exasperation. 'Would she be so sensitive? We aren't a couple of teenagers.'

'Yes, she is so sensitive. It's because of a past relationship that went tits up.' John scratches his stubble and twists his mouth to the side. 'Not sure if I should be telling you this.'

'Hey, you can't leave me hanging now you've started.'

John sighs. 'Okay, but you can't tell Anna that you know or she'll kill me.'

Ben rolls his eyes. 'As if.'

'Right, well, apparently, she was going to get married about ten years ago now. This is all second-hand from Anna, so I couldn't tell you all the detail. She and this Rick had been together ages and they thought they'd start trying for a baby. Lowena wanted to get married first – she's old-fashioned like that – and Rick agreed. Then he got a job in Hong Kong. He's an aerospace engineer and it was a post too good to turn down, apparently. He asked Lowena to come with him, obviously, but she said she couldn't leave her mum and dad behind, and Cornwall. Lowena adores the place. She's a homebody. Loves nothing better than walking the cliff paths and beaches.'

'Loved them more than Rick by the sound of it.'

'Must have. But then you could say that this Rick loved his job more than her. Anyway, since then she's had a few dates but nothing serious. She told Anna she's no time for men now. She doesn't want to get hurt again either and she can't be arsed going through all the rigmarole.'

'Rigmarole of what?'

'Dating and shit. You know.'

Ben did. He'd not been on one since Diana died, partly for that reason. Too long in the tooth to start all that again. But then there was something about Lowena... something that made him ask her out. As well as those gorgeous green eyes and tumble of dark hair, she had a genuine spirit. She felt like someone he could trust, and talk to about anything. But now, in the light of John's information, Ben can see she wouldn't be open to anything more than friendship. A shame, but probably for the best. 'Yeah.' He shrugs and heaves a sigh. 'Thanks, John. That's made things clearer. Guess we aren't right for each other after all.'

John's eyebrows shoot up to his hairline. 'Eh? You're just gonna chuck in the towel before you've even started?'

'Yep. Can't see the point in pursuing it.'

'I think you should give her a chance. You'd be good for each other. You might be just the man to make her realise love is worth having.'

'Jeez, you sound like a romance novel, mate.'

'And you sound like a coward.'

'Bit harsh.'

'You're just as scared as her, I reckon. Obviously, it's understandable after Diana, and then there's the other thing.'

'Other thing?'

'Your inheritance, as you prefer to call it. I suppose you worry that women might treat you differently if they knew about that.'

Ben nods. John is more perceptive than he seems at times. 'Yeah. I have to be careful.'

'Well, Lowena's your woman. She's not a gold-digger. Simple pleasures for that one.' John downs half his pint and then sits back with a self-satisfied smile on his face.

Exasperated, Ben's answer comes out snippier than he intends. 'But she's not interested, *is* she?'

With twist of his mouth John replies, 'You haven't given her a proper chance to say no. Try again, Ben. I've got a good feeling about this.'

Ben pushes a hand through his hair and considers his options. John's relentless optimism is giving him second thoughts. And it's true he didn't give Lowena a chance to turn down his offer the second time. He'd just assumed she'd not wanted much to do with him, or his boys. When he'd called, she might just have been tired, or in the middle of something. But does he really need all this angst at his age? Shouldn't it be more natural... and easier than this? He looks at his friend's hopeful face across the table. 'I don't know, mate. What if it doesn't work, even if she does agree to come out with me?'

'To quote the mighty Coldplay, "If you never try, you'll never know"...'

'Hmm.'

'So?'

Ben holds his hands up in defeat. 'Okay. I'll give it another try.'

Chapter Seven

S tanding to the side, Lowena appraises herself in her cheval bedroom mirror. She's ready for work, dressed in smart black trousers and a red figure-hugging V-neck top, and if it's not her imagination, she looks like she's lost quite a bit of weight. Particularly around her stomach. At only five-foot-three, as she'd hit forty, her love affair with cake and wine had started to tell, but due to her regular gardening activities, she's definitely dropped a good few pounds. The scales will reveal all, if she can find them. Probably shoved under the stairs in that big box of odds and ends when she first moved in. Her skin's got a nice healthy glow, the sun having caught her cheekbones and, in addition, threaded a few light streaks through her chestnut curls. Lowena's green eyes sparkle like two polished bits of sea-glass against her tan too. All in all, she's looking, dare she say it, a little bit attractive?

As she clears away her breakfast dishes and grabs her car keys, she idly wonders what she'll wear when Ben brings the boys round. He phoned again the day after his first call, and they'd arranged a visit for this weekend. Ben had been much more like his old self, but still no mention of a drink. That suited Lowena.

A little voice whispers, *So what does it matter what you wear on the weekend?*

Lowena instantly shuts the voice down. Tells it she wasn't thinking straight and that Ben's friendship is much more important to her than any 'might be' romance. Lowena realised the other day that her main aim in life was to become a friend to whoever needed one, and to do her best to enrich the lives of others through her love of books, and the garden of course. Apart from Anna, the young lads, Jack and Callum, would be the first to set foot on the hallowed turf since she took over the place. And, despite her initial worries, Lowena was sure that the experience would be a good one. She needs to be less proprietorial. Gardens are for sharing.

A quick tour of the garden before she leaves sends Lowena's spirits higher than the clutch of white clouds sailing across the sea of blue sky. The view from the end of the garden is as vibrant and bold as a child's painting. Yellow sand against an azure ocean, its edges trimmed with white rollers, brown paths ribboning the green swathes along the headland and a lone bench standing sentinel, just waiting for someone's company. Lowena had had that privilege only yesterday afternoon. Such a great place to think. She turns from the view and examines the rest of the garden. April is proving to be a gorgeous month and there are various shoots popping up everywhere. Last month produced a floral splash of sunshine in the shape of daffodils and crocuses against the half tumbled-down Cornish stone wall dividing her garden from a neighbouring field. A miracle, given the beds they sprang from were weed-infested and mostly in the shade of rampant brambles.

Thinking of miracles, as Lowena is about to step from the rickety path to her back door, her eye is drawn to a few green shoots in the patch of ground she'd sprinkled the seeds on from the magic box. Surely not. Though she'd made a wish, deep down, she had doubted there would be any germination. The seeds were so old. And already? It could only have been about four weeks or so ago that she planted them. Then her rational mind kicked in. Silly thing. These must be annual something-or-others popping up. But what are they? Lowena hunkers down and takes a closer look. Whatever they are, there's quite a variety. All very different leaves and shapes. She'll have to get a book from the library to try and identify them.

Driving to work along the narrow coast road, Lowena passes clumps of nodding daffodils along the grass verge and she nods back to them. The uplifting feeling she had wandering the garden is growing, and it's one of those days when you believe anything can happen. Something good. And this evening is Hayley's talk. Lowena has been a bit worried about it though. So far there's not been a lot of interest. Despite Lowena pushing the flyers on the front desk to every customer, quite a few had declined to take one. Lowena has taken some around the local shops, and hopefully people will have seen the posters on the door and walls of the library and just turn up on the night.

As she pulls up outside, her phone rings. 'Hi, Mervyn, how are things?'

'Things are good, I reckon. I managed to get quite a few of my friends to agree to come along to this art talk tonight. I know you were worried the other day.'

She was right. Good things will happen today! 'That's brilliant, Mervyn! Thanks so much.'

'You're welcome. Wendy Glanville's coming; she's my next-door neighbour. Then there's Nigel Carter – he's a mechanic. Always sorts my car out, nice man, sings in the choir. Milly Roberts, widow of my mate Stuart, and friend of my late wife's younger sister. She lives over by you in Treyarnon Bay. She's bringing her friend Janet, don't know her last name.' Lowena's bubble starts to deflate, but she bites her tongue. 'Then there's Zelah Williams, lives about a mile and half away – nearer you than me. I met her in the garden centre, not long moved here. I think she's what you'd call an eccentric. Dresses odd for her age, but nice enough. She's into growing herbs and stuff, and she's from St Ives, I think she said. Or was it St Mawgan? Anyway, the house in St Somewhere was getting too big for her now she's getting on in years. Moved here for a smaller place and a change, she said.' There's a pause and a sigh and Lowena hears a washing machine start a spin cycle in the background.

'Okay, Merv. That's great, I—'

'Mind you… Thinking about it, did she say it was because her mother was originally from St Merryn, and she was coming back to her roots? Or did her mother come from Zelah the village, hence the name, and her father was from here?'

Lowena didn't know. But she did know she was late opening the library and a young woman with a little girl had already arrived. The woman cupped her hands to the glass door and peered inside. Mervyn was still talking about Zelah's mother and would no doubt go on for ever if she didn't stop him. He was a lovely man, but my God, he could talk for England.

'That's brilliant, Mervyn. I'm thrilled you got so many to come along.' *Apart from Janet and Milly.* 'So, I'll see you all at seven this evening. Bye.'

After a busy day, Lowena pops back home to feed Conrad and herself. Then she gets changed into her gypsy dress, as she thinks of it. One of her favourites. A soft black cotton background, emboldened with pink velvet peonies and filigree blue forget-me-nots around a scooped lowish neckline, and ruched through with tassel ties. More tassel ties cinch in her waist and then the dress swishes in tiers to below her knee. After she put weight on, the dress was banished to the back of her wardrobe, but today it has barged its way past her more dowdy attire, demanding to be tried on. It fits perfectly. Lowena pairs it with tan leather boots and puts the finishing touches to her hair and make-up. The smiling woman in the mirror with the soft curls, sparkling eyes and curvy figure is almost unrecognisable as herself. But then she realises the greatest asset to her wardrobe lately is bags of confidence and a big dollop of happiness. Wearing those enhances her appearance better than any item of clothing.

———————

Lowena fusses over the seating, making sure each row of chairs is properly aligned and has enough legroom. In the kitchen, she puts cups on a tray with teabags and coffee, makes the squash, puts it in the fridge for after the talk, and puts the biscuits and cake on plates. There's enough of everything for around twenty people and she imagines around half will turn up, taking Mervyn's crew into consideration and the odds and sods who said they'd come in the week.

Hayley had been over earlier and brought a selection of her artwork, which they'd displayed on the wall in front of the chairs. Lowena thought it was stunning. Hayley is certainly a very talented artist and Lowena's even more excited about having her garden immortalised in oil or acrylic. Such an honour. As she's giving a last check on the chairs, in comes a sandy-haired man whom she vaguely remembered chatting to a few days ago about the talk. He's around fifty, dressed in black trousers, a blue shirt which complements his eyes, and a tan jacket. He's obviously made an effort, and Lowena's pleased the first Library Barn talk is being taken seriously.

'Welcome,' she says, offering her hand. His hand is smooth and soft. Not a manual worker then.

'Thanks.' He smiles. 'My name's Dan.'

'Lowena. I remember chatting to you before.' Sweeping her hand towards the chairs she adds, 'Thanks for coming and please take a seat.'

He does so and a few others come in. A young man and woman whom she doesn't remember seeing. They sit on the front row next to Dan, and before Lowena can introduce herself to them, a flustered Hayley rushes in, dressed in dark trousers and a tight-fitting floral top, showing off her stunning figure. Her hair's been straightened and hangs loose, and a lovely chunky turquoise necklace is revealed as she tucks a strand behind her ear. Lowena notices Dan do a double take and she hides a smile. Good job he's not standing, or he'd trip over his tongue.

Hayley slips her arm through Lowena's and takes her to one side. 'So sorry, but my stupid car's buggered,' she says as an opener. Her eyes are shiny and she's almost hyperventilating. 'I should have been here half an hour ago – had to get a taxi.'

Lowena puts a hand on her shoulder and says in a hushed voice. 'Hey. There's no rush, everything's ready. And I could have given you a lift; you should have called.'

'I didn't think. Nerves took over. It's ages since I've done anything like this.' Hayley sighs. 'Do I look okay?'

'Er, more than okay. You look stunning. Dan, the guy on the front row, was practically drooling just then when you breezed in.'

Hayley adjusts her shoulder bag while surreptitiously

looking at Dan. 'Really?' she says from the corner of her mouth. 'He's not half bad himself.' She grins and Lowena sees the nerves beginning to melt away.

'And please don't be nervous. Your work speaks for itself. It's stunning, just like you.'

Hayley surprises Lowena with a bear hug that nearly lifts her off her feet. 'That's exactly what I wanted to hear. You are totally lovely.'

'Why, thank you.' Lowena laughs and waves at Mervyn leading his entourage through the back doors. 'Now, go and make yourself comfortable, I think we're almost ready to start.'

Mervyn waves back and then flaps a hand at them all. 'Right, you lot. Hold up a minute. I want to introduce you to my friend Lowena who's the librarian here. She's a marvel with modern technology and a nicer maid you'd struggle to meet.' Mervyn's eyes shine with affection and Lowena's heart swells. She smiles and waits at the head of the gaggle of people, feeling a bit like the Queen at a command performance.

'We've got Zelah first.' Lowena shakes hands with a striking lady a little younger than Mervyn. She's tall and slight with a tumble of steel-grey curls to her shoulders, dressed in a hippy-style patchwork green and yellow velvet two-piece, the skirt reaching to her ankles. She's wearing what look like red Dr Martens under it. From her ears dangle two huge silver hoops, a diamond stud winks in her nose, and her lively blue eyes regard Lowena with interest. As she opens her mouth to speak, Mervyn cuts her off. 'She lives next door but two. Now, I couldn't remember if you moved here from St Ives, or what?'

'I moved from Penzance, Mervyn.' Lowena detects a hint of irritation in Zelah's reply.

'Oh?' Mervyn scratches his ear lobe. 'But you're originally from Zelah? That's why you got your name. You wanted to move back to your dad's roots because he lived here in St Merryn? Did I get that right?'

Lowena hopes Mervyn's not going to do these twenty questions with all his friends or they'll never get started. And Zelah looks like she'd prefer not to have the whole world listening in on her story. 'Sorry, Merv, but we should get started in a few moments. It's great to meet you Zelah.'

Zelah's eyes crinkle at the corners in a grateful smile. 'You too. I'll go and take a seat, I think.' As she passes, she pats Lowena's arm. 'Looking forward to this.'

'Right. Now we have Milly and Janet.'

Before Mervyn can launch into a long history of how he knows them, Lowena says stiffly, 'Yes, we've met. Please, ladies, do take a seat.' Milly looks as if she's going to say something, but Janet grabs her elbow and propels her away. Mervyn draws his brows together, and opens his mouth, but before he can quiz Lowena on her standoffishness, Lowena says to a happy-faced, mousy-haired man in his sixties with kind blue eyes, 'And you must be Nigel?'

Nigel shakes Lowena's hand. 'Pleased to meet you. Mervyn's told me lots about you.' Then he nods and takes a seat at the back in the middle.

'No Wendy, so far,' Mervyn says looking at the door and scratching his head. 'She definitely said she'd be here. Mind you, she's always bloomin' late.' As if he'd conjured her, a woman of a similar age to Nigel hurries in. She has blue eyes, wavy brown hair and an impish smile, busy energy radiating from her in waves.

'Hello, am I late?' she asks Mervyn and nods hello to Lowena. 'I've had to drop the dog off at my daughter's. He's more of a music lover than an artist.' Her laugh is infectious and Mervyn loses his grumpy face.

Lowena answers, 'No, you're just on time. Great to meet you, Wendy, I'm Lowena.' Wendy takes a seat and checking her watch, Lowena gives a thumbs-up to Hayley and goes to close the doors. As she does, two more people come in whom she's not met before, and hot on their heels comes Ben. What a surprise. He's very smart in dark jeans and a black and white checked shirt, and his hair looks still damp from the shower. His eyes flicker to hers and away as Lowena chats to the strangers in front of him.

As she ushers them through, Ben does the half-moon dimple smile and says, 'You look lovely tonight, if you don't mind me saying, Lowena.' Then his colour comes up and he looks past her towards where Hayley is checking through her notes.

What a totally unexpected compliment. What does she say to that? Lowena moves to the side and closes the doors. 'Thanks very much, Ben. I haven't worn this dress for ages, but it's one of my favourites.' He says nothing and continues to look at anything apart from her. 'Anyway, it's great to see you. I didn't realise you were coming tonight. Go and take a seat – Hayley's about to start.' Ben scuttles away sharpish and sits in the back row. Lowena can't work him out at all. One moment he's all warm and open, asking her out for drinks, the next he's all business-like, then he's complimenting her and simultaneously ignoring her. Very odd. She walks over to Hayley and gives her an encouraging smile. 'Ready for me to introduce you?'

Hayley nods and taps her bottom lip with her fingernails. 'Ready as I'll ever be.' Her smile's a bit wobbly but she looks pretty confident.

Lowena goes to the front and everyone immediately stops talking. Hayley's nerves must have jumped into her belly as she walked past, and she's glad there are only twelve people instead of twenty. 'Good evening everyone, and thank you for coming.' Oh God. Her voice sounds a bit warbly and her throat's got a tickle. 'Tonight's speaker is Hayley Porter, local artist and owner of *The Road to the Sea* in Treyarnon Bay. She'll talk for around twenty minutes. Then there'll be time for questions and answers, after which will be some light refreshment. Hayley will be here to answer any other questions during that time, and of course you are very welcome to look at the wonderful artwork that Hayley has here on display.' Lowena sweeps a hand at the paintings behind her. As she turns back to the group, she notices Janet pull a peevish face and whisper something in Milly's ear. Milly shakes her head and rolls her eyes. Lowena will have to keep her eye on that one. 'So, without further ado, here's Hayley.'

All smiles, Hayley takes Lowena's place and there's a smattering of applause led by an enthusiastic Mervyn. As she talks, Lowena wanders past the chairs and down the other way, where she sits on a side chair. Hayley's talk is confident, lively and informative. Her passion for art is alive in every word and the group is held spellbound. Apart from Janet, predictably. She spends most of the talk with her face screwed up like an old sprout and more huffs and sighs than a leaky airbed. It's a wonder Hayley's not put off, but she's either oblivious or very good at ignoring distractions. Ben keeps catching her eye and they share a brief smile each time. It's all a bit weird, so Lowena makes an effort to keep her eyes to herself for a while. This weekend will be very odd if he behaves like this when he brings Callum and Jack over.

After the talk, Lowena's making sure everyone has a drink and Hayley goes around with the biscuits and cake. There's a convivial atmosphere and a low hubbub of conversation as people mingle and look at the artwork. Lowena allows herself a pat on the back for organising her first event, and is thrilled that it all seems to be going so well. Dan thanks Lowena for his tea and waves at Hayley, pointing to the largest seascape on the back wall. It's of Treyarnon Bay at sunset and absolutely gorgeous. 'Hi, is this one for sale, Hayley?'

Hayley puts the tray of biscuits down and gives him a big smile. 'Yes, they all are.'

Dan nods and peers at a little leaflet with the prices in. 'Four hundred and fifty. Hmm.' He puts his head on one side, looks at the painting and strokes his chin. 'I shouldn't really. But it's an original, not a print, yes?'

'Yes, none of the ones here are prints.'

Lowena watches them chat and if she's not mistaken notices a spark of attraction flashing back and forth on their words. A movement at her side and a polite cough. It's Milly with Janet standing to the side, arms crossed, face set. Wonderful. 'We just wanted to say how much we enjoyed the talk, Lowena. And to say I hope you have forgiven us for our childish behaviour the other day,' Milly says, her kind face earnest, her forehead furrowed. 'We are very sorry, aren't we, Janet?' Milly gives her friend a dig in the arm.

Janet pulls her chin back and clucks her tongue, and turns her gaze to a small painting of a country lane in autumn. Lowena thinks she's behaving more like a teenager than a woman in her seventies. 'I'm not sure Janet looks very sorry at all,' Lowena says with a sigh. Then she turns her back on the old goat and treats Milly to a big forgiving smile. 'But thank you for taking the trouble to apologise, Milly. Let's forget all about it now. Would you like some more tea?'

Janet's arm thrusts between them, empty cup in hand. 'I wouldn't say no.'

Lowena's about to say how rude she thinks Janet is, when Zelah comes over to them. 'What a wonderful evening it's been. So many interesting people to meet too,' she says to Lowena and smiles at Janet and Milly. Lowena quickly introduces them all and Zelah continues, 'Hayley is an extremely talented artist. I think I might buy that little one called *Sunrise on the Sand*. Utterly stunning.' Zelah fluffs her long grey curls and a whiff of patchouli oil puffs through the air.

Janet harrumphs and folds her arms across her black no-nonsense blouse. 'The price certainly stunned me. A hundred quid for a bit of daubing on a postage-stamp canvas? Must have taken her all of ten minutes.' Her gaze sweeps the length of Zelah and back as if she's something unpleasant washed up on the beach.

'Hmm. I doubt that very much... Not an art lover, Janet?' Zelah narrows her eyes. She puts her head to one side and her large hoop earrings catch the light.

'Not especially. I don't mind a nice print, but wouldn't pay more than twenty quid for one. Too much pomp and fuss associated with these so-called artists if you ask me.' Janet's gimlet stare swivels away to fix on Hayley who's still chatting with Dan. She sniffs and folds her arms. 'All that nonsense she talked about art being for everyone, indeed. Everyone who has a fat wallet, more like.'

Zelah turns her back on Janet and says, 'Thanks so much for organising this, Lowena. It was wonderful. I'll go and get that painting before Janet here beats me to it.' Then she laughs and squeezes Lowena's arm before making her way across the room towards Hayley and Dan.

Janet's mouth drops open as she watches Zelah join the others and she clucks her tongue in disbelief. 'Cheek of her! And what's she come as, anyway? It's not bloody Halloween.'

Lowena's fed up to the back teeth with Janet, but as she whirls round to verbally sharpen them on the old witch's windpipe, Ben taps her on the shoulder. 'Hi, Lowena, saw you with Zelah. I was chatting to her and Mervyn earlier. Did she mention the herbs?'

'Herbs? No.' Lowena tries to avoid Janet and Milly's eyes. They are hanging on Ben's every word, probably imagining he's going to drop down on one knee and propose.

'Well, she and Mervyn are big gardeners. And what Zelah doesn't know about herblore isn't worth knowing.'

Janet elbows Milly and says in a stage whisper, 'My comment about Halloween wasn't far of the mark then. Must be a bloody witch.'

Milly rolls her eyes and shakes her head at the ceiling.

Ben gives Janet a puzzled frown and continues, 'So anyway, I told them all about your garden and that my boys are coming to give you a hand this weekend. I wondered if Zelah's expertise might be of interest?'

Lowena hadn't considered growing herbs, but it was a nice idea. She doesn't want to continue the conversation with Janet listening in though. 'Would you excuse us, ladies?' she says and slips her arm through Ben's, leading him to the far side of the library. Let the old mares gossip about that one. 'Sorry to drag you off, but that Janet one is poison on legs.'

Ben laughs. 'I did rather get that impression. She's done nothing but scowl and grumble all evening.'

'Yeah. She'll certainly be grumbling now.' Lowena glances back over her shoulder. Sure enough, Janet's mouth is running ten to the dozen and her laser stare is homed in on Lowena and Ben. It's a wonder they haven't burst into flames. She wonders why Janet is always so grumpy and rude. Maybe something awful happened in her past to make her so bitter and twisted. Or maybe she was just one of life's miserable grumps. Turning to him she says, 'Herbs. Yes, a nice idea, I've been meaning to get a book on them.

I'll have a chat with her. And I've been toying with the idea of inviting Mervyn over to see my plot, as I know he can get a bit lonely and he adores gardening.'

'Yeah. His eyes lit up when he was talking to me about his love of growing things from seed, and Zelah chipped in about the healing properties of this, that and the other. The whole conversation was really uplifting, you know?'

Ben's expression looks uplifted now. His half-moons are dimpling and the green flecks in his eyes look like blades of grass in spring. Lowena realises he's stopped talking, yet she's just staring at him, comparing his eyes to grass and thinking about... What exactly was she thinking about? Her mind has gone blank to anything apart from him. It's as if everyone else has vanished and there's just them, his eyes drawing her in, the set of his jaw, his smile, the way his hair falls on his forehead. Then panic sets in because he's starting to look less uplifted and staring at her as if she's an exhibit in a curio shop. And no wonder.

'I have a great idea!' Her sudden explosion of words sends his eyebrows skyward. 'I've been thinking of having a kind of house-warming, or a garden-warming more like. Just for a few friends, and later in the year when it's warmer. But you know what? I think it might be nice to do it this weekend.' She looks away from Ben's surprised face and around the library at everyone chatting and thinks what a wonderful and warm atmosphere there is. And before she can stop herself, she walks to the front of the room and raps a tea tray on the back of a chair.

Into the expectant silence and curious expressions, she tips, 'Hello again, everyone. What a wonderful evening we've had. Thanks again to Hayley.' Lowena turns to Hayley and begins a round of applause. 'Now, I know a few of you love gardening, or simply being in a garden. So, I'm opening mine up to anyone who feels like popping along on Saturday, about two-ish? Do bring a bottle of something and I'll make some food.' At this point, her stomach flips and Lowena starts to wonder what the hell she's doing. What seemed like a wonderful idea a moment ago is fast losing its appeal. Everyone is looking at her and there's no choice now but to plough on. A nervous laugh escapes her. 'Nothing fancy! And my garden is far from finished. In fact, it's a bit of a jungle.' The nervous titter is joined by a bit of arm flinging.

'Do you want a hand to get it shipshape?' Mervyn asks, his face eagerness personified.

No. Not really. In fact, not at all. *God, what have I done?* her mind yells. Her mouth has other ideas. 'Yes, the more the merrier! Many hands and all that. Okay, I'll write down my address and put it on the front desk. Please put your name down if you're coming.'

Lowena walks to the desk and the conversation starts up again. What the bloody hell was she thinking, inviting all these people to her garden? It was as if a madness had temporarily taken over her mind and body. Okay, yes, she did truly believe that gardens were for sharing, but not with so many. She'd nearly snapped Ben's head off when he'd first suggested his boys came to help. Now she'd invited the whole world and his wife. She glances over to where Ben had been standing, but he's nowhere to be seen.

Chapter Eight

Working part-time certainly has its benefits. Today is Lowena's day off, which is a godsend as there is no way she could have faced going into the library. Heck, she doesn't even want to get out of bed. Sunlight pokes a few fingers through a gap in the curtain and strokes a honey line across her face. In no mood to be reminded of the time of day, she groans and pulls the quilt over her head and tries to stop her tortured senses opening the box containing last night's ridiculous actions, and bemoaning them for the hundredth time. What on earth had possessed her? One moment she was having a perfectly lovely conversation with Ben about herbs and uplifting feelings, the next she was inviting everyone at the talk to her house. Madness.

Thoughts of Ben make her punch the pillow, turn over and let out a long sigh. He had buggered off pretty sharpish yesterday. Not surprising, really. Lowena feels she must have hurt him because of the way she'd reacted when he'd offered Callum and Jack's help, and then there she was, inviting half of Cornwall. Plus, the fact it was the same day he was supposed to be coming over with them. Would he still come? Lowena would have to ring him and see how things were. During the long spells of wakefulness in the night, analysis of her crazy behaviour had flitted to a number of explanations, eventually settling on one which seemed most favourable. She pulls the quilt free of her head as she's beginning to cook under there and runs it through her mind again.

Lowena had been overcome by a desire to share her wonderful garden with her fellow man. Hayley's talk had been about the love of art, the freedom of expression, lifting one's eyes from the day-to-day to look at the world through an artist's eye. Seeing the 'ordinary' in a new light, and appreciating the subtle nuances and beauty in colour, form and texture. Allowing time to appreciate the majesty of a wave on the ocean, or marvel at a bird in flight, and all the little things that make up the whole. These are the things that make a difference in our lives. It follows that Lowena had seen an opportunity to do just that, hadn't she? To bring the community together in nature and to make new friendships, forge amity across age groups, gender and backgrounds. Lowena smiles. Based on all that, she decides she's done a good thing. The garden party will be great. Fun. Memorable.

Tossing back the quilt, she springs from the bed and slips on her dressing gown. It's almost ten o'clock and she's wasting her day. At the window, she draws back the curtains and looks out over the garden, and beyond to the sleepy blue ocean. A seagull turns a lazy wheel across the sky, and a light breeze wipes a few troublesome clouds from the face of the sun. Another lovely spring day. Lowena's heart soars with the seagull for a moment, then follows its steep trajectory south as it plummets from view. Who's she kidding? An annoyingly honest voice pushes its way to the front of her consciousness, rolling up its sleeves, and wearing an expression that would give Janet's a run for her money. It informs Lowena that she didn't make the grand gesture last night for noble reasons at all. She made it because of something else entirely. Something she's unwilling to allow out of its secret place, up and out into the sunshine. A voice of reason cuts in on the dance, carefully unlocking that place and spelling out why Lowena rashly invited everyone. On some subconscious level she'd been protecting herself against Ben. If there were more people there, there'd be less chance of her making a fool of herself with him. Her bird's-nest hair and pyjama-clad reflection sigh in agreement. 'Oh, shut up!' she tells them, and stomps downstairs.

After her grumpy cat has been placated with a late breakfast of tuna, Lowena makes herself a strong cup of tea and an indulgent bacon and egg sandwich. Unhealthy food when she's in a tizz always makes her feel a bit better. As she's wiping the last bit of runny egg yolk from her plate with the bread, her mobile does a tap dance across the table. Catching it just before it leaps onto the kitchen tiles, she tells herself that she must remember to turn vibrate off. Oh good, it's Hayley.

'Hi, Lowena, you okay to chat?'

'Yeah, it's my day off.'

'Excellent. I was wondering if you'd like me to make a start on the painting at your place on Saturday? Another time would be fine if you think it might be a bit too hectic with everyone there.'

Lowena pulls the bit of paper, with the names of those coming, across the table towards her. Dan, Wendy, Mervyn, Nigel, Zelah, Hayley, and horror of horrors, Janet and Milly. Lowena's sure that Janet put Milly's name down, as the names are written in the same bold hand. Why they want to come is beyond Lowena. They're hardly what you'd call kindred spirits. Probably because they're nosy parkers who want to spread lots of gossip about the place. So, eight in total. And if Ben, Callum and Jack come, that makes eleven. Oh God. She's just remembered she invited Anna and John. In fact, she hadn't, it was Anna who had first come up with the whole idea on the phone the other night. Great. That made thirteen. Unlucky for some. 'Um…'

'What does um mean?'

Lowena sighs and flicks the paper onto the floor. 'Um means I don't think it would make a difference one way or the other. It's going to be a complete disaster.'

'Oh? Why do you say that?'

'Because I don't know half the people coming. Those I do know are like chalk and cheese, and bloody Janet is an evil witch who will make it her job to ruin everything! And I'm worried what they'll do to my lovely garden. I don't want people hacking at it every which way, without so much as a by your leave.' The whine in her voice is embarrassing and it sets her nerves on edge. She tries to blink away tears of frustration.

'Oh, love. That's not good. Do you want to pop over to talk about it? I'm in the shop, but it's quiet and I have a cream cake with your name on it from Truscott's bakery.'

'How can I resist such a wonderful offer?' Lowena sniffs and wipes her cheeks. 'Thanks. See you soon.'

The Road to the Sea is at the end of a windy little path that leads to its namesake. It's a smallish shop, but the big picture window and blue and white stripped awning above the silver lettering give it a seaside appeal, which must make it very welcoming to people walking past to and from Treyarnon Beach. Inside, the walls are a painted a stylish light teal, upon which hang many seascapes and scenes of the Cornish countryside. There's an old-fashioned tinkly bell as the door opens, and the smiling face of Hayley behind the pinewood counter ties up the whole experience with a warm, characterful ambience.

'I adore this place!' Lowena says, closing the door behind her and doing a quick three-sixty to make sure she's missed nothing. She has, by the front door. 'Oh, my goodness. Look at these pebbles pretending to be crabs! How clever.' The pebbles are realistically hand painted with tiny shells for legs and bigger ones for pincers. She picks one up from the display table and decides it will look exactly right on her living-room shelf at home. In fact, she thinks she'll buy two. Hurrying them over to the desk, she gives Hayley a hug and asks, 'Can I please buy these, Shopkeeper?'

'Call them a present.' Hayley waves away her money.

'Thanks, but no thanks. You have a business to run, and you said you've been quiet.'

Hayley's protest is flapped away, so she takes the sale and comes from behind the counter. Today she's wearing a cotton dress the same colour as the walls and her hair is twisted into a high bun. 'Now, young Lowena, time to have that coffee and chocolate éclair while you tell me all about it. Come through to the back. It's comfier upstairs in my flat, but I have to listen out for customers.'

Lowena's unsure how much of 'it' there is to tell. Some information hasn't been admitted properly to herself even. Some, she thinks, is just nerves or feelings of foreboding about her garden guests, unfounded or otherwise. One thing is for certain, she could use a friendly ear or two. 'Chocolate éclairs are my favourite. Drooling already.' Lowena follows Hayley into a little back kitchen, not dissimilar to the one at the library, and flops down in a white plastic garden chair. The air's full of the smoky aroma of good coffee, with sweet chocolate undertones from the cakes. Bliss.

'Okay, tell me what's bothering you.' Hayley sets a mug of coffee and a plate in front of Lowena on a small red Formica table and pushes the open cardboard cake box towards her. Inside are two éclairs and two custard slices.

'Custard slices too! What a choice.'

'Have both,' Hayley says with wicked smile and licks a dollop of éclair cream from her finger.

'Both! I couldn't possibly... could I?' Scraping her wind-blown curls into a scrunchie, she takes a big bite of the custard slice.

To answer that question, Hayley puts the éclair onto Lowena's plate and grins. Then through a mouthful of cake she says, 'Your hair looks nice in a ponytail.' She holds up a chocolaty finger. 'Not that it normally doesn't.'

'Really? I only put it up to avoid caking it in, well, cake!' Lowena always thinks she looks a bit shrew-like without hair around her face.

'Yeah. Shows those green sea-glass eyes off.' Lowena flushes at the compliment. 'Okay, spill the beans. You'll feel better with it all off your chest.'

Lowena thinks about this as she sips at the scalding coffee. Where to start? The beginning – the proper beginning – is too far away, hidden under too many feelings, and maybe not relevant. She's only ever shared all of it with Anna, and her mum knew bits. Besides, all that is water under the bridge and she doesn't feel like getting her feet wet. So, she decides to start with last night and see what happens.

'I was kind of buoyed by your talk about art being uplifting... and all the stuff you said about art being good for your spirit and how it's for everyone. There're a few things I feel like that about, too. My garden, the Cornish coast, my daft cat Conrad, oh, and books of course...' Lowena takes a break and eats more of the custard slice and lets her thoughts drift.

'Hello?' Hayley waves a hand in front of her face. 'I hope there's more 'cos I'm struggling here.'

Lowena laughs. 'Sorry, miles away. Yep. Anyway, I was chatting to Ben about Zelah and her herblore, and I suddenly thought it would be a great idea to invite everyone over. You know, because of the sharing thing, and the fact it had been such a great evening. It felt like a proper community event, you know?'

'I do. It was a big success, thanks to you.' Hayley makes a start on her second cake.

'No. You, mostly. But I helped and so did Merv.' Lowena takes a swallow of coffee and contemplates the éclair.

'And now you're wondering if you've done the right thing? Because of miseries like this Janet, and you're worried they will take over your garden, make it into something unrecognisable?'

'Yes, I stupidly said they could all muck in and "help" when Mervyn asked last night. The idea was already a bit overwhelming, so I said the first thing that came into my head. I'm such an idiot.'

Hayley dabs her mouth and lightly taps Lowena's hand. 'You're not.' She sits back watching Lowena over the rim of her coffee cup, her pretty olive-green eyes missing nothing. 'But I'm getting a feeling you're only telling me half a story.'

Was she? Of course. Less than half. Is she going to make it the whole? Lowena sighs and under Hayley's steady gaze she feels something inside start to unlock. Little bolts sliding back, catches flicking open, until the reason she invited the whole of Cornwall to her home is revealed in all its dubious glory. Naked under the light of truth. 'Okay... The truth is that I think my emotions got the better of me. I was talking to Ben, as I said...' Lowena stops as she catches a knowing look in her friend's eye. 'What?'

A mysterious smile. 'Nothing.'

'It's something. What's on your mind?'

Hayley puts her hands up. 'Well, I did wonder if Ben had something to do with it... There's definitely something going on between you.' She wiggles a forefinger back and forth.

'Going on?' Lowena's voice resembles the sound of a dog's squeaky toy when it's snapped up in its jaws, and a rush of blood heats her cheeks.

'Yes, it's obvious you like each other from your body language when you're together.'

Lowena wonders if Hayley's been taking notes from the lovely Janet. 'Well, I...' She takes a deep breath and blurts, 'It's all very odd. When we first met, we got on great. I thought he was a nice guy, caring, and very passionate about his local community, but that was all.' Lowena's blush deepens. 'Okay, seeing as I'm baring all, I *did* think he was attractive. Then we had a bite to eat together at the library, and he opened up to me about his youth work, his wife who died, his kids and stuff.' Then she tells Hayley about the being asked out for a drink fiasco, complete with earwigging Milly and Janet, the awkward phone call, and about his odd hot and cold behaviour ever since.

'Hmm. Not sure what to make of that.'

'You and me both.' Lowena demolishes the last of her éclair and washes it down with the remains of her coffee.

'Refill?' Lowena nods and Hayley brings the coffee pot over. 'I'm wondering if he doesn't know how to behave around you now.' She sloshes coffee into Lowena's cup. 'You know, after you made it clear that any drink would be just as friends, and your reluctance to accept his offer of help from the boys.'

Lowena inhales the steam from the coffee and ponders on this for a few seconds. 'Possibly, but why did he tell me I looked lovely last night, one minute, and then practically ignore me another?'

'Maybe he's trying to switch off his feelings, but they keep popping up from time to time...' Hayley does the knowing look again. 'Maybe your feelings are doing the same.'

Opening her mouth to protest, Lowena snaps it shut again. 'Perhaps. In fact, I think me rushing away from him and doing the grand invite was to stop myself from saying something silly to him. He was standing really close to me and giving me this intense stare. I was thinking how stunning the flecks in his eyes were and as green as new grass, or something ridiculously romantic. My heart was beating really fast and I just had to get away, before I made a fool of myself. And if I invited loads of people to the garden, there'd be less chance I'd say something inappropriate to him.'

Hayley frowns. 'Inappropriate? What are you so afraid of? You clearly like each other and you're both single.'

'I was hurt very badly once. And once was enough,

thanks. Since then, I have been happy on my own. And right now, my life is so full. I've got my new home to get sorted, my job, my garden and the wonderful ocean on my doorstep.' She smiles at Hayley. 'And lovely new friends like you to keep me company. A man would just complicate it all.'

Hayley wrinkles her nose. 'I reckon that guy who hurt you has a lot to answer for. I'm not saying a woman can't be happy on her own, but you said yourself it's because of him that you won't get involved again.'

'I did?'

'As good as.'

Lowena hesitates then sighs. Might as well tell the whole story. 'Yeah, I suppose Rick was the reason. We were together seriously for seven years and I thought the sun rose and set with him. We decided to get married and start a family, then he got this fantastic job offer in Hong Kong. He was an aerospace engineer on a good wage, but the salary would almost have doubled if we'd moved over there. Rick said it would be the perfect place to start a new life and family with no money worries, and a lifestyle we could only dream of here.' Lowena shakes her head as a rush of memories silence her words.

'I'm guessing you didn't want to leave your beloved Cornwall?' Hayley puts her hand over Lowena's.

'Exactly. My parents and friends too. Rick didn't seem to understand that life was about more than money and lifestyle. He said I was set in my ways and lacked ambition. We parted acrimoniously, I'm sad to say. Rick said I didn't love him enough, if I'd prefer to stay here instead of making a new life with him. Couldn't I see he was following his dream? I said the same back to him. He laughed at me… Said I had no dreams, just a sad, boring little life.'

'Nice. Was he always so materialistic?'

'No… Well, yes, a bit. But the Hong Kong job offer really changed him. Maybe he showed who he really was for the first time.'

'Sounds like you had a lucky escape.'

'Yeah, but it almost destroyed me. We'd been together so long, since school really. Apart from a break of three years when he went to university. After that, I promised myself that was it… No more men. I did relapse a few times, went on a couple of disastrous dates, mainly because I didn't give them a chance. But it's been years since Rick left, and until Ben popped up, I have been fairly happy to be single.'

'Fairly?' Hayley asks, narrowing her eyes.

'Don't miss much, do you?'

'Nope.'

'Now and again, I *have* wondered what it would be like to find someone, "the one", you know?' Hayley nods. 'One who's perfect for me, a soulmate, who knows me inside out, who would never turn out to be a shit kind of a "one".' Lowena laughs. 'I even made a wish that I could find such an elusive creature on a magic box a little while ago.'

Hayley frowns. 'A magic—'

'Don't ask.' Why had she shared that? Dear God, Hayley must think she's mad.

'Ben might be the one?'

'No. He's just a lovely man who's being friendly and I'm reading all sorts of rubbish into it. Stuff that isn't there. I need to put my silly crush – because that's what it is – out of my mind and continue with my life. And what a life I have. I'm so lucky, Hayley.'

'So, you're happy?'

'Yes.'

'You might try telling your face that, then.'

This makes Lowena laugh. 'Yeah, well, there's still the matter of the garden party or whatever the hell it is on Saturday to worry about.'

'Simple.' Hayley sits back and folds her arms. 'Cancel it.'

'I can't do that.'

'Why not?'

'Because it will make me look rude.'

'It needn't. I'm sure we could come up with a good reason between us as to why you have to put it off to a later date.'

Lowena thinks about this and is very tempted. Then an image of her mum's frowny face surfaces. The kind of frowny face she put on when, as a child, Lowena tried to put off doing things that were a bit difficult. *You have to tackle problems head on, maid. No point in running away, because you'll have to face them eventually.* 'No. I'm not a coward. I'll still have it, but I need to think of a plan to make sure my garden isn't ruined.'

'Good girl!' Hayley slaps the flat of her hand on the table. 'I'll help you. And if Janet so much as looks at anyone the wrong way, I'll help you chuck her into the Atlantic!'

As Lowena wipes away tears of laughter, she realises how lucky she is to have a wonderful new friend like Hayley living round the corner. Chatting with her feels like a sticky tangle of cobwebs has been spring-cleaned out of her head. Lowena knows exactly what she must do now. She'll ring Ben later and check he's still coming on Saturday. Hopefully, if she stops behaving like a crazy person, he will still be her wonderful new friend too.

Chapter Nine

D an looks out of his window at the squabble of
starlings on the bird feeder at the end of his garden.
There's enough food for them all, why they can't see that?
Maybe it's instinct. Fight for your patch, be top dog – or
bird, in their case. Dan knows quite a few humans with the
same ethics, but thankfully he'd left them behind in the
frozen north. Sometimes he misses his old life though.
Leaving the police early was the hardest thing he's ever
done, despite the nasty starlings he'd had to deal with on a
day-to-day basis. Criminals never thought there was
enough food for everyone. Mostly because in their world
there wasn't. Live by the sword and so forth – kill or be
killed. Dan shrugs off unwelcome memories with a growing
sense of melancholy, and collects his breakfast dishes. What
he needs is a brisk walk on the beach.

Treyarnon Bay is one of his favourite places and, living
in St Merryn, one of his closest. Dan is looking forward to
the weekend so he can see Lowena's garden and meet

Hayley again too. Last night really gave him a lift, because since moving from Sheffield almost six months ago, he'd hardly made any friends. Truth was, he'd made none. He told himself that was because he didn't go out to work, or anywhere else, to be honest. Apart from the weekly shop. What did he expect? People to come knocking on his door and asking him if he was coming out to play? The wonderful seascape he'd bought last night was hanging above his fireplace, and if he really concentrated, he could smell the salt air and feel the wind ruffling his hair. Dan smiles. Time to sample the real thing.

On the beach, Dan strides forward with long loping steps, chin set against the stiff uppercut of the breeze, his chest full of fresh air, and a glimmer of hope. Nevertheless, despite his efforts to lose it, the past trots like a determined stray, just a few paces behind. What was he thinking, moving here on a whim, just because the family used to come down here when he was a kid? Those days were full of blue skies, endless summer sun and crack-of-dawn fishing trips on the rocks with his beloved dad, while back at the caravan, his mum and sisters cooked a full English for their return. Those days were long gone. Dan can't remember the last time he'd gone fishing. Since those heady days he'd grown up, joined the force, got married, had two kids, got divorced and left his job under a cloud. His life, when potted and condensed like that didn't have much to show for it. There were some highlights however. He'd gone into the police to make a difference and until that last fateful case, he had always thought he had. In fact, he knew he had. The baddies had been caught, most of the time, and he'd been able to sleep at night with a clear conscience.

Dan stops and watches a couple of youngsters dip a fishing net on a long pole into a rockpool. A girl and a boy, around ten and twelve, probably brother and sister. A little way off, two adults wave at them. They release a dog that hurtles towards the kids along the golden sand, faster than a cloud's shadow. The girl screeches as the boy chases her with something in the net. The dog joins them, leaping round the girl on its hind legs, its yap harsh and strident in his ears. Dan wonders if the youngsters from the future will look back fondly on days like this. Days when they had the rest of their lives waiting to unfurl like a rolled-up carpet. Days when love was unconditional and when fun, laughter and adventure were constant playmates.

Turning his back, Dan leaves the beach and climbs the cliff path, with each step trying to raise his mood with positive thoughts. Annoyingly, they are far away over the ocean, out of his grasp, swept away on an outgoing tide. Dan notices a bench to his left on a patch of springy green turf right on the edge of the cliff. The perfect place to rest, get his breath and gather his thoughts. A bit of serious contemplation is needed, self-assessment. No more harking back. The future is what matters.

As he sits, the wooden slats creak and shift slightly under his weight, and he stretches both arms out along the back rest. To his right, the path rises gently following the headland; to his left, the beach shelters under the curve of a hill dotted with a few houses and, stretching ahead to a china-blue horizon is the ever-changing swell of the

Atlantic. Immediately calmer, Dan uses his old DS skills, methodically organising his thoughts into logical order. Okay, what useful things has he got now? A house not too far from the sea, no stress, freedom to do most of what he wanted – whatever that was; he'll come back to that one – enough money in the bank to see him through if he's careful, thanks to his occupational pension, and a grown-up son and daughter who still quite like him, despite his ex-wife's attempt to sully his reputation. And it won't be long before he becomes a granddad.

Dan's attention is taken by a yellow kite attempting to be flown by the same kids he saw earlier with the fishing net. The kite goes up and falls, up and falls, until it eventually just hops along the beach like a wounded bird. The dad of the family runs up to them, waving his arms about and shouting something. Dan's too far away to hear, but whatever he said must have worked, because the kite suddenly soars up into the blue like a sunburst. Up, up and up it goes, then it takes a nose dive and crashes. Like his marriage, really, Dan thinks. Nearly twenty-five years and nothing in common when the kids left. Apart from broken dreams and a shorter path to the grave than there used to be.

He exhales and closes his eyes. Then he finds a Werther's Original in his coat pocket, pops it in his mouth and tells himself to stop thinking about negative stuff. 'Himself' isn't listening, however. Sandra had felt the same about the demise of their marriage, but she had said they should work at it, as they were too old to start again. What kind of a premise was that to stay together? Dan had gone along with her though. He hadn't had the energy to fight. Then, instead of the promotion he was after, he'd left his job. She'd hated that. Told him he was spineless and a coward. He should get back on the horse; everyone makes mistakes. Things had fast become intolerable between them, and she'd agreed to the divorce and to sell the family home. Sandra had let everyone know that the split was ALL his fault though, and she'd never forgive him.

The kite goes up again and Dan ties his troubles to the tail string. It's no good sitting there mulling over the past; he's already decided the future is what matters, so now he has to make it true. Maybe he'll start with little things. Go fishing, make some bread, perhaps get some paints and have a go at expressing 'the inert creativity that we all have within us', or whatever it was that the lovely Hayley had said last night. Dan has no idea if he'd be any good. His last attempt had been as a schoolkid, but he remembers that he liked mixing paints to make different colours, sploshing them on the paper and seeing what happened. Dan smiles as he watches the kite climb higher. His life is like that blank piece of paper now – he can do anything he likes and see what happens.

Dan's first splosh on the paper involves a detour from the carpark via a little row of shops at the top of the lane. He remembers the name of Hayley's shop was *The Road to the Sea* and that it wasn't too far from the real thing. Before he'd set off from his car, Dan had wondered if Hayley would think he was a bit forward, just showing up at her place of work like that after meeting her only the night before. Would she think he was some weird stalker type?

But this isn't enough to turn his feet back around; he needs to be more spontaneous and braver. Show Sandra that he isn't the coward she thinks he is. Not that she'd ever know, but it could help Dan do bolder sploshes.

Hayley is in the shop, her back to him, sorting some small prints on a stand. She has her hair in a bun and is dressed in light blue, or is it turquoise? Whatever it is, it suits her. Dan pretends to look at various displays in the front window, while surreptitiously keeping an eye on her movements. *No, not at all stalkerish, Dan...* Taking a deep breath, he pushes open the door and whacks a smile on his face. A smile which, hopefully, says 'friendly and warm', not 'crazed serial killer'. The tinkle of the bell makes Hayley turn, and her eyes widen in momentary surprise. Either that, or shock and horror at seeing him standing in her shop, stalkerish with a rictus grin stretching his chops.

'Dan, how nice of you to pop by.' Hayley comes over and touches his shoulder lightly. It feels a bit awkward, and Dan has the impression that she had been going to give him a peck on the cheek but thought better of it.

'Hope you don't mind. I was just walking on the beach and remembered that your shop was up the road.' He drags his gaze from her stunning eyes before she really does think he's a stalker, and scans the artwork. 'And what a wonderful shop it is. So many great pieces to choose from.'

'Thanks. And thanks again for buying that seascape last night. Have you found a place for it yet?' She leans one arm on the counter and smiles at him.

Dan thinks she looks more relaxed now, which helps a knot of apprehension unravel in his chest. 'I have. It's up over the fireplace already and I can't take my eyes off it. I could stare at it all day.' There's a silence in which they bounce a smile back and forth between them for a short while, until Dan realises his is fixed and is desperate for some words to unfix it. Hers or his, he doesn't mind which.

'Would you like a cuppa?' Hayley asks.

Thank God. 'Oh, that would be nice. But only if it's no trouble.'

'Course not. Come through.'

An hour has passed in what seems like a few minutes. The awkwardness that followed him into the small kitchen earlier has left. In its place there's a warm atmosphere, full of laughter, easy conversation and shared snippets of each other's pasts. Dan drew a brief sketch of his previous job, his divorce and his children, although the reason for leaving his job was airbrushed over. She had presented a similar etching of a successful business in London, no children, a broken partnership in both senses of the word, and a hope for a new life in Cornwall. In these respects, they were quite similar. Their conversation has come to a natural end for now, and she has to tend to the shop, but Dan finds he doesn't want to leave. He could stay here all afternoon listening to Hayley and maybe talking to her about his new ambition to dabble in 'sploshing'.

As he follows her out, an idea pokes him in the belly and dares him to repeat what a little voice whispered in his ear a few minutes ago. The words are in his mouth, and on the springboard of his tongue as he pauses by the door to say goodbye. Just as he opens his mouth to release them, Hayley says,

'Well, thanks for coming over, Dan. I enjoyed our little chat – we must do it again before long.'

'I was thinking the same. In fact…' *Come on, Dan, do it for God's sake!* 'Would you like to go for a drink tomorrow? Or any night suiting you, really.' *There. He'd done it.*

Hayley does the eye-widening surprised look again, which he doesn't know how to take. But she puts him out of his misery by saying, 'That would be lovely. Tomorrow is good for me.' Then she throws in a big, warm, non-awkward smile and kisses him goodbye on the cheek.

Dan whistles to himself as he strides down the road to the sea and the carpark. And by the time he gets into the car he's added a chuckle or two. Things in life might just have started to look up.

Chapter Ten

Morning has slipped from the day, its departure sending longer shadows across the lawn. Lowena hadn't noticed it leaving as she'd been too tightly wound – a bit like a clockwork toy set on high speed. It's the day of the garden party and her nerves are doing circuits in her belly. She prepared much of the food for the garden party this afternoon herself, but thankfully, Anna and Hayley are due in an hour. Lowena wipes her hands on a tea towel and looks at the long pine kitchen table groaning under platters of freshly baked sausage rolls, quiches, cooked chicken pieces, pasties and cakes from Truscott's, and enough hummus to fill the holes in the plaster in the downstairs shower room.

Anna is bringing soft drinks and crisps, peanuts and fresh crusty bread. Hayley is bringing a selection of cheeses and a seafood rice salad. Both refused payment, but Lowena will figure out a way of slipping some money into their bags. Their help this afternoon will be invaluable. It will also be interesting to see how Anna gets on with Hayley. Lowena thought she detected a hint of jealousy over the phone in her oldest friend's responses, when she'd told Anna how wonderful her new friend Hayley was. Lowena puts her hands on her hips and sighs at the food. Will there be enough for everyone? A feeling she is missing something keeps nagging at the back of her brain. Salad... She'll make a salad or two, then it all should be perfect.

As Lowena chops tomatoes for the salad, she thinks about her telephone conversation with Ben the other day. His tone was calm, polite and friendly (if not as warm as it once was?), and he'd mentioned he'd still be coming today with Jack and Callum. The way she'd rushed away from him at the talk and invited the whole world hadn't been mentioned. Lowena was going to raise it and check that he'd not been offended that there'd be one or two more here than they'd originally arranged, but had bottled it at the last moment. Sleeping dogs and all that.

The salad made, Lowena shoves the container into an already packed fridge and an unwelcome lightbulb moment swings a bright arc through the muddle in her mind. Booze. That's why she wondered if they'd have enough. She'd forgotten the booze! Damn it! She has no time now to go shopping. Yes, she'd told people to bring a bottle, but what if they didn't? Anna and Hayley will be here any second, so it's too late to ask them. John? No, stupid, he'd be coming with Anna. Who does she know well enough to ask to pick up some wine and beer on the way? Merv? Hmm. He'd probably get Guinness and Lambrusco. Then she reminds herself that she's stereotyping, and for all she knows he might be a wine buff. Chances are he isn't though… Okay. Ben it would have to be.

A few minutes later, Lowena ends a surprisingly easy call with Ben just as the doorbell rings and Conrad comes with her to answer it. Well, he comes to be nosy and to trip her up by the looks of it – tail up in a brush, weaving in and out of her ankles and feet like some furry feline heat-seeking missile. 'Conrad, stop!' she says as she flings open the door. Anna is the first to get the full force of his impact as he pounces on the leather tassels hanging from her red and black cowboy boots.

Anna scoops him up before he can climb into Hayley's carrier bag at her feet. 'Come to your Auntie Anna, sweetums.' Turning to Hayley she says, 'Conrad loves his auntie, don't you, hmm?'

Lowena smiles at her two friends but says nothing. Anna's never really shown much more than a passing interest in Conrad before.

Anna tickles him under the chin, smiles at Hayley and continues in the high-pitched baby voice, 'But then I *have* known him since he was a tiny weeny kitty, haven't I, precious?'

Lowena is surprised at her uncharacteristic show of affection. Then suddenly realises that Anna's establishing her place in the pecking order. She's signalling to Hayley: *I have been Lowena's friend for ever, we share a past, I know her inside and out; you are just a newcomer.* Dear oh dear. Are we in the school playground? But then, Lowena has to acknowledge this is what Anna can be like sometimes. Bossy, domineering, but with a heart of gold to boot.

'Hayley, Anna, come in,' Lowena says, picking up Anna's carrier bag. 'Let me give you the grand tour.' She gives them both a quick hug and they follow her inside.

At the start of the grand tour, Anna asks, 'This is your first visit to Kittiwake Cottage then, Hayley?'

It's only Anna's second, Lowena thinks.

'It is, yes.' Hayley puts her shopping bag down on the floor in the kitchen and smiles.

'Then let me tell you you're in for a real treat. The garden has one of the most spectacular views I've ever seen. Lowena bought the place on the strength of it, didn't you, love?' Anna tips Conrad onto the table and folds her arms.

Hayley mirrors her pose. 'Yes. I've heard all about it. I can't wait to commit it to canvas.'

'Ah, yes. Lowena did mention something about that. Nice,' Anna says in a dismissive tone and follows Lowena through the living room. 'Lead on, Lowena!'

———————

Back in the kitchen again, Hayley sighs and says, 'I am almost speechless. What a lovely home you have, Lowena. And I've only seen the garden and view from the window, but Anna is right. Spectacular!'

'I'm always right.' Anna flings her arms to the side theatrically and grabs the kettle. 'Okay, who's for tea, or something a bit stronger, possibly?

'I'm afraid it will have to be tea until Ben gets here.' Lowena tells them about her oversight. 'And where's John, by the way?'

'Oh, he went for a walk on the beach. Said we girls would get on faster without him.' Anna fills the kettle and gives Lowena a cheeky wink. 'Now, tell us all about the lovely Ben and you. There's a sparkle in your eyes whenever you mention his name.'

Hayley is the only one who knows about her feelings for Ben, such as they are. And Lowena avoids her eye as she replies to Anna, 'Eh? Don't be daft. There is no spark, and certainly no me and Ben.'

Anna raises her brows and clucks her tongue. 'So why have you gone scarlet, then?'

'I haven't!' Lowena turns away and gets cups out of the cupboard, wishing her cheeks would stop doing an impression of a forest fire. She clears some food away to make a space on the table while the fire's doused.

'You have. Come on, let's be knowing.'

'There is nothing to know,' Lowena says, pouring boiling water into the cups. 'He's a very lovely man who cares about the lives of his youngsters and about his community and I like him as a friend.' Lowena's glad her cheeks have calmed down, probably because it's the truth. More or less. A little voice muscles to the front of her consciousness insisting she likes him more than that and she knows it. Dismissing it, she takes the mugs over to the table. 'Let's sit here and have this cuppa and then we'd better crack on with the rest of the stuff you've brought.'

'Great subject change, Lo,' Anna says. 'What do you think of Ben, Hayley?'

'He seems nice,' Hayley replies, sitting down at the table with Lowena. 'Not that I've said more than two words to him yet.' Then with a flourish, she pulls a small sketch pad out of her bag. 'I thought we could do that rough plan we talked about the other day for the garden. If we go outside in a mo, you could talk me through your ideas, and I'll do the sketch. Then we'll pin it up where everyone can see, and you can explain what you think people could do today. Just a little list, so they don't go off hacking everything about like you were afraid of.'

'What a brilliant idea!' Lowena says. 'That would be a weight off my mind if people could see my vision for the place.'

'What is your vision?' Anna asks.

'Let's go outside now, and I can draw it as you speak,' Hayley says enthusiastically, taking her sketch pad and cuppa to the back door.

Anna sighs and in a resigned tone says, 'I'll stay here and put the crisps and peanuts in bowls, shall I?

Lowena wants to tell her to lighten up but instead replies, 'Thanks, that would be so helpful!'

Once in the garden, Hayley lowers her voice and inclines her head towards Lowena. 'I hope I haven't done anything to annoy Anna. I feel like there's a bit of a frosty atmosphere around me.'

'Yes, I've noticed. I think she's a bit disgruntled about the way you and I get on. Silly really. She's not normally like it, but I think she misses me. We worked together and lived near each other for so long, saw each other every day. I relied on her so much after Mum died, and I've neglected her, to be honest, because I've been so busy. Maybe she feels like I don't need her, now I have a new life and new friends, which is not true. I should make more of an effort when I've got a bit straighter in my work and homelife. The cottage still needs quite a bit of work. And the garden.' Lowena casts her arms wide. 'Well, you can see how much work *that* needs!'

'I can. But I can also see why you love it so much. There's a sense of calm and peace here. I could feel it as soon as I stepped outside.' Hayley taps her pencil on the corner of her pad. 'Okay, go for it.'

Now Lowena is on the verge of seeing a plan for her garden on paper, rather than in her head, she finds the jumble of ideas that were half formed and fuzzy round the edges suddenly become crystal clear. Standing at the top of her long, wild patch of jungle, Lowena takes a breath of sea air and the words pour out of her so fast that Hayley's pencil becomes a charcoal blur over the page as she tries to keep up.

'A round herb and veg patch to the right here, with a path of pebbles through the middle which will lead to the main path running through the whole garden until it reaches the end and the view. Over to the left there will be roses, then an arch over the path in the middle will have honeysuckle or maybe jasmine. I'd love a pond to the left just off centre with maybe a small bench so I could watch the wildlife, while the breeze puffs the scent of jasmine and honeysuckle at me on warm, balmy evenings.'

'Okay, slow down a bit,' Hayley says with a laugh. 'Are you keeping the old hedge overlooking the view?'

'No! God knows why the old owners let the damn thing grow so high. Okay, I know you have to have something to stop people toppling over the edge onto the beach, but that bloody hedge obscures everything, especially if you let it get out of hand. Which they tend to do.'

'You could do with a low Cornish stone wall and a raised viewing platform. Maybe even build a wooden pergola over it with a scented climber growing up it,' Anna says from behind them. She's got a mouthful of peanuts so it takes a while for the whole message to filter through. 'Could do with a few little trees or bushes to stop some of the wind off the sea too.'

Lowena turns round and flings her arms around Anna in a giant bear hug. 'Oh my God, that's perfect! Thanks so much, you clever, clever thing!'

Anna steps back and coughs a few half-chewed peanuts onto the grass. 'You trying to bloody choke me, woman?' She wipes her runny eyes on the back of her sleeve, thumps her chest and takes a deep breath. 'Okay. Think I'll survive.' Then she laughs and everyone joins in.

'I must say that's an inspired suggestion, Anna,' Hayley says, scratching a few quick pencil strokes across her page.

'It is bloody wonderful!' Lowena says. 'I've been thinking for ages what to do about the view while making it safe too. A raised pergola and a wall. Genius.'

'Genius,' Hayley agrees.

Anna's bright blue eyes crinkle at the corners as a big smile lights her face. Running her fingers through her copper bob, she says, 'I'm glad you like the idea. But I must say, it's obvious what was needed really.'

'To you, maybe. It would have taken a month of

Sundays for me to dream it up,' Hayley says, dotting the pencil hard onto the pad and shoving it behind her ear.

'Me too,' Lowena says with a smile, noticing how Anna is practically preening.

A beaming Anna steps up to Hayley and says, 'Let's be seeing the plan, then.'

Hayley turns round the pad and holds it up for them both to see. 'Oh my God!' Lowena yells.

'Wow! I love it!' Anna shrieks.

And then everyone talks at once for a while about colours, flow and architecture, as if they're on a gardening make-over show. Lowena watches her two friends laughing together as they stick their heads through the gap in the hedge to take in the view. She thinks Anna's over her grumpy phase thanks to Hayley, and the garden of course. The garden brings the best out in people.

Chapter Eleven

E veryone arrives at once and the garden is buzzing with conversation, laughter and bonhomie. There's a variety of tools leaning against the shed courtesy of Mervyn, Jack and Callum, a trestle table courtesy of Ben full of food and drink, a stereo playing classical music courtesy of John, and a little tray of herb plants brought by Zelah, who at the moment is holding court with Jack and Callum on the healing properties of mint. Today her ensemble includes gold wellington boots, yellow and black leggings and a floaty orange top dotted with silver stars.

Lowena and Anna are rushing about making sure everyone has a drink until Milly catches Lowena's arm and says, 'Can Janet and me take over for a while? You must have other things to be doing.'

Janet hovers at Milly's shoulder, stuffing her face with a sausage roll, and looks about as interested in helping as she was in Hayley's artwork. Lowena hands the tea tray to Janet and says in her sweetest voice, 'That would be lovely, thanks so much, Janet.' Janet takes the tray but can't reply as she has hamster-cheeks full of pastry. 'There's another tray over there. Milly, could you put some plastic cups on it and see if anyone would like a soft drink?'

'I'd be delighted. I love to keep busy and be of help if I can.' Milly smiles and hurries off in the direction of the tray.

Before Lowena does her little spiel about what people can or can't do to her garden, she must go and introduce herself properly to Callum and Jack. She only said hello earlier as lots of people were talking to her at once as they arrived. Ben had been hovering behind them and just given her a quick smile. They are still talking to Zelah, so she hurries over and waits for Zelah to finish. Jack's tall, broad, dark-haired and brown-eyed. Callum's got fair, curly hair tied up in a ponytail, he's not as stocky, and is blue-eyed. Both boys are tanned, wearing old jeans and T-shirts, and look very at home in a garden. 'Hi, Lowena, I was just talking shop with these two lovely boys. Seventeen and they know so much already!' Zelah says, beaming at them. 'I wish all youngsters knew about the importance of growing things and being part of the soil, as it were.' Zelah swishes a hand towards the ground and her bangles click-clack together.

'It's great to meet you, boys,' Lowena says sticking her hand out. 'I'm so grateful that you're giving up your free time to help out like this.'

Jack and Callum shake hands with Lowena and Callum says, 'It's our pleasure. There's nothing like getting to know a new bit of ground and ripping the shit out of a few weeds.'

Zelah tips her head back in a fruity laugh. 'Oh, I do love you two. You make me feel young again.'

'You are young, Zee,' Jack says. 'Well, you're not. You're old, obviously.' A wink at Zelah. 'But young in the head, if you get me?'

Lowena hides a smile as Jack is being very earnest, while Zelah hoots again. 'I do get you, boy. You're a tonic and no mistake.'

A few moments later, Lowena taps a spoon against her glass and immediately the garden falls silent as everyone looks at her.

'Thanks so much for coming all of you, and welcome to my garden. My assistant Hayley will demonstrate her fabulous plan. She's committed my half-baked dreams and ideas for this space to paper, and there they are!' Lowena does her best big smile and casts an arm towards the shed, where Hayley has attached the drawing of the garden she did earlier.

There is a ripple of applause, followed by a few oohs and aahs as people take a closer look, and Hayley takes a theatrical bow as she's congratulated by the assembled group.

'So,' Lowena continues. 'I know that many of you kindly offered to help get this show on the road, and I'd be very grateful if you would be mindful of the plan. Perhaps today just doing the bare minimum, such as pulling weeds, trimming the hedge, perhaps some light digging of borders and the like. Hayley will be painting the view for now, and I think the plan is to add the finished garden around it afterwards.'

Anna sticks her hand up from the back as if she's a kid in class. Lowena chuckles and nods for her to speak. 'I'd like everyone to know that the raised pergola was my idea.' She places a hand on her chest and flutters her eyelashes comically. 'So if anyone knows of any woodwork handyperson, then please tell me. We need to make sure it's the perfect kind of wood in type and colour to really frame the view as you walk towards it down the path.' Anna makes a square of her forefingers and thumbs and squints through at the distant view. 'We also need it to be hardy, as the wind coming off the Atlantic is very unforgiving.'

'I know a few handymen,' Mervyn says. 'Nigel over there for one.' He nods at Nigel who looks very embarrassed at having all eyes on him.

'Well, I'm a mechanic by trade, and—'

'And a bloody good woodsman too. Don't hide your light under a bushel, Nige,' Mervyn says with a grin.

Nigel's round face glows like a bashful emoji, though it's pink, not yellow, and his blue eyes twinkle as he clears his throat. 'I'll be happy to have a chat to you about it, Anna.'

'Marvellous!' Anna says, already making her way over to him.

'I'll make a start on the light digging,' Mervyn says.

'I'll have a look at the herb garden. See what the soil's like and make notes on what will grow best where,' Zelah says. 'I can plant the ones I brought, and might even do a little sketch. Won't be as good as Hayley's, but I can have a bash.'

An unintelligible muttering comes from the direction of

Janet, but she looks around as if it had nothing to do with her when people turn to look her way.

'We'll do the hedges and maybe dig the foundations for the wall,' Jack says and Callum nods in agreement.

The remaining people look a bit unsure, so Lowena says with an encouraging smile, 'You don't all have to know exactly what you'll be doing – play it by ear. And there's enough weeding for a month, if in doubt.' Lowena wonders if all this doesn't sound a bit cheeky. People might think she's taking advantage. But then they did offer. Actually no, Mervyn did. Lowena's heart sinks. Maybe people are just here for a nice afternoon and now feel obliged to help.

There's a bit of a lull, until Mervyn says, 'Come on then, you lot. Let's get cracking!' They don't need asking twice, and soon the garden is a hive of activity.

Lowena needn't have worried, as almost everyone seems to be enjoying themselves. Even Janet and Milly are making themselves useful by offering refreshments. Janet is the almost everyone, because she still looks like a bulldog chewing a wasp, but at least she's doing it. Wendy and Nigel are weeding with Anna, and Mervyn's digging. Zelah, on her knees, is poking about in the ground with a trowel, while the breeze is making steel-grey streamers of her hair and knotting one strand around the other. Dan's standing over by Hayley as she paints, ostensibly clipping back some brambles, while mostly gazing adoringly at her when she's not looking, and Callum and Jack are making short shrift of the hawthorn hedge as if they're hewing a path through the Amazon rain forest.

Ben and John, though obviously enjoying themselves,

are the only ones doing nothing. Nothing on the gardening front, that is. They're mainly busy drinking and eating, sitting side by side on the crumbling wall, with a bottle of beer in one hand and a pasty in the other, having a good old chin-wag.

Just then Zelah catches Lowena's eye and beckons her over. She sticks a hand in the air for her to help her up, and then brushes earth from her colourful leggings. 'Now, my dear,' she begins, with a furrowed brow and a raised forefinger as if she's telling Lowena off. 'This is where you wanted the herb garden, yes?'

'Yes… I think so. Why, is there a problem?'

Zelah shakes her shaggy mane. 'Not at all. In fact, quite the reverse, as you do already have some wonderful seedlings sprouting up.'

'Seedlings?'

'Yes. You do *know* what seedlings are, right?' Zelah's thick brows part and rise, like a seagull's wings in flight.

'Yeah, of course. I don't know what these seedlings are, I mean. I didn't plant anyth—' Suddenly an image of her scattering the seeds from the magic Tintagel box pops into her head and she says, 'Actually, yeah. I *did* sprinkle some seeds from an old container Mum had. I never expected anything to grow though. I noticed them a few weeks ago, but thought they were what the previous owner had planted. Then I've been so busy since, I forgot about them. I reckon they're most likely to be what the previous owner put in, not the seeds I scattered about.'

'Hmm. Apart from the mint over there, which shoots up like grass every year,' Zelah points a finger at the ground near the hedge, 'most of what's growing looks to have come from seeds recently sown. A miracle really, given you've not started them in the warm.'

Lowena's heart squeezes as a warm rush of love for her mum floods through her. *Miracle.* There's that word again. It always seems to be associated with the Tintagel box. 'Wow, what have I got?'

'Well, it's hard to be absolutely sure at this stage, but definitely Chamomile, Valerian, Hyssop and what looks to be Fennel. All *very* early and doing incredibly well.' Lowena is awestruck. The seeds she sprinkled all came from the same paper package, and looked the same. How could they be different plants? Zelah puts her hands on her hips and looks at Lowena. 'If I were you, I'd perhaps put a little polytunnel over them for now, just to protect them from any lingering overnight frost.'

'Polytunnel?' Lowena feels totally unprepared to be a gardener, and thinks she's beginning to sound like a parrot.

'Yes. Don't worry, I'll send you a link later. The local garden centre will have some.'

Zelah's friendly wink and smile put Lowena's mind at rest. She'll be able to get on top of it all with a little help from her friends. 'Thanks, Zelah. I'll need to ask for your wonderful wisdom and advice until I get a handle on all this,' Lowena says.

'That's what I'm here for.' Zelah smiles again and then her attention's taken by another clump of little plants just to the side of the herbs. 'My goodness, maid. I've never seen these growing so early... it can't be?' Zelah hunkers down and strokes the leaves of the little green shoots, speaking to herself. 'Maybe this was a cutting from before. It wouldn't have taken outside a greenhouse in a seed tray... least, I don't think so.'

'What are they?' Lowena asks, bending over.

'If I'm not mistaken, I'd say they were dahlias.'

A lump of emotion bobs in Lowena's throat and tears prickle at the back of her nose. Dahlias had been her mum's favourite flowers. 'Oh... wow, Mum,' she says to the sky. Blinking away tears, she sees that Zelah's looking at her quizzically. 'Dahlias were...' The feeling that her mum is here standing beside her in the garden is so strong, she can't finish her sentence.

'Aw, love. Your mum liked them, eh?' Lowena can only nod. 'Then I reckon she planted them for you. Take comfort in that.' Zelah gives Lowena's arm a squeeze and wanders over to talk to Jack and Callum.

'Can't take your eyes off her, can you?'

Ben shuffles on the stone wall, and not just because his bum's getting uncomfortable. 'Eh? Who?' he asks John with a sidelong glance, though he knows the answer already.

'Don't give me that,' John snorts and takes a swig from his beer bottle.

'Zelah?' Ben grins. 'Yeah, she's sure one attractive older lady. And she's getting on really well with the boys.' He finishes his pasty and wipes his greasy hands on the wall.

'You know who I mean. I've noticed you've been giving

each other a wide berth too. That in itself speaks bloody volumes.'

'If you mean Lowena—'

'*If* I mean Lowena, he says.' John puts his head back and laughs raucously and Janet sniffs in disdain as she stomps past him. 'Stop pissing around and admit it.'

'Hey, keep your voice down,' Ben hisses, feeling his colour come up as Anna looks over at her husband curiously. John shakes his head and gives him the hard stare. 'Okay, yes, I might have been looking, but it's going nowhere.' Ben decides to update his friend on what's happened – or not happened, more like – since they met in the pub. He knows John won't shut up until he does. 'At the library the other night I told her she looked stunning. It just came out when I least expected it. I was thinking it, but hadn't meant to say it, so I felt a bit stupid.'

'Why? Women like to be told they look stunning, surely?'

'Do *they*? Yeah. All women are the same. They all like their appearance to be randomly commented upon, approved of, as if they're some prized dog at Crufts.'

'Eh?' John looks at Ben and scrubs his hand over his hair in puzzlement. Ben gives him a withering glance. 'Oh, don't go all feminist on me, you know what I mean.'

'Hmm. Well, this was just out of the blue and random, and I think she was so shocked she didn't know what to say to start with. But she thanked me for the compliment and I made a sharp exit as soon as I could.'

'Right. So, if she'd been offended she wouldn't have thanked you, would she?'

'I don't know. Perhaps she was being polite and thought I was a complete tosser.'

'Has anyone ever told you that you overthink situations, Ben?' John asked, patting Ben's shoulder as if he were a pet dog.

'You have. Loads.' Ben shrugs John's hand off and takes a swig of his beer.

John chuckles. 'So, what happened next?'

'After Hayley's talk, things seemed more natural between us. I was telling her about my conversation with Zelah, what she knew about herbs and stuff, which Lowena seemed interested in. But then she just sort of zoned out, started staring into my eyes and her cheeks turned a bit pink.'

'She went pink?' John, strokes his stubbly chin with thumb and forefinger. 'Hmm. This is promising. She might have realised she fancied you, or something.'

Ben snorts. 'Then why did she go all weird, run off and invite everyone here today? I made a quick exit after she did that. I mean, it was just meant to be me, Callum and Jack. I was already wondering if I could make an excuse about them, so I could turn up here on my own. How stupid was I?'

'"Wondering." That's your trouble, mate.' John jabs a finger through the air at Ben. 'You're *always* wondering, and overthinking. You should have *done* something before now. In the pub the other week you said you'd give it another try with her. But what have you *actually* done? Turned up at the library, complimented her and then buggered off before the end of the evening. Just because you *thought* she was offended, or acting weird around you.'

Ben sighs and considers this. Perhaps John's right. But then John's not a widower who's been out of the dating game for a thousand years, is he? He's someone who always knows the right thing to say to people. 'It's all right for you. You've got more confidence than me.'

'You've got loads but don't realise it. Look, mate, I know it can't be easy after Di, starting again, but you've got a lot to offer a woman. And I don't just mean your colossal fortune.'

'Yeah. And as I mentioned last time we met, what if she finds out about that? She'll act different around me, bound to. Anyone would. Might decide all of a sudden that she wants to marry me and have my babies.'

'Babies?' John laughs. 'She might have left that a little late.' He drains his bottle and looks askance at Ben. 'I told you before, money doesn't impress her. She's down to earth, a real good egg. But to be honest, if you think she's a shallow gold-digger out for what she can get, then it's probably for the best that you leave her the hell alone. She's been hurt before, as you know. I wouldn't want to see that happen again.'

Ben realises he's talked out of turn. John's so rarely snippy with him. He feels like a proper shit to imagine Lowena as out for what she can get. Truth is, Ben's not sure if he can trust anyone. How can a person not be affected by that amount of money in some way? It's only human. Ben always tries to put himself in other people's shoes. And he knows if he was dating someone who had millions of

AMANDA JAMES

pounds in the bank, then he'd be affected by it. It would change the way he reacted to her, wouldn't it? Or maybe he wasn't as nice as Lowena. Who knows? So what now? He either tries again properly with Lowena, or he stays away from her, and women in general, for ever. Full stop. Ben would like a normal relationship based on how someone feels about him as a person, without the complications of his wealth encroaching on that. But is that even possible now?

He turns back to his friend. 'I'm sorry, John. I know you're right. Lowena's lovely. She's the first woman I've even considered starting something with since Di... It's not easy to decide what to do, that's all.'

John squeezes his arm. 'Hey, I get it. I do. But why should she find out about the money? It won't come from me. And you said that apart from me, there's just your kids who know the truth. You can get to know her properly, and tell her about the dosh only when you're sure it's working.'

Ben's inclination is to always be honest and upfront about things, but John's got a point. He's about to answer, when he sees Lowena making a beeline for them along the rickety path. 'She's coming over,' he whispers to John. But John's already standing up.

'Yeah, so now's your chance. I'll make myself scarce.'

'Hi, Ben, having a good time?' Lowena says as she stands over him, a hand shielding her eyes from the angling sun.

He stands, folds his arms, then thinks that might look defensive, so he unfolds them again and puts his hands on his hips. But then that could look aggressive, so he shoves

140

his hands in his trouser pockets and tries his best smile. 'Great, thanks. This garden is everything you said it was and more.'

'Thanks. It is rather wonderful, and it will be even more wonderful after today. Isn't it brilliant that all these people are here mucking in?' Lowena turns, tosses her chestnut curls over her shoulder and gesticulates at everyone. 'Look at this crowd, people from different walks of life, ages and personalities all working the land together. Perfect.'

As she's talking, Ben can't take his eyes from one particular member of the crowd right now and thinks she's quite perfect too. The sun's picking out a few lighter threads in her hair, her curvy figure is accentuated by a floaty soft-green top, nipped in by an elasticated waist, that complements her eyes, and the tight blue jeans certainly accentuate her... Oh God. Has she caught him ogling her bum? Ben turns his face into the salt breeze to cool his cheeks, points over to where Callum and Jack are at work and says, 'It is, I agree. The boys are in their element, and there's a great community vibe going on.'

'Yeah. The boys are lovely. Thanks so much for asking them to help. And sorry I was a bit sniffy about it at first.' Lowena gives him a smile and Ben has an urge to kiss that full, perfectly shaped mouth. 'I felt protective of my garden, until I realised gardens are for sharing. My mum always used to say that the power of nature, growing things, nurturing, is so therapeutic. Necessary to the well-being of all of us really. We sometimes don't realise how important being close to nature is. Some of us aren't lucky enough to have a garden either.' Lowena opens her arms wide and chuckles. 'Certainly not one as fabulous as mine. And I'm definitely no expert, but I'll learn from my friends.'

'You will. And don't apologise. I totally understand what you mean – though I'm hopeless at gardening, hence the pasty and beer corner.' He holds up his empty bottle with a sheepish grin. 'I only have some shrubs around a patio at mine – it's very uninspiring. I've been thinking of getting another house nearer the sea, so I'll choose one with a better garden.'

'Lovely. Well, if you're wondering what you can be doing, I'm sure Anna will instruct you on the art of weed pulling. I'm going to do a bit of that now too, if you want to join me?' She stretches past him to collect the empty beer bottles from the wall and an intoxicating waft of perfume finds Ben's nostrils.

Ben does want to join her. He can't think of anything better. *Do it now while nobody is around before she walks away. Ask her out. Go on. Do it!* Swallowing down a lump of apprehension wrapped in a coating of fear, he begins, 'Lowena. I was wondering if—'

'Bloody hell,' she says at the same time, waggling the beer bottles in his face. 'I forgot to pay you for the booze I asked you to get earlier. I meant to ask how much it was when you came in, but I was busy and distracted at the time.'

Great. That went well. 'Oh, forget it. It wasn't much.'

Lowena's beautiful sea-glass eyes grow round and she shakes her head. 'Two packs of beer and three bottles of wine isn't nothing.'

'Call it a house-warming. Or a garden-warming.'

'That's very kind, Ben, but I couldn't.'

Ben thinks she looks like an earnest kitten. A very cute earnest kitten. Hmm. What was he saying to John about sexist comments? 'Seriously, it doesn't matter.'

'Look, I know you're hardly strapped for cash, but I always pay my way.'

What the hell? Alarm bells strike up a discord in his ears and the cute kitten image scampers away up the garden path. 'What do you mean by me not being strapped for cash?' His tone is accusatory, but he's not in the mood to be polite.

Lowena's mouth turns down at the corners and a puzzled frown knits her brow. Her tone matches his. 'Eh? Well, I mean that it seems you don't have to worry about money much, you know, with you donating the barn and the way you help out financially with the youth projects and stuff. I just assumed you were... comfortable?'

Ben places his hands on his hips. Is she hiding something? Does she know about his money? 'What have you heard?'

'Pardon? I've heard nothing.'

'Yeah, you must have.' If John's told Anna, she'll have told Lowena. Damn him!

She takes a step back and folds her arms. 'Ben, I have *no* idea what you're on about. You told me the first time we met you had an inheritance, so that's why you were able to take early retirement and do something that really made you happy.' Lowena looks at him with concern, but he doesn't let his frown slip. 'Look, I can see I've offended you, but I honestly didn't mean to.' Her eyes look a bit teary, but he doesn't care.

'If you say so.'

'What's that supposed to mean?' She blinks her eyes furiously and sets her jaw.

Ben thinks about what to say next. He could confront her properly, ask her exactly what she knows about his finances, or he could just walk off and forget the whole thing. And definitely forget any romantic notions he'd had about this woman in the first place. She might be genuine, but there's something nagging at him. His money is obviously at the forefront of her mind, or why mention his inheritance? What if he was right after all? And John's certainly not heard the end of this. No. It was all a stupid idea anyway. He'd be better off by himself.

'Nothing. Forget it,' he says, and strides off to talk to Callum and Jack. Maybe he can convince them to leave early, because he wants to get as far away from Lowena as possible.

Chapter Twelve

Lowena's in her shed pretending to sort some gardening tools while trying not to cry. Everyone outside is having a great time, all mucking in together – even Janet is pulling a few weeds. But now, because of Ben, her day's ruined. She can't understand what the hell is wrong with him. They had been getting along really well, hadn't they? He'd being doing the half-moon smile, and looking at her with longing in his eyes... or was she misinterpreting the signs as usual? No. There *had* been the same atmosphere between them as in the library that day. So, what went wrong? It was obviously when she'd mentioned his money. But it was no secret – hell, he'd told her about it himself the first time they'd met to discuss the library barn.

Lowena puts down a pair of secateurs and sits down on an upturned bucket. She'd told herself before and she'd have to tell herself again. This crush or whatever it is has to stop. The idea that he could be simply a wonderful friend is just a lie that her brain lectures her heart about. Her heart appears to listen, takes notes even, but then throws itself at Ben whenever they meet. But he's making her miserable, and today shouldn't be a day for misery. It's a day for joy and laughter. Someone comes in the door behind her and Lowena rubs her eyes, jumps up and turns round, hoping her face doesn't look like a puffy old tomato.

'Hey, Lowena, what's wrong?' Hayley asks. The puffy tomato face was a giveaway then. Hayley pulls Lowena to her and gives her a big hug, which is enough to set the tears off again.

'Oh nothing. I'm being silly.'

Holding her at arm's length, Hayley looks into her eyes and says, 'Whatever it is, it's not silly. Sit down and tell me about it.'

Lowena pulls a tissue from her sleeve and blows her nose. Then she sits back down on the bucket and heaves a sigh. Hayley sits cross-legged on the floor in front of her and does an encouraging smile. 'Okay, it's Ben. Again.' She gives a little laugh. 'That rhymes.' Lowena tells Hayley all about the argument and her total bafflement over his behaviour.

Hayley fiddles thoughtfully with the beads in her plaits throughout and purses her lips. 'I'm buggered if I know the answer to this one, Lo. Maybe he doesn't like people mentioning his money... but what did he mean by asking you what you'd heard?'

'I have no idea. Maybe there's more to his money than meets the eye.'

'What?'

'Again, I don't know. So, that's me done now with him. It's too hurtful and the rest of my life is so positive right now. New friends, a great job and this wonderful house and garden. Ben can bugger off. Been there, done that, etcetera.'

'Hmm.' Hayley's olive eyes narrow knowingly. 'I've been wondering what happened to "I just want to be friends, I'm happy on my own"?'

Lowena sighs. 'Yeah, I know what I said. And I did mean it at the time, but whenever Ben appears, I get a skyful of butterflies showing up in my belly, and all ideas of friendship go out the window.'

'But that obviously means you like him. Why don't you go and talk to him? Find out exactly how he feels?'

'No way.' Lowena instinctively knows that it would end badly if she did. She's too emotional for one thing, and her brain is winning over her heart right now. 'We will stay as friends, in fact not even friends if he carries on being such a Jekyll and Hyde character. I can't be doing with it.'

Hayley smiles. 'Let's just see how it goes. Maybe things will take their course without any input from you.' Then she glances through the door and does a little wave at someone.

Lowena follows her gaze. 'Ah, waving at Dan, eh? Now that's a *proper* romance in the making, and no mistake, Ms Hayley Porter.' She giggles and gives Hayley a playful push on the shoulder.

Hayley grins. 'I wouldn't go that far but...' She covers her face and speaks through her fingers. 'Promise you'll keep this to yourself?'

'Yes, of course.'

'We have seen each other – a date, if you like.' Hayley looks at her friend for a reaction.

'Ooh, that's great! You are perfect together.'

Hayley holds both palms up to Lowena. 'Hey, steady on. It was just one date.'

'But there'll be others. *I can feel it in me water.*' Lowena affects a broad Cornish accent just like her gran used to have, and laughs. She's so thrilled for her friend, but a tiny part of her wishes she had the same relationship with someone who cared. More than a tiny bit, if she were honest. 'And he's like a puppy dog with you. I saw him worshipping you from afar when you were painting earlier.'

'Oh, stop it.' Hayley's colour comes up and she flaps a hand in front of her face a few times.

'Aw, well I'm thrilled for you, mate. Couldn't be happier.'

'Early days, but thanks, Lo. I think it might work out with any luck. We are quite different, but we make each other laugh and we have some shared interests too.' Hayley gives a little shake of her head. 'Apart from bloody fishing. Dan was on about us going the other day, but I hate to think of those poor little fish flopping about in a bucket or whatever, and then being bashed on the head. Turns my stomach.'

Lowena laughs and then suddenly remembers her dad's old basket. Dan might want it – beats it languishing in the shed unused and gathering dust. She tells Hayley to mention it to Dan. 'If he wants the basket, tell him to grab it before he leaves.'

'Are you sure? It was your dad's.'

'Yeah. I couldn't bear to throw it out when I cleared Mum's place, but if I know it's going to a good home, that's great. Dad would have wanted it to be used.'

'Thanks, I'll mention it.' Then Hayley notices the Tintagel box on a low shelf and points to it. 'That's a gorgeous box. So delicately carved.' She gets up and goes over to it, picks it up and traces her fingers over the grooves of the tree inlaid into the wood.

'Yeah. That's the magic box I told you I made a wish on, about "finding the one". Guess it didn't come true after all.' Lowena couldn't believe how sad that thought made her. Stupid, given it was just an old box wrapped in a few old wives' tales. 'Why don't you make one?'

Hayley looks at her. 'What? A wish?'

'Yeah. For you and Dan.'

'Nah. Seems daft.'

'Yeah, you're probably right. It's only got a tiny bit of dust left in it anyway.' Lowena goes to take the box and put it back on the shelf.

'Err, not so fast,' Hayley says, her eyes twinkling. 'It can't hurt, can it?'

Lowena smiles and tells Hayley about her mum making a wish on it for a baby after trying for so many years to conceive, and Lowena was the result. 'She called me her miracle baby.'

'Aw, that's so lovely. Okay.' Hayley closes her eyes and holds the box to her chest. 'Here goes.' After a few moments she smiles and hands the box to Lowena. Then she nods through the door where Wendy and Nigel are chasing about the garden. Wendy's been snipping back the hedge with some clippers and now she's shrieking like a banshee, pretending to snip Nigel's bottom with them.

'They're having a great time by the looks of it,' Lowena says, with a chuckle.

'Yeah. Mervyn was telling me that they went to school together, and had a bit of a teenage fling. After school they drifted apart and married other people, but it didn't work out for either of them. So now they're divorced, met again at my talk at the library, and look to be rediscovering their youth.'

'How sweet. It's heart-warming to see people having fun together.'

Hayley smiles as she watches Wendy and Nigel rolling on the ground play-fighting like a couple of kids. 'It is. Maybe love grows in gardens too.'

'Maybe it does,' Lowena says, following Hayley out into the sunlight. To herself she adds silently, *For others, but not for me.*

Janet's done enough skivvying and gardening for now. Bloody slave labour. God knows why she agreed to come to this 'fun thing' with Milly, and it's about time she had a rest and another bite to eat. She washes her hands at the kitchen sink and considers having a bit of a snoop around the rest of the cottage, to see what she can find out about this Lowena. Because Janet would bet the farm that she's not all sweetness and light. That's all a front. There's more to her than meets the eye.

Bugger. That Anna woman has just come in to wash her hands too, so there's no chance of that. Janet forces a smile as Anna says thanks to her for handing the towel over. Then she grabs a pasty and a bottle of beer and legs it down to where a few garden chairs sit overlooking the view.

Thankfully, nobody else is in that area right now, so she won't have to make any more small talk. Hayley the 'artist' has left her easel at last. That one definitely knows how to avoid work, Janet thinks, as she flops down on a chair and sinks her teeth into the crumbly, rich pastry. As she chews, she glances at the painting on the easel to her left. A watercolour by the look of it. Such as it is… Daubs of green and blue, wiggles and blobs. Janet's great niece could do better, and she's only ten.

'Hi, Janet, enjoying the view?' Mervyn asks, drawing a chair up alongside her and plonking himself down with a huff and a groan. 'By 'eck, my old knees will feel this tomorrow.'

Marvellous. Now she has to make more conversation, when all she wants is a rest and a snack. Through a mouthful of pasty she says, 'Yes, maybe you should go home for a lie down. A man of your age doesn't want to do too much.'

'A man of my age?' Mervyn raises his bushy white brows at her in surprise. 'I'm not much older than you.'

He bloody well is. 'You must be six years or so?'

'I'm eighty.'

Janet sniffs. 'Six years, as I thought.'

'Always wondered how old you were. Now I know.'

The crafty twinkle in his grey eyes tells Janet she's been duped. Not that she could give two hoots about who knows her age. 'Hmm. Bully for you.'

'I could do with a sit down too.' A voice that Janet can't quite place says behind them. Oh, good. More folk to disturb her peace.

'Pull up a chair, Zelah, this is the oldies' club.'

Zelah. Yes, of course. Marvellous.

'Less of the "old", I'm younger than you, Mervyn.'

'Not by much, I'll bet.' Mervyn does a conspiratorial wink at Janet which she deflects with an eye roll.

'I'm seventy-six.'

'He's four years older then,' Janet says, to steal Mervyn's thunder. 'And I'm seventy-four. Just so we all know, like.'

Zelah laughs and drags another chair over. She sits down next to Janet and pulls a sandwich and cake wrapped in a napkin out of her huge canvas sack which passes for a bag. Might as well have a pillowcase on a bit of rope, Janet thinks. 'What a wonderful place,' Zelah says with a sigh and gazes out across the ocean.

'Hmm. I bet it's cold in winter though.' Janet takes a swallow of beer and gestures out to sea with the bottle. 'What with the wind whistling off that, right under your front door.' She thinks Zelah does a bit of a huff at her comment. But it could just be her taking a bite of sandwich.

'Nice work if you can get it,' Milly says, walking over to stand in front of them. 'What happened to weeding and chopping back, eh?' She laughs and leans over to rest her hand on the back of Janet's chair.

'Better door than a window,' Janet grumbles and makes a show of craning her neck around Milly's body to see the view.

'Oh, stop moaning. I'll join you for a minute if I can find a chair.'

'There's one next to the shed,' Mervyn says. 'Shall I get it for you?'

'No, stay put, Mervyn. A man of eighty needs his rest,' Janet says with a wink.

'I'll be back with the chair and a snack in a mo.' Milly eyes the food Zelah and Janet have. 'Can I get something for you, Mervyn?'

'A pasty if there is one, please.' Then he goes after Milly to collect the chair anyway.

'I had a pasty earlier, and lovely they are too,' Zelah says. 'But all this gardening and chatting makes me hungry.' She glances at Janet's full cheeks. 'You too, eh?'

Swallowing the mouthful, Janet replies, 'I was a bit peckish, but I can eat for England and not put an ounce on.'

'It wouldn't hurt if you did. What with you being so tall and slim, like,' Zelah says with a smile.

Janet can't decide if she's being complimented or criticised, so keeps quiet.

Milly comes back, carrying a tea tray with a selection of sweet and savoury food and a pot of tea with four cups. She nods at the food and sets the tray on the ground. 'Just in case anyone wants anything else.' She straightens up and puts her hands in the small of her back and looks at them all. 'Cuppa?'

Janet swills the last of her beer and nods with the rest of

them. And they all sit in companionable silence, apart from commenting on the view and the pleasant weather for a few moments, while drinking tea and munching. Janet's still munching too. Cake mostly.

'Those two youngsters, Callum and Jack, are wonderful,' Zelah says. 'They know so much about gardening already, and they've had such a poor start in life. It's a fantastic project that Ben has up and running.'

'Hmm,' Janet says, not at all taken in by all that malarkey.

'What's "hmm" mean?' Zelah asks, a little sharply.

Janet lowers her voice and looks over her shoulder to check that no one can hear. 'It means that I don't trust these young offenders. How do we know what they're really like? They could pretend to be nice. You know, chatting, finding out about us, where we live, if we're well off, live alone and everything. Then when they've got enough information, they come and burgle us. I refused to speak to them earlier.' Janet folds her arms and sniffs. 'Just walked off as if I'd not heard. They won't fool me.' Zelah looks ready to interrupt so she holds up a finger. 'And I'm mentioning them to the Neighbourhood Watch. Better to be safe than sorry.'

'For goodness' sake, woman,' Zelah hisses. 'They aren't young offenders; the group's for disaffected youth. Ones that have been on the edge of trouble maybe, or struggling at home or school. And even if they *had* been young offenders, they're here to help their community now. Hearts of gold, the pair of them.' She bangs her cup down on the arm of her chair and glares at Janet.

Janet's shocked by the fire in that glare. Zelah's normally

kind blue eyes are chips of steel right now. Well, she can bugger off. 'So *you* say. I prefer to be less trusting than some. I've been taken in by people before – once bitten.'

Zelah huffs at her and gives her head a disparaging shake, which annoys Janet even more. The rest of them shake their heads too, so she continues, 'And that Lowena's no better than she ought to be. She's hiding something, I reckon. I only came here because Milly wanted me to come with her.' Janet folds her arms and stares calmly out at the far blue horizon, waiting for the inevitable barrage of questions.

'What on earth are you on about?' Milly asks.

Janet turns to face her and opens her mouth, but Mervyn gets there first. 'Lowena? Hiding something?' he asks, with a deep frown.

'That's nonsense!' Zelah says, her eyes glittering with anger.

'It's not nonsense,' Janet says, glaring at them all, warming to the fight. 'Tell me how an unmarried woman of her age can afford this place, on a part-time pittance? How she can afford to splash the cash on pasties, booze and everything too? She's in it with that Ben, I reckon, and those scoundrel boys he has in his so-called schemes. He's like a modern-day Fagin and she's bloody Nancy!'

The rest of them all protest at once, and a stern voice from behind her asks, 'Are you talking about Lowena?'

Janet swivels round to see Anna, arms folded, her eyes the twins of Zelah's. Ha! She doesn't scare Janet. 'Yes, I am, if you must know.'

'What an awful thing to say about a wonderful woman

who always does her best for everyone. She threw this garden party to bring everyone together, to try to forge a sense of community, and your malicious gossip can't be further from the truth.'

'Well said,' Zelah says. 'And those lovely boys are far from scoundrels!'

'I'm shocked at you, Janet,' Mervyn says.

'And I'm appalled. You've said some pretty nasty things in your time, Janet, but this…' Milly, flabbergasted, raises her hands and lets them fall to her knees with a slap.

Janet feels like a naughty child in class, but won't be bullied into just accepting this rubbish. 'You'll all be sorry when I'm proved right,' she says, avoiding their accusing eyes.

'If you think so little of our host, why are you here?' Anna asks, with quiet anger.

'I came with Milly. She's daft enough to be robbed blind if I'm not here to protect her.'

Milly's mouth drops open and her soft brown eyes shine with unshed tears. 'You've gone too far this time, Janet. If you don't mend your ways, I want nothing more to do with you.' Milly picks up her bag and hurries away up the garden.

Mervyn says nothing, just stands up and follows Milly. Anna does the same. And Zelah stands up and glowers down at Janet, the sea breeze whipping her hair about her head. 'You need to get your act together, madam. You're carrying the weight of so much anger and bitterness, it's a wonder you can actually walk.' Then her expression softens and she twists her steely curls up into a clip. 'But, if you

need to talk to someone about it, I have good listening ears.'
She nods once and follows the others.

Alone with only her anger, the view and her thoughts
for company, Janet ponders on Zelah's words. Who the hell
does she think she is? Saying those things to her? Janet's not
angry and bitter all the time. Just looking out for law-
abiding citizens. She tells it like it is. Not like bloody Zelah,
floating about like some latter-day hippy, all wise and
gentle-natured. Talking about healing herbs and rubbish. It
suddenly strikes Janet that Zelah might be in on it with Ben,
Lowena and those two teenagers. She might be supplying
that wacky baccy grown in her garden – or in her house
actually. Janet's read in the Sunday papers about cannabis
rooms full of lights and heaters. She certainly wouldn't put
it past Zelah. Nobody would suspect a woman of her age
doing that, would they? The perfect cover. Maybe those
young wasters sell it for her and take a cut. And maybe
that's why she moved from Penzance – because the
neighbours suspected her.

'You all right on your own here, lovely?' A woman with
wavy brown hair and a friendly smile steps in front of Janet,
blocking her view. Janet vaguely remembers her from the
library talk and she's seen her larking about here with a
man, chasing him round. Shameful for a woman of her age.
And why do people call each other 'lovely' nowadays?
Shop assistants do it, people on the phone, now this woman
here. They don't know each other from Adam. Too familiar
for Janet's liking.

'Yes, thank you,' Janet says and turns looking pointedly
past the woman out to sea. Hopefully she'll take the hint.

But the woman sits in one of the vacated chairs. Marvellous.

'My name's Wendy. You're Janet, aren't you?'

'Hmm.'

'It's been a lovely afternoon, hasn't it? Great garden.'

Janet's in no mood for small talk, and it's about time everyone knew about what's going on here. 'Hmm, not really. Not sure of the company, to be honest.'

'Oh?'

'Yeah. That Lowena, I reckon she's a bit shifty to say the least; probably up to criminal activity with that Ben fellow and those teenagers. But I won't go into detail. Hold onto your purse is all I'll say.' Janet folds her arms and twists her mouth to the side. 'And that Zelah, well. The least said about *her* the better.'

Wendy frowns and looks concerned. 'Really? I don't know Lowena very well, but I can't see her doing what you said. And what's Zelah done?'

'Apart from swanning about as if she's at Woodstock? Plenty, I think. She's into all this herb stuff. I think there's particular herbs she's interested in.' Janet taps the side of her nose. 'Illegal ones if you get my meaning.'

'My God, you've done it now.' Milly's anguished voice comes from behind. Janet turns to see her old friend arm in arm with Zelah, whose mask of horror tells Janet they have both obviously overheard everything she's said to Wendy.

'Done what?' Janet says, trying to brave it out. She's done nothing wrong really, has she? Okay. Maybe she ought to have investigated further before voicing her suspicions, but...

'You know what!' Milly snaps. 'We came back over to talk to you, to try to see why you're saying these horrid things, but that's it now. I'm leaving and I don't want you to follow me. We are finished, Janet.' She jabs a stabby finger at Janet. 'No longer friends. And do *not* try to phone me!' Zelah says nothing, just gives Janet a sorrowful look, then the two women turn and walk away.

Wendy makes some excuse and goes too, and Janet feels as if her heart's been wrenched out and chucked into the Atlantic. She's never seen Milly so angry with her in all their sixty-nine years of friendship. Releasing a slow breath, Janet stands up and brushes down her cream linen trousers. There's a stain on the thigh – must have been the chocolate cake. Milly has that special stuff that gets stains out; she'll ask her—

Oh. No, she can't now. Annoying tears press at the back of her eyes and she angrily scrubs them away. Time to leave this awful place. Gathering her things, she pushes past Lowena and Hayley as they come out of the shed and strides into the lane. It's not far to walk home, and things will look better tomorrow. Milly will come round in the end. She always does.

Chapter Thirteen

I t's been quiet in the library this afternoon. Lowena puts it down to the lovely April weather, and the weekend tomorrow. Sensible people will be out walking on the beach and playing in the sunshine. Though a bit jealous, in a way, Lowena's glad to be in the peace and cool of the library barn. The morning had been pretty full on. Rhyme Time with the toddler group was lively, to say the least. She still had 'Wind the Bobbin Up' as an earworm, and if the wheels on that bus went round her head one more time, she'd scream. Still, being busy had stopped her from dwelling on Saturday's garden party disaster. Anna and Hayley had pointed out that the only disaster was Janet and Ben, and that the rest of the time had been wonderful. They were right, Lowena supposed, but it still hurt.

Lowena pushes a little trolley of returned books to place back on their correct shelves down the aisle. While her mind is mainly on the task, little tendrils of sadness keep twisting themselves up into her consciousness, trying to spread miserable thoughts about Ben and Janet. Lowena sighs. The trick is to think of all the positive points of last weekend. Everyone, apart from the two unmentionables, had really enjoyed themselves, got to know each other better and the garden had been practically transformed in such a short time. Many hands really did make light work. Zelah had bonded with Callum and Jack, Milly too. Mervyn had been in his element, giving advice and encouragement and Anna and John had learned loads from Zelah about herb growing, as had Lowena. She is overjoyed with the new plants that had somehow grown unaided in the herb patch against all odds, and the dahlias of course.

Lowena smiles as she replaces *Pride and Prejudice*, one of the most borrowed books in the library. Love never gets old in books, or in real life, it seems. Romantically, Nigel and Wendy seem to be going from strength to strength, as do Hayley and Dan. Hayley had told Lowena, after everyone had left the garden, that she felt the Tintagel box really did have the magic of King Arthur, or perhaps Merlin, because Dan had taken her hand as she'd been painting the view, and told her she made him happier than he'd been for a long time. 'It was only ten minutes after I'd wished on the box – so it must be magic,' she'd said with a wink.

Lowena isn't at all sure about that, unless it's just her who doesn't get to benefit. So much for the legendary words – whoever had the box would be blessed with a beautiful garden, bountiful crops and love of their fellow man. Lowena hacks back a tendril of misery and tells herself off. She *does* have a beautiful garden, bountiful crops and love of her fellow man. Just not Ben's and Janet's.

Lowena had been totally shocked when Anna and Zelah had filled her in about Janet. How could the woman have said such awful things about her? About Ben, the boys and Zelah? Lowena had known the woman was a proper curmudgeon, but such malicious gossip was one step beyond.

Back at her desk, Lowena checks the computer to see if any books are overdue and tries to keep her mind tendril-free. It's absolutely futile agonising over others' behaviour. There is nothing she can do to control it, but she can control her response to it. They both needed putting right out of her mind. Janet is a sad, bitter woman who deserves pity, really. Lowena might find some from somewhere, eventually, but she's fresh out right now. And Ben? Ben is a man with whom she thought she'd made a connection. Turns out she was wrong, and that is that. He obviously has some issues, but Lowena isn't the one to iron them out. She has her own issues, thank you very much, and they are best left unanalysed if she wants a happy life. She was happy before he came along, and she'd be happy now he's gone again.

Humming 'Wind the Bobbin Up', Lowena wanders into the kitchen to make a cuppa. Her spirits are on the rise and she's successfully batted away any more negative thoughts. Perhaps tomorrow she'll walk to 'her bench' by the ocean and have a little picnic.

'Lowena. Can we talk?'

Whipping round, she sees Ben in the doorway and nearly drops the milk carton 'I... er...' She's so shocked her words won't cooperate.

Ben tries a half-moon smile but it doesn't work as he's

obviously nervous, evidenced by the raking of his hands through his dark curls and the shifting of his weight from one foot to the other. He thrusts the palms of his hands at her and says, 'Look, I know you must be angry with me, and rightly so. Hell, I'm angry with me. In fact, I've been furious with myself since Saturday.' Again, the half-moon, which stays a little longer, before it's obscured by the tortured, dark clouds in his eyes. 'And I wouldn't blame you if you told me to "do one" as the lads say, but I hope you won't. I need to explain my awful, irrational behaviour. Will you listen?'

Lowena leans her hand on the sink for support. Will she? She doesn't know. What would be the point, as she's not sure she could actually trust him again? How does she know that he won't switch from Dr Jekyll to Mr Hyde again, just when she least expects it? Ben's wearing the expression of an expectant child, a child who knows he's done wrong and wants forgiveness. He also looks like an incredibly attractive man in his salmon-pink shirt that's open at the neck, revealing the beginnings of dark chest hair. She's drawn into his hazel-green-flecked eyes and has to give her head a little shake to get her thoughts in order. Taking a breath, she says, 'I'll give you a few minutes, but I am quite busy.'

'Oh, I didn't mean here. This is your place of work and I've just turned up unannounced. No, I'd like to explain over a drink, if that's okay.'

Is he for real? 'You suggested that once before, remember? Didn't happen.'

'I know. I know. And that's my fault. All of it is.' He

swallows so hard his Adam's apple bobs. 'Please, Lowena.' Ben folds his arms for a second, then puts his hands on his hips, until finally he lets them hang by his sides like a couple of pendulums.

Lowena is divided. Does she need any more upset? But he does look contrite. As she's about to answer he interrupts.

'I'll beg if I have to. On my knees.'

He makes as if to do just that, until Lowena holds a hand up. 'No. That won't be necessary. Okay, where and when?'

Ben's dark clouds are swept away by a sunlit smile. 'Tonight? Here in St Merryn or nearer you?'

'Here's fine.' Lowena knows if she has to drive, she won't be tempted to have more than one drink. 'How about The Cornish Arms at seven-thirty?'

'Perfect. We could have a bite to eat too?'

Lowena sighs and folds her arms. 'Don't push it.'

Lowena's sitting at a corner table wondering if the yellow dress with red poppies of her mum's was a good idea. She'd been meaning to wear it since she cleared her mum's things, before she'd sold the house, but until tonight, she'd never got around to it. As she idly searched along the rail in her wardrobe earlier, it had 'spoken' to her, as Anna often said about clothes. At home, the dress had seemed the perfect choice to show Ben what kind of a woman she was. Bold, confident and sassy. But here in the pub, all she feels is a bit showy-offy and loud. A couple of women in their thirties and done up to the nines, chatting at the bar, flick a disparaging eye over her once or twice. So Lowena sits well back in her seat and folds her arms over the bright flowers on her chest. Perhaps she's more of a shrinking violet than a bold poppy after all.

The clock on the wall ticks down to seven-thirty and Lowena shuffles in her seat. Why did she get here fifteen minutes early? It feels more like fifteen hours since she walked in. The soda and lime she's been nursing is almost finished, and she might need a wee very soon. Maybe she has time to go quickly before Ben gets here, otherwise she'll be shuffling in her seat while he's explaining the reason he behaved like a pantomime villain last week. While she's in the loo, Lowena can check her hair's still in the tortoiseshell clip properly – it feels like it's dangling off – and make sure her poppy-red lipstick isn't on her teeth as well. Grabbing her bag, she stands up, just as Ben walks in looking like a guy in an advert for aftershave. Tall, lithe, his eyes cat-like, hair ruffled by the fresh night air, he might even be walking in slow motion. When he sees her, he raises a hand and points at the bar with a questioning eyebrow.

Lowena raises a hand back, points to the soda and lime on the table, then at the Ladies' sign and rushes towards it. #MimeArtistsRUs. She hopes he got the message and isn't following her. In the loo she wishes she'd not agreed to come. Everything feels wrong, awkward – especially the dress. It looks like she's trying too hard, and that's the last thing she wants Ben to think. He's the one that should be trying too hard after the way he behaved. Lowena knows she would have felt comfier dressed in her black jeans and any one of her smart tops. Too late now though. While she's sorting her hair out, which has indeed escaped the clip at the back, in come the two women who were looking down their noses at her a little while ago. Through the mirror, Lowena notices one nudge the other and they openly both give her the once-over again. Well, really!

'I hope you don't mind me saying about your dress,' the one with platinum-blonde hair and red lips says. Lowena dreads to think what she's going to say, but paints on a questioning smile. 'Only me and my friend Julie here couldn't help commenting on it when we saw you in the bar, could we, Jules?'

Julie, the sharp-faced, dark-haired, I-made-my-eyelashes-from-a-spider's-legs one, nods in agreement. 'We couldn't, Kayleigh. It is just fabulous!'

It is? Lowena tries to stop her jaw from hitting the sink.

'So retro! Is it vintage?' Kayleigh asks, taking a step forward to peer more closely.

'Erm. Well, yes. It was my mum's and she wore it in the 60s.'

Julie nods. 'I knew it. That's quality, that is. Pure quality.'

'Yeah. You look like a bloody film star in that,' Kayleigh says. 'Doesn't she, Jules?'

'She bloody does, Kay. What with her dark curls and red lipstick. And those stunning green eyes. A bit like Jaqueline Bisset in the 60s. I did a film studies course at college,' Julie adds, with pride in her voice.

Both women look at Lowena expectantly, big smiles on

their faces. Well, how wrong can a person be about wearing this dress? She feels her spirits lifting almost as fast as her confidence. 'Thanks so much, both of you. I don't really wear such bold prints, but this one just spoke to me from the back of the wardrobe.'

'It'd be at the front of mine!' Julie says with a bray of laughter.

'And mine!' Kayleigh agrees. 'If you ever want to sell it, I'm your woman. Julie and I run a little retro boutique in Padstow called Days Gone By. Pop in some time – I'm sure you'll find something you'd like.'

'I'm sure I would,' Lowena says as the women wave goodbye and go into their respective cubicles. 'Thanks again!'

Lowena walks back into the bar a different woman. The shrinking violet has gone, and bold, confident and sassy is back. It's ridiculous how much those few compliments have changed her mood. She shouldn't have to be validated; nevertheless, those kind words were very welcome. Now, Lowena can face Ben as the woman she intended to be when she first set out that evening. There he is, sitting at her table. Next to her glass of soda and lime is a large glass of red wine and he's taking a sip from a pint of beer. The wine's a bit presumptuous of him, isn't it?

He stands up when he sees her walking towards him and his eyes appreciatively sweep over her 'Hi, Lowena. You look absolutely gorgeous.'

Unusually, Lowena doesn't experience a rush of heat to her cheeks because of his compliment and admiring glances, but instead feels calm and in control. 'Thanks, Ben.

You don't look so bad yourself.' She sits opposite and nods at the wine. 'I don't remember asking for that.'

His smile drops. 'Oh. I remember that's what you were drinking on Saturday and went for it. I can get you something else if you'd like?'

'No, this is fine. I had decided on no alcohol tonight as I'm driving, but one will be okay, I think.' She says 'Cheers' and takes a sip. Ben smiles and then an immediate silence settles between them, as thick and impenetrable as mist on Bodmin Moor.

Lowena's about to say something inane about the weather to break the deadlock, but Ben beats her to it. 'Okay, I'm just gonna spill it all, come right to the point and hope that you'll understand. It will be a miracle if you do, to be honest, because I'm not sure *I* understand me sometimes. But I had a talk to John after the garden party, and we hammered it out until I had something resembling a semi-coherent theory. That okay?'

She's glad he's riding on the elephant in the room, sooner rather than later, and settles back in her seat. Half of her is dying to know his story, but the other is running out the door. What if it's something really awful? Is she ready for a dark kind of revelation? Lowena makes her lips form an encouraging smile and she says, 'Fire away. I'm listening.'

Ben heaves a sigh and folds his arms. Then unfolds them, picks up a beer mat and turns it round and round with his two forefingers on the table. 'So, you're the first woman I've been interested in getting to know since Diana died,' he says to the beer mat. Then he looks up to gauge her reaction. Lowena nods and makes her face neutral. 'Until I met you, I'd resigned myself to living alone for the rest of my life. I mean, I'd been very lucky. I'd had many happy years with the love of my life, so I thought there was no way the universe was going to be that helpful in future. But turns out I was wrong.' He holds his hands up, and his eyes go wide. 'Oh, don't get me wrong. I'm not saying I'm in love with you or anything, before you run out screaming, but I am very attracted to you and think you're a very lovely person. Someone whom I'd like to get to know better.'

Lowena gives him a genuine smile this time. She finds his honesty refreshing and starts to relax properly for the first time that evening. And he deserves something in return. 'Okay. I'm with you so far. And I'm glad you want to get to know me. I must admit I felt the same about you when we had lunch that time in the library. But I pretended I didn't. You see, my past can get in the way too sometimes. I'll tell you about it when you've finished your story.'

Ben nods, stops turning the beer mat and looks at Lowena the whole time he's speaking with an intensity she finds a little disconcerting, yet comforting too, as he's showing how important this all is to him. 'Right. As well as deciding not to have a relationship with anyone else, for the reasons I said, I also missed Di so much. She loved me for who I was, not what I had or did.' He laughed. 'But then, when we met, she had no choice because I had nothing. Poor as a church mouse.' He looks quizzical. 'I wonder why church mice are seen to be poorer than other mice? You'd think they'd have more access to money, wouldn't you? What with the collection plate and all.'

Lowena cracks out laughing at this. These are the kinds of thoughts she has. 'You would. Maybe the church cat takes it all.'

Ben laughs too and takes a pull on his pint. 'The thing is…' Then he stops and smacks his lips as if he's tasting the words in his mouth. 'Another reason I decided to stay single is because I have to be very careful… If I want someone to love me for who I am, not what I have, I mean. To an extent, I didn't think that would be possible anymore. You see, a year after Di died, I came into some money.' He shakes his head. 'I'm not being honest. I didn't come into some money; I won the bloody EuroMillions.'

Lowena's jaw drops, and she sucks up a dribble of wine before it slides down her chin. 'Oh… wow. I wasn't expecting that.'

'Neither was I. I couldn't believe the number of noughts on the cheque for a few days. Still have to pinch myself when I see the bank account.' Ben scrutinises Lowena's face closely.

What does she say next? She's dying to ask how much, but thinks it will be a bit rude. 'Er… well, I can see why you would be a bit wary of people.' Though in a way she couldn't, because who would actually know, if he keeps it secret?

Ben puts his head on one side and does the half-moon. 'You're the first person not to ask how much I won. Mind you, only three people know the truth.'

'It's up to you if you want to tell me,' Lowena says, taking a sip of wine. She's not playing silly games.

'It was twenty million.'

Lowena manages to keep the wine from dribbling this time, but it's a close call. 'Blimey!'

'I know. It was a shock, and I wasn't sure if it was a good shock or not. Who needs that kind of money, for God's sake? To be honest I'd not really considered winning. The lottery was just something I did. And not very often either. But in the end, I decided it was a good thing, because I gave my kids some, funded the schemes I run and left teaching, of course. It gives me so much freedom to do a hell of a lot of good in the community.'

'Yes, I can understand all that. It would have been a huge shock. Who are the three who know?'

'My kids and John. I gave him a bit of help too with his business. Not a huge amount, or Anna would have been suspicious. At first I offered him a lot more, but he said he liked to pay his way and stand on his own two feet. He also said that having a load of money might change things between him and Anna, cause arguments. Said they had a good marriage and he wanted to keep it that way. I totally got where he was coming from and told him that if he was ever in need, he'd only to say the word. I also told him he could divulge to Anna that I'd had an inheritance but not how much.' Ben stops, draws his hand across his chin and his cheeks turn a bit pink. 'That's what was wrong with me at your party. I was convinced he'd told Anna and she'd told you. It upset me so much because I really like you and I thought...' He sighs and looks at the table.

Lowena's temper is bristling for release at the thought that he imagined she was after his money. It would be a bad idea though as she can see he's contrite. However, she has to say what's on her mind. 'You thought I was after your money.' It's a statement, not a question.

Ben gives a sheepish nod. 'I did. Well, at least I thought you knew about it. Later that day I had a word with John and he told me in no uncertain terms that I was way off beam. He said he'd never betray our friendship like that, and also that even if you did know about the money, you were no gold-digger. The whole thing nearly broke our friendship and we've been mates since school. I was so ashamed at my behaviour. If I'd not been so taken with you, I'm sure I wouldn't have reacted as I did.' Ben's eyes dart to Lowena's and away. Then he clears his throat and gives her a hard stare. 'But that's no excuse. I'd be very grateful, and forever in your debt, Lowena, if you'd accept my sincerest apology.'

Despite the gravity of the situation, Lowena wants to smile because of his very earnest expression and old-fashioned turn of phrase. Managing to keep her face straight, she says, 'I'll think about it. And I do understand to an extent. But John knows me well. I have never been, nor will I ever be, impressed by money. I have no desire to be rich. All I want from life is to be happy and to help others if I can. I think you have the same goals in life – that's why we hit it off in the first place.'

'Yes. I completely get that now. I was just confused and mixed up with bits of my past hooking up with my future and the idea that I wanted to be taken at face value. I tried to put myself in your shoes. If I knew you'd won the lottery I guessed I might behave differently towards you. There'd be a big wadge of money in the space between us – blocking normality out, shaping the direction of our relationship before it had even begun.' Ben slides his eyes to hers and away. 'Plus, I didn't want to be hurt. Pathetic, I know.'

Lowena wants to give him a hug. He's being so honest and truthful, no matter how vulnerable that makes him. Maybe this can work after all? She touches his knee and smiles. 'Not at all. I can identify with that... If you like, I'll tell you my story?'

Ben shuffles in his seat and looks unsure. Then he says, 'Thing is, I might know some of it. I want to be truthful from the start... I asked John what he knew about you one night when we went out for a drink. He only told me bits and bobs, because he didn't get the full story from Anna.'

Lowena takes a sip of wine, curious to find out what he thinks he knows. 'Go on.'

'Well, I know you were serious with a guy called Rick and he went to work abroad. You stayed here... and it put you off trusting men in the future, or wanting another relationship. I hope you're not angry. But I can't sit here and pretend I don't know anything about you.'

He's honest to a fault, she'd give him that. 'Hm. That's more or less it in a nutshell. Rick didn't understand why I didn't want to leave here – the country, my parents, friends. Said I had no ambition and no dreams. Didn't I realise how much money he'd make out there? He pretty much messed my head up, as we'd been together so long.'

Bed nods slowly. 'Right. No wonder you were wary

174

about my advances.' A half-moon bashful smile lights up his face. 'If you could call them that.'

Considering how much she should reveal, Lowena smiles back and then takes the bull by the proverbial. 'I'll see your honesty and raise you a naked truth. I was wary only because I wanted to get you know you better. In the same way as you wanted to get to know me better.' Lowena takes a big gulp of her drink to muster up some courage. 'You're the first man I've really been interested in "romantically" for a very long time.'

The half-moons swell to full, and joy dances in his warm conker-coloured eyes, the little flecks of spring grass shimmering above the glow of his cheeks. 'So, we are very similar, in that you're the first one I'm interested in, and so am I for you, after a long relationship. And we're both worried about getting hurt.'

Lowena shrugs. 'Pretty much, it seems.' She's pleased they've both been able to share their feelings in such a straightforward way. And there's none of that awkwardness often present between them. Nor is there any embarrassment or doubt. For the first time Lowena feels they have moved on. Gone through the gate from a narrow and muddy footpath into a wide-open sun-speckled meadow.

They stare at each other for a few seconds and Lowena starts to get a bit hot under the collar. If she were wearing a collar of course, not this low-cut 'retro' dress. Her imagination keeps offering up a picture of her leaning across the table and brushing her lips across his sensuous mouth.

Breaking her train of thought he says, 'Can I suggest, if you're willing of course to forgive me, that we start to get to know each other on a more regular basis? Take it slow, always be honest with each other, and see where it leads?'

This is exactly what Lowena would have said, if he hadn't. 'Sounds good to me. And yes, I think I can forgive you about the gold-digger thing. Despite not caring two hoots about having loads of money, as Rick found out, I can see how maybe some people might. That essentially would affect their view of you, and your whole relationship, should you enter into one with them.' God, now who was sounding old-fashioned? Maybe she should get a fan out of her bag to cool her cheeks.

Ben stretches his hand across the table and covers hers with it. It's warm and strong and his elegant long fingers slip through hers and a little tingle starts in her wrist. Lowena gives his hand a squeeze to let him know she's happy with his 'advances'.

'Lowena, this evening has gone so much better than I thought it might. I'm over the moon that we've got everything out in the open. When can we do this again?'

An idea takes shape quickly in her mind's eye. Two people having a picnic on a bench, gazing out over an ocean vast and blue, getting to know each other under a turquoise sky dotted with seagulls. 'How about Sunday? I could make a picnic and we could go for a walk by the sea?'

He squeezes her hand and grins. 'What a brilliant idea.'

Chapter Fourteen

The elements are against Janet as she sets off for the café and baker's shop in Treyarnon. She's seen two crows flying backwards, racing each other and the stiff breeze, while her best navy and pink scarf is doing its best to blindfold her. At least she's got her new stout walking boots on. Nevertheless, Janet doesn't want to get them messed up, so she kicks a pebble out of her path and side-steps a muddy puddle. As she stomps along, she thinks again about her promise to Milly, made under duress the other day. Janet's determined to honour it, but the idea of apologising to Lowena and that crazy air-head Zelah sticks in her craw. She can't quite get her head round the fact that Zelah had made matters so much worse afterwards, telling Lowena everything that happened and then filling Milly in on it all.

Janet swallows a knot of emotion as she recalls her old friend's declaration that their friendship would not resume until she had apologised. Milly's words had reflected her cold, distant stance. Janet stared vacantly at the road in front of her but in her mind's eye she could see an image of Milly and hear her hurtful words echoing in her ears.

'I saw the very worst of you at Lowena's party, Janet.'

Milly had emphasised the word *very* and narrowed her beady brown eyes at Janet in the hardest stare, until she'd had no choice but to look away. Those eyes had made her feel like a naughty child. An unwanted child that everyone tolerated and never invited to birthday parties. Janet had considered telling Milly to bugger off and who needed her friendship anyway? Only for a second though, because unfortunately, Milly is the only friend she has. She could make more, of course, but she can't be bothered.

Janet harrumphs and kicks another pebble. Since when did giving people an honest opinion amount to being the *very* worst in a person? Aren't individuals allowed to have a point of view these days? It's all that political correctness malarkey. You have to consider everyone's feelings before you even open your mouth, in case you might offend them. God forbid that someone might be offended. How could they possibly carry on with the rest of their lives? Janet snorts. People today are too mollycoddled. In her day if you were offended, you'd say so, and give as good as you got. Folks need to toughen up a bit. Stop being snowdrops or whatever it is. No. Snowflakes, she thinks. She would have to google it to see what it actually meant. But basically, lots of people these days are a lot of bloody wimps.

The inside of the café smells like coffee, pastry and cinnamon and despite having breakfasted less than an hour ago, Janet's stomach craves an apple turnover with double cream and a pot of Earl Grey. As she closes the door behind her, a gust of wind assists the scarf in its blindfolding mission, and it isn't until she's disentangled it that she sees Lowena sitting at a table tucking into a bacon roll. Can she back out and do a runner, as the young ones say? No. She's already been spotted, and Lowena's stare is a replica of Milly's. Great. Okay, nothing for it. Order the food and ask if she can join the woman. Get the damned apology out of the way and then there's just old Hippy Drawers left to tackle.

Lowena's stare looks no less hostile as Janet walks towards her table bearing the tray of goodies. 'Hello, Lowena. I know I'm not your most favourite person right now, but if I could join you, I'd like to say I'm sorry.'

Lowena raises an eyebrow and pushes her plate to one side. 'Sure. Make yourself at home.'

Janet thinks her tone's bordering on the sarcastic. Those unusual green eyes of hers are guarded too and her normally smiley mouth is a grim line. Oh well. Here goes. 'Thanks.' Janet takes her things from the tray and leans it against the table leg, where it promptly slides to the floor with a clatter. Janet's heart is clattering too and she hates the way she's already on the back foot. The unwanted child. Sitting down, she pours her tea and takes a sip while considering how to begin. 'The thing is, Lowena... I was just thinking out loud really at yours last week. I didn't mean any harm, and I'm sorry if I upset you.' There. That was enough, even for the frailest snowflake, surely?

'Ri-ght.' Lowena draws the word out, fluffs her mass of unruly curls and gives Janet another unwavering stare.

'What you're actually saying is, you're sorry if I was upset, but you're not sorry that you said those things. You were just voicing your thoughts about me, and about Zelah too?'

Janet feels she's been drawn into a trap. 'Er, well kind of. But it *was* only my opinion.'

Lowena shakes her head and blows heavily down her nose. 'So, you think I'm in cahoots with old Fagin Ben and the boys are robbers? Zelah's a willing accomplice and supplies us with weed? And the reason you think this is because I'm a woman in my forties, who has no husband to provide for her and a house by the sea, therefore my income is obviously ill-gotten.'

Hearing it laid out like that, Janet thinks it does sound rather nasty, and if she were in Lowena's shoes she wouldn't be best pleased. But then again, Janet wouldn't be involved with anything untoward in the first place, would she? Torn between apologising again, saying she'd let her imagination run away with her, and saying *yes, that's what I thought all right, what have you got to say about it?*, Janet takes another sip of tea until she gets herself untorn. Milly is more important than a misunderstanding with a relative stranger. She says, 'I'm not sure what I thought at the time. Perhaps what I said isn't the case. I do tend to say things first and think after. Maybe I have an over-active imagination.' Janet tries a little laugh, but cringes at her submissiveness. It's not in her nature.

'*Perhaps* what you said isn't the case?' Lowena says, and shakes her head again. 'No, it certainly is not. Ben is one of the most caring men I have ever met, and those boys are trying to turn their lives around. They've been dealt a rubbish hand and Ben's helping them achieve their goals. And me? If you really want to know, I sold my house and my mother's, after she died last year. I had a few savings, and so did Mum. Therefore, I was able to buy my house here without the help of a husband. I know that must be very hard for you to comprehend – you know, a woman like me, managing to live a reasonable life without a man behind her.' Lowena's eyes have become the colour of holly leaves and her anger is almost palpable. 'And as for Zelah, she's a wonderful caring person too who is learned in herblore. Historically, people, women in particular, though I know you seem to think as a gender we're dependent on men, have used various plants and herbs for good health and well-being, and I for one am grateful for the help she's giving me in my garden.'

Lowena hasn't bothered to lower her voice, and Janet's aware of the flapping ears of the two women at the next table. There's only them and one other couple in the place, and apart from the metal clink of spoon on ceramic, and the shuuusssh of the coffee machine, it's silent. Janet feels a tide of embarrassment rush up her neck as she considers Lowena's words. Maybe she was a bit rash. Maybe she should have found out more before rabbiting on to everyone like she did at the garden party. Why didn't she? *Maybe because you wanted to sound important, Janet. As if you knew things. Things that they would want to know.* Lowena pushes back her chair and picks up her bag. Oh God. She can't go yet, or Milly will find out the apology didn't work! Janet leans forward and lowers her voice, 'Look, Lowena, all I can say is I'm sorry. I didn't want to upset you.' This time what she says is true. She does feel sorry.

'Okay, Janet. Let's put it behind us, hey?' Lowena smiles as she shrugs on a coat the colour of sunshine. The smile isn't sunshiny though. It's forced and her eyes dance away from Janet's. Before she leaves, she leans down and says in Janet's ear, 'But please think about the feelings of others before you say stuff in future. Maybe you can even think of nice things to say instead. It will make you feel better too if you do, I promise.' Then she pats Janet's shoulder and heads for the door. Once she's gone the conversation starts up again and Janet digs her fork into the apple turnover. Unfortunately, she's completely lost her appetite.

Later that day, Janet is disconcerted to find herself torn again. Being torn is a rare thing for her, and twice in one day is most unwelcome. Janet normally knows exactly what to do and why. Her gut is almost always right, and she makes sure she follows it without hesitation. Today her gut is constantly changing its mind. The dilemma in question is whether to track down Zelah and get the apology done, or leave it for another day. Originally, she'd plumped for getting it over with. She had never been a ditherer and a putter-offer, though the apology this morning hadn't gone at all well. And if she were honest, which she was, mostly, but not always with herself, it had rattled her slightly.

Janet pottered around her kitchen cleaning things that didn't need it, making tea she didn't drink and mulling her decision over until she could stand it no longer. She'd given up on her gut and decided to toss a coin. Heads she'd find Zelah, who, according to Milly, walks the top path through the wood and meadow, gathering herbs on an afternoon. Tails, she'd do it another time. Janet looks at the shiny tenpence piece balanced on her thumb and forefinger, and gives it a flick. Her gut squeezes as heads is revealed. More kowtowing to practical strangers waits in her immediate future. But at least her decision is made. On with the new walking boots, scarf and maybe her new red woolly hat as well, because a glance through the net curtains at the battered daffodils on the patio tells her the wind hasn't given up yet. Not by a long chalk.

After half an hour searching for Zelah, Janet feels like the daffodils. The bright spring sunshine that had at least tempered the wind this morning had gone off to play elsewhere, and an assembly of charcoal clouds had swept in over the fields nearby, a bit too close for comfort. Janet wonders if Zelah might actually be at home, like sensible people ought to be on this inclement April afternoon. And it is a Saturday. Milly didn't say anything about gathering herbs on a weekend. She snorts. Herb gathering. Why didn't the woman go down to Boots for her remedies, like everyone else? Because she delights in being different, Janet thinks. That's why she wears that ridiculous diamond in her nose. Who wears those things in their nose when they're in their seventies unless they want to be noticed? And the long straggly hair, jewellery and floaty clothes. Attention-seeking is what it is. Janet had decided she'd have a short hairstyle once she'd passed the fifty mark. Her mother had always said women who have longer hair in their later years look like mutton dressed as lamb. And she was right. Mind you, Janet did wear a little light make-up, but nothing too outlandish. It wouldn't do.

Thinking of outlandish, around a bend in the woodland path, coming towards Janet out of the bluebells, strides the woman herself. Today, Zelah's a flash of purple frock-coat and baggy green velvet trousers stuffed into yellow wellingtons. Her crazy hair is partially hidden under a red fedora, and a wicker trug over her arm contains trails and stems of various plant life in greens and russet. Janet thinks she looks like something out of a Sunday-night suspense drama. A drama about a crazy old witch living in a wood who everyone thinks is the baddie, but turns out to be a red herring. When she spots Janet, Zelah stops. Stares. Janet exhales and stomps towards her. *Let's do this.*

'Afternoon, Zelah,' she says, forcing a smile.

Zelah's mouth twitches and she nods at Janet's head. 'Matching hats.'

Janet frowns. An odd greeting, and a red woolly hat is hardly the same as a flashy fedora, is it? 'The colour perhaps.'

'Hmm.' Zelah flings an arm at the woods. 'Not seen you along here in the wilderness before. Just out walking?'

Zelah's staring at Janet's legs, which is most disconcerting, so she turns to the side and gazes out over the fields. 'Yes, lovely views.' Her peripheral vision shows Zelah's eyes are still focused on her legs.

Zelah speaks to them now. 'I reckon I have just the thing for your knees.'

Janet's head snaps round. 'My knees?'

'Well, your right one. You favoured it as you came down the path.' From her basket she pulls a bunch of green fern-like leaves. 'Take this yarrow and make a cuppa with it. Or eat it in a salad. Brilliant as a tonic and a wonderful anti-inflammatory.'

Janet is gobsmacked. She's had problems with her achey knee for a fair few months now, but is amazed that Zelah could tell she's having problems by watching her walk. There's no way she's taking any bloody herbs though. God knows what might happen. The old witch might be trying to poison her for all she knows. 'Yarrow? Never heard of it.' Janet sniffs and keeps her arms folded to make sure Zelah doesn't try and force the leaves into her hands.

'Not surprised. Most people don't know that they have a pharmacy growing all around them.' Zelah points behind her at a field adjoining the woodland. 'There's a lovely load of it in yonder pasture. Folks have been using it for centuries.'

Yonder pasture? She's even talking like an ancient crone now. 'Hmm. Well, I'm not used to such things and my knee's not that bad anyway.'

Zelah's mouth forms a tight smile. 'As you wish.' She puts the yarrow leaves back in her basket. 'I'm having some bramble leaf tea when I get home, 'cos I'm getting a sore throat. You're welcome to join me?' A wink. 'I have ordinary tea if you think I might poison you.'

Janet's gob is smacked once again. Maybe the woman can read minds too. Perhaps she really is a witch? But what astounds her more than this is Zelah's offer of tea at her house. After all the horrid things Janet said about her at Lowena's party, and she's not even had time to apologise for it. That's why Janet's here after all. Maybe she could pluck up courage on the walk to Zelah's? 'I don't want to put you out,' she says. Though she's not entirely sure why. It annoys Janet when people respond to her offers of refreshment in this way. Another favourite is, *Only if you're sure*. Why wouldn't a person be certain in their intentions before offering tea, coffee or whatever? Or, *Only if you're having one*. As if the host would offer refreshment and not have one themselves. British politeness is very hard to fathom.

'Of course not. I wouldn't have offered otherwise,' Zelah says, bending suddenly and plucking a few dandelion heads from a clump by the hedgerow. 'Okay, so you coming, or what?' She stuffs the heads in the trug and sets off along the narrow path without waiting for a response.

Janet follows on behind with a sinking heart, wondering what she's let herself in for.

Zelah's house is at the end of a country lane surrounded by fields. It's a bit ramshackle and in need of a spruce-up, in many ways like Lowena's place. The garden is nowhere near as big as Lowena's, but it's full to bursting with things growing. What things, Janet has no idea. She had a lawn once, but had it paved. She can't be doing with constantly mowing and weeding out daisies. There are only three patio tubs allowed. At the moment there's lavender in one, a rose of some sort in the other, and daffodils in the last. They were all bought for her by Milly, otherwise she wouldn't bother. She's always getting scolded by Milly for forgetting to water the damned things anyway. Janet likes to be practical. Patios are for enjoying on warm summer days with the crossword and a pot of tea, possibly a glass of wine, if she's in the mood.

In the kitchen, Zelah waggles a cup with a smiley yellow face on it at Janet and says, 'Sure I can't make you a cup of yarrow tea? It will do your knee a power of good.'

'Ordinary tea will do just fine, thanks.'

'Suit yourself.' Zelah bustles about like an over-active bumble bee, opening drawers, cupboards and a packet of biscuits. 'I was going to offer you some of my home-made biscuits, but they have a variety of healing herbs in. And seeing as you have an aversion'—Zelah twists her mouth to the side as if she's tasted something bitter—'we'll stick to Jaffa Cakes.'

Feeling the need to set the record straight, Janet replies, 'I don't have an aversion as such.' Though this is exactly what she has. 'I'm just careful what I eat and drink... I mean, I have no idea what affect that yarrow might have on me.'

'No, that's clear. Nevertheless, I'm betting it would have a beneficial one. I'm experienced in these things after all my years of helping people. But never mind.'

Janet's beginning to wish she'd never accepted Zelah's invitation. The atmosphere in this little yellow and green kitchen is far less cheerful than the décor. In fact, it's a bit frosty. Janet bites into a Jaffa to fortify herself. She needs to apologise and get out of there as soon as she can. Duty done, she can then tell Milly, and get back to normal. Swallowing a mouthful of tea, she says, 'I meant to say earlier. I am sorry if I upset you at Lowena's the other week. I often speak without considering the feelings of others.'

Zelah, who's just put a whole Jaffa in her mouth at once, gobbles it down. Then she locks her cool blue eyes onto Janet's. 'Apology accepted. I would like to know the reasons for your malicious comments, though. Because you must have them. I've only known you five minutes, but apart from today, every time I've been in your company, I've found you to be unkind, stand-offish and downright rude.' Janet's eyebrows shoot into her hairline. Charming! Zelah's bluntness could stun a bull elephant. There's not an ounce of awkwardness in her voice or expression. Shocked, Janet just sits there like a chastised child as Zelah takes a sip of tea, puts her head on one side and softens her expression. 'As I said to you at Lowena's, you're carrying a weight of anger and bitterness, and I'd like to know why.'

A rush of indignation brings a fire to Janet's cheeks. How bloody dare Zelah sit there, coolly making comment on her as if she's an authority on everything? Janet clenches her hands so hard that her fingernails dig into her palms and she has to take a few deep breaths while she considers her response. Janet knows what she'd like it to be. A swift slap across Zelah's stupid face. But then Milly would never be friends with her ever again. A riposte of a few cutting remarks would bring a similar situation. What to do? It's not in Janet's nature to let people bully her. Because this is what this old witch is doing, isn't it? Hiding her true nasty side behind a benign smile and pretty eyes. Pretty eyes? Has she? Janet shakes that thought away and pushes her mug to one side on the kitchen table.

'I'm not sure I'm very happy with what you've said to me. In fact, you could be seen as downright rude yourself.' Janet sets her jaw, congratulating herself on how she made her feelings clear without going over the top.

Zelah throws back her head and laughs out loud. A throaty laugh that's uninhibited, full of mirth and altogether genuine. When Janet heard her laugh like that before, she'd assumed it was theatrics. An 'everyone look at me' type of laugh. But no. Zelah's eyes are moist with merriment and she dabs at them with a tissue while muttering, 'Bloody hell, Janet. You certainly surprised me there. I expected you to go bananas.'

Janet gives her a withering look. 'So you were trying to push my buttons, as the youngsters say?'

'Not as such. But in some ways I'm similar to you. I say what I think... though in my case it's because I genuinely do want to help you if I can.' Zelah holds a silencing finger up, as Janet opens her mouth to speak. 'You're going to say you don't need helping, and actually, you have to be going now, thank you very much.'

This is more or less exactly what Janet had been going to say. A harrumph escapes her lips instead, so she purses them to make sure no expletives escape by accident.

Zelah fluffs her steely locks and sends a sweet smile across the table. 'I promise it will help to talk. I'm a big fan of talking – sharing my feelings. Sometimes all the sad thoughts from my past twist up inside me, like underwear in a duvet cover after a fast spin cycle.' She chuckles. 'If you want to untangle your washing sometime, I could help you. I could share my story with you too. We could do it now, if you like? But I'm thinking... you're not quite ready.'

'Not quite ready' is an understatement. Feelings and stories about the past are best left well alone, Janet has found. She keeps hers under lock and key in a dark and seldom-used room of her mind. There's no telling what would happen if light was switched on in there. She pushes her chair back and stands. 'No. And I'm not into all this sharing my feelings stuff. But thanks for asking. Now I really do have to get back. Thanks for the tea and biscuits, Zelah.' Janet manages a tight little smile and almost sprints for the door.

On the way home, a ray of light filters under the door of the dark, seldom-used room, and allows an idea to shine at the forefront of her mind. Might it be nice to talk to someone about things? The way her life has turned out. The way it's not the one she dreamed about. It doesn't fit her properly. It never has. It pinches, pulls across the shoulders, digs in across her chest so hard sometimes Janet thinks it might crush her. But then the life she dreamed about was impossible when she was young. And now? Now it is too late. Far, far too late.

As a consequence, Janet always feels left out of things. Her life never seems to quite measure up to that of others. Lowena, Mervyn, Milly, Zelah, all of them seem to be having a marvellous time. They seem to have that elusive thing that humanity prizes above all else, the thing we all strive for: happiness. If she's totally honest, Janet's never been what she'd call really happy. Contentment has been an uphill battle too. Maybe that's why Janet lashes out at the others. Imagines the worst of them. Perhaps she wants to diminish their stature, so hers feels bigger...? Janet stops walking. Where the hell has all that come from? Her insides feel jumbled and tied in tight knots. It's all that bloody Zelah's fault, poking around in Janet's head, suggesting she share her feelings, and this, that and the other. Well, Janet's not for sharing anything with the old witch, or with anyone else come to that. Not now. Not ever.

Chapter Fifteen

Dan's not been as happy as this for years. In fact, apart from when he held his children for the first time, he's never been as happy. Maybe in the early days with his ex-wife he felt content, but there were no fireworks. No platoons of River Dancers in his heart every time he saw Sandra. Dan assumed these silly portraits of love were only to be found hung on the walls of romance novels, or on the big screen. Content was normal. Fireworks were the construct of the idealist; the sugar-coated dream of what love should be like. Not how it really was. Dan has changed his mind about all that. He's had to. Because as soon as Hayley walks into a room it's Bonfire Night and New Year's Eve rolled into one.

Despite the fireworks and heart-bursting happiness, the idea that it can't last has been hovering over him like a thunder cloud for the last few weeks. Dan's mum often used to say there were more storms than blue skies in every life, unless you were blessed by the angels. Furthermore, she said angels didn't bless the likes of them. Cheerful soul she was. Perhaps his thunderclouds are inherited from her. Either way, Dan knows that he must tell Hayley the real reason why he left the police. He wants no little shard of untruth festering away in his consciousness. Little shards have a way of burying into the quick of you and cutting off your lifeblood. Hayley deserves honesty; he wants no secrets between them. Secrets tend to drive wedges between people.

The picnic is ready, and as he sees Hayley's car pull up outside, he slips a bottle of champagne into the cool bag. There's no special occasion, apart from a picnic on the beach, but that's special enough. As he passes the hall mirror, a glance at his reflection tells him his sandy hair could do with another comb and he's buttoned his green and white checked shirt skewwhiff. The phrase 'punching above his weight' is no stranger to him, but Hayley seems to like him. She likes him a lot. Maybe he'll tell her the three little words he's been dying to say over the last month.

The other night, as Hayley lay next to him after making love, her warm body moulded to his, her head on his chest, he'd almost managed it. But as he'd opened his mouth to say the words, she'd mentioned something about her paintings, and the moment had passed. Thinking of which, Dan is stunned with his own painting efforts. Once he'd told Hayley of his ambition to put paint to paper, she'd gone all out to encourage him. She had given him a few pointers, but mainly he'd managed by himself. His sploshes weren't half bad at all. Hayley had said how amazed she was at his natural flair and creativity.

'Hello, handsome,' Hayley says now, as she sweeps in on a cloud of that intoxicating perfume, she always wears, a vision in pink and violet. On anyone else, braids full of pink and green beads, a pink floaty top with bells on the hem and violet shorts to the knee might look a bit saccharine, but Hayley looks good in absolutely everything. Also in nothing at all. Dan smiles as a sneaky image of her naked slips into his thoughts.

'Hello, the most beautiful woman in the world.' Dan lifts her up and spins her round, kissing her passionately as he sets her back down.

She laughs. 'What a welcome! And I hope you're ready, 'cos I could eat a donkey. Been really busy at the shop and not had time to stop for lunch today.' She hugs him and buttons up her denim jacket.

Dan nods, points to the picnic bags and grabs his car keys. 'All set. It's getting a bit nippy out, so I was wondering if we should take a blanket?'

'A blanket, on a lovely May evening in Cornwall, right next to those beautiful Atlantic rollers?' Hayley folds her arms and frowns.

'Er…'

A big smile tells him she's pulling his leg. 'God, yes. Better make it a warm one.'

The huge golden sweep of Constantine Beach is still peppered with a healthy number of dog walkers, surfers and families, even though it's past seven in the evening. The sun will be thinking about going to bed in just over an hour, but people are obviously making the most of the beautiful scenery. At the foot of the dunes, Dan unpacks the picnic and Hayley attacks the cold, spicy chicken, coleslaw, salad and new potatoes as if she's not eaten for weeks. Looking like a greedy hamster, her cheeks packed with food, she moans, 'Oh my God, Dan. Did you make this coleslaw yourself?'

'I did. I also cooked the chicken marinated in seven herbs and spices.' He rummages in the bag and pulls out a fresh bread stick. 'And I made this baguette too. Want some? I have a little pot of butter in the cool bag.'

'Wow! A woman could get used to this.' Hayley gives him a lascivious glance from under her lashes. 'Everything you do, you do spectacularly well. So far, you have ticked all my boxes.'

'I aim to please,' Dan says, moving in for a kiss, but she stuffs some bread in her mouth, closes her eyes and moans with pleasure. Champagne time, he thinks.

When he pulls the bottle out and hands her a plastic glass, her eyes grow round. 'Champagne? Blimey, you really are spoiling me. What's the occasion?'

This is it, Dan. The perfect opportunity to get those three little words out there. He takes a deep breath, raises his glass to her and says, 'Being on a Cornish beach, on a sunny evening with a woman I— Ouch!' A football smacks into the side of his face and his glass drops to the sand.

'I am SO sorry!' yells a young man with three children in tow, running towards them up the beach. 'I kicked it and the wind took it. Are you okay?'

The three children, all probably under twelve, gather round the man who is presumably their dad, wide-eyed and red-faced. Dan sighs and rubs his cheek. 'I'll live. Don't worry.'

The man apologises again, and after they've gone, Hayley comes over and puts the cold butter pot on his cheek. 'That must have hurt,' she says, tenderly kissing his lips.

Although it did sting, Dan waves her away with a smile. 'Hey, it's a graze from a football. I'm absolutely fine.' He notes a tone of irritation in his voice because the special moment with Hayley has been lost – again. As she puts the butter back in the cool bag and pours him more champagne, he realises it's for the best though. Because the other thing he must tell her needs to come out *before* he tells her how he feels. Her reaction to that will be everything.

Hayley bites into a strawberry and gives him a tight smile. 'You okay, Dan? You seem far away.'

'I am. I've got this crappy confession to make about why I really left the force. It's been on my mind since we started seeing each other properly. I have deep feelings for you, Hayley, so I need you to know everything about me.'

Her expression grows serious and she wraps the blanket around her shoulders. 'Okay. Sounds a bit worrying, but I'm all ears.'

For a few moments, Dan looks at the ocean and the pink and yellow fingers of sunset already stroking the horizon. He takes a deep breath. 'My last case involved a missing teenager, Kelvin Grant. He was sixteen, into drugs, crime, all sorts. He'd been known to us since he was twelve. I led the investigation and was on the trail of a local gangster, Carl Morris, nasty thug. Kelvin had been dealing for him, but kept some of the money by all accounts. I'd had Morris in and grilled him, but he had an alibi. Watertight. His snivelling little minions lied for him, rallied round. But I knew he'd done something to young Kelvin. Convinced of it. I couldn't prove it though.' Dan takes a moment as unpleasant memories smack into his consciousness like a wrecking ball.

Hayley reaches out for his hand. 'God, Dan. I can tell this is eating you up. You don't have to tell me.'

'Yeah, I do.' He squeezes her hand and lets go. 'I had released Morris, but we had another lead. A grass. Someone with an axe to grind tipped a colleague off about Morris. He had a secret lockup on the other side of town that only a few knew about. All sorts of stolen goods were in there. I asked a couple of officers on my team to check it out, but they didn't do it immediately. This grass had made stuff up before... Anyway, they waited until the next morning... and it was too late.' Dan blinks away a terrible image in his mind, an image that haunts his dreams, and downs his drink in one.

Hayley covers her mouth and speaks through her fingers. 'Oh God. Kevin was found... in the lockup?'

He nods and pours another glass. 'Yeah. Tied up and beaten. Coroner said he'd only been dead a few hours. If my officers had gone when they should have, he'd be alive now.' Dan feels an ocean of grief tighten across his chest. 'It was my fault, Hayley.'

She shakes her head in disbelief. 'But why? You told the officers to go. There's no way you can be held responsible!'

'I was their boss. I should have double-checked, made sure they went straightaway. But I didn't.'

'Did you double-check on everyone all the time, to see they'd done their job?'

'Well, no. There weren't enough hours in the day to—'

'Exactly.' Hayley shuffles along the sand and wraps the blanket around them both. 'Stop beating yourself up for other people's mistakes.'

'The thing is…' Dan takes another deep breath and forces the words out. 'The thing is, Kelvin was black. The black community were up in arms, said we were racist. Said that if Kelvin had been white, he'd have been found in five minutes. It wasn't true, of course, but I couldn't live with myself. I took early retirement and got out. Sandra said I was stupid. Said I was a coward to bow to public pressure like that, and it made me look guilty. But it wasn't like that. No matter how I tried to justify it, the buck stopped at my door. A young lad died on my watch. Time for me to go.'

Hayley is silent for the longest time. She just stares out at the ever-changing sunset and says nothing. Dan is about to ask her what she thinks, when she says, 'Did you never consider they could be right? That white kids might have been treated differently? Kelvin was a black youth, well known to you. He was up to all sorts, so what were you expected to do? He'd be off his head somewhere and come home soon enough. Kids like him always land on their feet.'

Dan's stomach turns over and he shifts away slightly, turns to face her. 'You think I was racist?'

A sigh. 'No... course not. You wouldn't be with me if you were, would you? But it's a well-known fact that the police are institutionally racist. It's built into the system, the culture.'

He puts his head in his hands. No. He had been slightly worried about Hayley's reaction because of her heritage, but he hadn't expected this. 'The officers just made a mistake, that's all. And I should have checked. It had nothing to do with race. I can see why you'd think so, I suppose.'

Hayley snorts. 'Because my dad's black? Ri-ght. Yeah. Just a knee-jerk response without any thought or consideration, that's me. Totally uninformed and clueless.'

Dan's surprised by the bitterness in her voice. Hayley moves away and tosses the blanket at him. 'Hey, I didn't mean that,' he says. 'Look, I knew these officers. Both good lads, never knew them to be racist, or use racist terms or language.'

She stands up and folds her arms, glowers down at him. 'Doesn't mean to say they weren't. They might not have been intentionally racist. As I said, it's part of the culture. I grew up in London, saw plenty of it from the Met. Stop and search, all sorts. So, don't make out I'm naïve.'

Hayley's anger sparks his own. 'I wasn't! I was telling you why I really left the force. That I was ashamed that a young life was lost because of my incompetence. It had nothing to do with the colour of his skin.'

Hayley shakes her head. 'I'm not saying it did with you, Dan. I'm just surprised that you won't even consider the possibility your officers had preconceived ideas about

Kelvin, exactly because of who he was.' Her expression softens. 'Look. Our life experience dictates our perceptions... and we have very different life experiences, Dan.'

Dan looks away, feels his heart sinking faster than the sun over the ocean. This wasn't at all the way he'd imagined a picnic on the beach with champagne to be. There was no more happy atmosphere in which to launch those three words he'd been saving up. She was right, they had very different life experiences, but they weren't different enough to alter things between them, were they? To ruin everything? Hayley's faraway expression and hunched body language worried him. Please don't let her end it over this. A misunderstanding. Why the hell did he have to tell her any of it! He could have just kept quiet. Bugger the clean slate and honesty, if it means she no longer wants him. Maybe let the thing lie now. He asks, 'It's getting chillier. Want to go back to mine? Watch a movie, something on Netflix.'

'Not tonight, Dan. I'm a bit tired.' Avoiding his eyes, Hayley starts to quickly gather everything up. 'Lovely food by the way. Thanks.'

Polite and cool. She's acting like a stranger. Dan picks up the bags and they walk to his car in silence. He can't think of anything to say. He's worried that whatever he does say will be the wrong thing. On the short drive back, they talk about which spices he used for the chicken and she says again how much she liked his cooking. But to Dan it feels as if something's broken. Something important. At his house Hayley helps him take the picnic things in then she drops a peck on his good cheek before opening her car door. 'Thanks again for the picnic, Dan.'

Dan goes to take her in his arms, but she ducks into the driver's seat and closes the door. Through the open window he says, 'Want to do something tomorrow?'

Hayley's eyes look anywhere apart from at him, and she starts the engine. 'I'll call you. Night, Dan.'

With a heart like lead he watches her drive away, and wonders if the important and broken thing will ever be fixed.

Chapter Sixteen

Sometimes there's nothing better than sitting with your feet up in a garden in the sunshine on a gorgeous afternoon, cuppa in hand, biscuit barrel on the table, watching the world go by. Lowena sighs with contentment, selects a dark-chocolate digestive and crunches into it. Bliss. At the end of her transformed 'jungle', Nigel's making great progress with the pergola on the raised platform he built last week, and seems to be thoroughly enjoying himself. Nigel's partial to a cuppa and biscuits too, and Lowena's made sure he's readily supplied with both, plus sandwiches and pasties every time he comes over.

Lowena can hardly believe how her garden has changed. In the few months since the party, Jack and Callum have finished the Cornish stone wall, helped clear the weeds and created all the separate areas in accordance with Hayley's plan. Mervyn has popped over from time to time, though she sees him at the library more often. He's getting on so well with his grandson Matthew who arrived from

Australia last week. It's great to see the old gentleman so happy. And Zelah, who pops over quite often, has instructed Lowena in how to make good use of all the wonderful herbs growing from the seeds sprinkled from the magic Tintagel box. Putting them in salads, teas and cakes is second nature to Lowena now. Milly and Janet have visited once or twice, which is nice, though Janet is very quiet these days. Quiet is preferable to her previous persona, but it's as if she's had her spark removed, which Lowena can't help thinking is a little sad.

The wonderful late-spring sunshine has opened a riot of flowers and brought shrubs to life over the past few weeks. The intoxicating scent from the three rose bushes hangs heavy in the still air, the climbing jasmine too over the rustic arch over the path. Lowena can hardly wait to plant the honeysuckle at the base of the pergola when it's finished. After the great start her friends gave her, she's now managing the whole garden by herself. It's hard work, but rewarding. She must have inherited her mum's green fingers after all.

Getting up from her garden chair, thoughts of her mum still in her mind, Lowena wanders over to the dahlias. They're such wonderful and vibrant flowers. And Lowena has them in a variety of colours – bold orange, yellow and red. How they got here is uncertain, but Lowena knows her mum's alive in every petal. A tickle on her ankle makes her jump. Conrad's tail. 'Conrad. Where did you come from?' She kneels down to fuss him, but he darts off into the grasses and shrubs, probably after an unfortunate shrew.

That cat loves the garden as much as she does. He's always off exploring.

As she stands and brushes down her jeans, Ben with his halfmoon smile slips quietly into her thoughts as he often does these days. Trips to the cinema, dinner, walks on the beach, picnics on the bench, have all become part of Lowena's new landscape. It's a landscape she loves and would now be lost without. This both alarms and thrills her, in equal measure. How has she become so quickly dependent upon his presence for her well-being and happiness? Echoes of Rick's desertion and the transformation of a man she thought she knew into a cruel stranger are never far away. Lowena tells herself that Ben would never let her down, but 'once bitten' is the answer that whispers a reply in the night. Can she let herself be happy without worrying, for once? Lowena is going to have a damned good try.

This weekend might be the best time for trying, because she's going round to Ben's for dinner. He is making Beef Wellington and homemade apple crumble for pudding. Last week he'd told her to write down three favourite dishes with puddings on little strips of paper, and Lowena had to pick them out of a cup. He's always doing lovely things like that. And while they've been taking things very slowly over the last few months as agreed, Lowena feels that Saturday night might be the night to speed things up a bit. She'd almost suggested he stay over last week, but she'd chickened out at the last minute. The reason for this was that it had been a very long time since she'd had a man in her bed and Lowena had panicked. What if she'd lost the knack, or made a mess of things?

Anna had provided a listening ear and soon Lowena was feeling better about herself. Anna had reassured her and told Lowena that she was a confident, attractive and strong woman any man would give their right arm to sleep with. This had led to a hilarious conversation about why anyone would want someone else's right arm, and what on earth would they do with it? Remembering it now, Lowena chuckles to herself, but spins round as she hears footsteps behind her.

'What's so funny? Let's be knowing,' Hayley says, walking down the path. She's hugging a flat square shape under a sheet to her chest, wearing green dungarees, a checked red shirt and a curious expression.

'I was just thinking of a silly conversation I had with Anna the other day.' Lowena smiles and eyes the square shape. 'What's that and what brings you here this fine afternoon?'

A beaming Hayley carries the object over to the garden table, sets it down and points at it. 'This brings me here this fine afternoon, and this'—she deftly unwraps the sheet—'is what it is!' With a flourish, she reveals a stunning canvas of Lowena's ocean view. 'Whaddya think of your present, my dear?'

Lowena can hardly speak, her heart's so full it's blocking the release of words. It's as if she's actually looking at the view right now, it's that real. Through a frame of yellow honeysuckle, the bold brushstrokes blend a mix of deep ocean blues with shades of green as iridescent as a beetle's wing, and vibrant as lime zest. White horses gallop across a biscuity sand while a golden sun rides the skies on a swirl of cloud. Eventually she says, 'It is incredible. Beautiful. Stunning. My God, the waves actually look as if they're moving!' Lowena throws her arms around Hayley and squeezes her so hard she squeals. 'Thank you. Thank you so much. I adore it!'

Hayley laughs. 'I'm so glad. Now can I have my ribcage back before you stop my breathing?'

Lowena laughs too, lets go of her and picks up the canvas. 'I'm not sure where it should go. Come in the house with me and we'll test it in every room.'

After a tour of the house, they decide on the chimney breast in the living room. There's a hanger already there and once it's in place the two women stand back and admire it for a few moments. 'It's in the right place,' Hayley says.

'Yeah. It feels like it's happy there.'

Hayley looks askance. 'Not sure paintings have feelings.'

'This one does,' Lowena says with a laugh. 'Fancy a cuppa?'

'Um. Not sure I have the time; it's my lunch hour, but I'm supposed to be rearranging the shop this afternoon. I thought it looked a bit tired and sad the other day.'

Despite Hayley's explanation, Lowena thinks there's something else. As they went around the house, she'd seemed a little absent, her mind occupied elsewhere. Something's bothering her friend. In fact, the description she gave of her shop could be applied to the owner. 'You have half an hour at least, and I bet you've not actually had lunch.'

'No. But I'm not that hungry.' Hayley looks out of the window and sends a faraway stare to the sky.

'You'll be hungry when you taste my ham, tomato and special secret ingredient sandwich.'

Hayley looks at Lowena, and a quizzical smile tips up one side of her mouth. 'Special secret ingredient?'

'Yup. I can't tell you what it is – you'll have to taste it to find out.' Lowena does puppy-dog eyes and turns down her bottom lip. 'Pretty please.'

'Okay, I can see I'll get no peace until I do.'

While Lowena makes the sandwich, the conversation in the kitchen has been mostly about Lowena and Ben, the garden, the library, in fact everything to do with Lowena and nothing to do with Hayley. Every time Lowena's directed the chat away from herself, she's found she's been deflected back again, like Groundhog Day. Hayley's obviously reluctant to talk about what she's up to. Most specifically her and Dan. Now, as they sit opposite each other at the table and bite into their sandwiches, Lowena's determined to find out what's making her friend unhappy.

Hayley says through a mouth of sandwich, 'This is a gorgeous ham and tomato sandwich, but what's the special secret ingredient?'

'There isn't one. I just said it to make you stay for lunch so I could find out what was the matter with you.'

Stopping mid-chomp Hayley says, 'That was sneaky. And what do you mean? There's nothing the matter with me.'

Lowena can tell that's not true. She's gone a bit pink in the cheeks and can't hold her gaze. 'Every time I ask about you and Dan you deflect my questions. What's going on?'

Hayley puts her sandwich down and looks as if she's going to deny it but then takes a sip of tea. She lets out a deep sigh and then, 'We had an awful disagreement at the beach. It was a lovely evening; we had a picnic with champagne and I felt very close to him. I'd the feeling he wanted to tell me something important...' She shrugs and sighs again.

'That he loved you?'

'Possibly, I don't know. It's a bit soon after all... but then a guy kicked a ball up the beach and it hit the side of his head – totally ruined the moment. After that, the whole atmosphere changed and he said he needed to tell me the real reason he left the police.'

'I thought it was early retirement.'

'Me too. Well, it was, but because of a particular incident.'

Lowena listens while Hayley tells her about an incident which he couldn't live with, involving the death of a black youngster, officers who should have acted more quickly but didn't, and the consequent accusations of racism. They'd fallen out because Hayley had suggested that perhaps Dan could have considered his officers might have been racist in their inaction. He'd taken it personally and they'd parted on frosty terms. Wow. Lowena isn't sure what to say or think about it all. She can see both sides of the argument. 'Hmm. That's tricky... Not sure why it ended so badly though? Is Dan likely to be someone who ignores racism right under his nose like that?'

'No.' Hayley puts her head in her hands and mumbles to the table, 'I never said he was, just that he could have considered racism might have been at play. Maybe even unconsciously.' She tosses her head back and gives Lowena an intense stare. 'He implied I was naïve and being knee-jerky because of my colour. So, I reminded him I grew up in London, and had witnessed first-hand police harassment of black youths. I never suffered myself, but friends of mine did. And...' Hayley picks her mug of tea up and wraps her hands around it. 'And my poor dad suffered more, but I didn't mention that.'

Lowena can tell Hayley's holding back tears so reaches across the table for her hand. 'Want to tell me about it?'

A sniff. 'I don't know if it will do any good. The past can hurt when you dig it up from its resting place and drag it out into the daylight for no reason. I'm not going to tell Dan about it, so what's the point?'

'It's up to you. But it might help?'

'Okay... As you know, my dad is black and my mum is white. You will meet them as they're coming down for a week in June. Anyway, back in 1973 when Mum was pregnant with me, they were walking back from the theatre one summer evening and cut through a park and playground. Three white youths who were drunk and larking about on the kids' swings saw them and ran over, blocking their path. They poked Mum in the belly, called her all sorts of disgusting names, called my dad the N-word and said he should fuck off back to his own country. Dad tried to guide Mum past them as he knew he stood no chance against three, but they tripped him up and gave him a vicious beating.' Hayley stops and wipes her eyes.

Kicking herself for persuading Hayley to dredge up the past, Lowena says, 'Oh, Hayley. I'm so, so sorry. No wonder you were upset with Dan's dismissal of the officer's possible racism.'

She shakes her head. 'No. Sadly, that's not the whole story. After they'd finished with Dad, the youths had wandered off to the grass beyond the playground and were still larking about. Mum helped Dad up and they saw a couple of coppers in the street opposite. Mum left Dad on a bench and ran over to them and explained what had happened. The coppers came over and looked at Dad, then at the yobs over on the grass. They wandered over to them and had a chat. Mum said they were laughing and joking with them. The yobs went on their way and the coppers came back to Mum and Dad. They said the lads had denied it, and there were no witnesses, so no point in taking them in for questioning. That was that. They left. Didn't even offer help to get Dad home. He could hardly walk. Took them an hour to get back and they only lived five minutes away.'

'Oh my God. That's terrible.'

'Yeah. Mum said they looked at Dad as if he was something they'd scraped from their shoe. Her too.' Hayley shakes her head. 'And I have lots of stories like that from friends and family. I could write a book.'

'But if you told Dan all this, it would help him understand why you were so upset the other night. He must have been pretty shocked when you flew off the handle like that with little explanation.'

'It might. But no… I don't think we're right for each other. We're from different backgrounds, with different views on the world. When I knew he'd been a copper I had some reservations; now I realise I was correct.'

This is awful. Lowena knows they are right for each other – it's obvious to anyone who sees them together. They just need to talk it through, to see why they clashed so much the other night. Dan was hurting over the death of a boy on his watch; his guilt at that was eating him up. Hayley was hurting because of what happened to her parents all those years ago, and the racism she'd witnessed. There was no wonder it had ended in fireworks. Trouble is, both of them tend to be a bit stubborn, Lowena's found. 'I don't think you were correct, love, and I hope you can find a way forward. Honestly, you and Dan are so good together.'

Hayley turns away, her pretty olive eyes swimming in tears. 'We were, but I'm afraid that's all gone now. He wants to see me, but I keep putting it off. It's for the best.'

No matter how Lowena tries to change her mind, Hayley remains resolute. What a shame. After Hayley's gone, Lowena potters around the garden unable to settle to anything. She remembers the day of the garden party and the look of adoration in Dan's eyes as he watched Hayley painting the view. Surely that can't be allowed to be thrown away. Hayley adores him too. It's obvious, or she wouldn't be so upset. Maybe Lowena can do something. But what?

In the shed, Lowena grabs the watering can and then notices her dad's old fishing basket still at the back by the plant pots. Maybe it slipped Hayley's mind to ask Dan if he wanted it. A spider dangles down in front of her eyes on a silken thread, along with a solution to Hayley and Dan's problem. Hooking the spider to one side, she slides the basket out and carries it to her car. A note of apprehension follows her, reminding Lowena that her mum said never to meddle in other people's business, unless it was absolutely necessary. Lowena dismisses it, deciding this is worthy of meddling. And anyway, it's not really meddling, is it? It's just telling a few truths.

Chapter Seventeen

As the evening creeps towards night, in the soft apricot light, Ben on 'her' bench looks like he's in a scene from a film. A lone man, handsome, contemplative, gazes out at the last vestiges of sunset across a vast sleepy ocean. A woman strolls up the coast path towards him, her dark curls lifting on the breeze, the sage denim jacket she's wearing perfectly picking up the colour in her sparkling eyes – or she hopes it does – and the roses in her cheeks giving her a fresh windswept complexion. She's been collecting a few bits of sea-glass from the beach, and soon the man and woman will go home together. It's there that Lowena's imagination stops, because she doesn't want to get ahead of herself. Joining Ben on the bench, she slips her hand into his and rests her head on his shoulder.

'Got what you were after?' he asks, dropping a kiss on her hair.

'Yeah. You're what I'm after,' she says, squeezing his hand.

'That's just because I made you Beef Wellington.'

'True. And hopefully we can have the apple crumble when we get back, now we've walked off the main course.'

He laughs and they sit together in comfortable silence while the sea shushes the shingle, and from a rock, a lone seagull screeches to the sky. Over dinner she'd told Ben about Hayley and Dan and that she'd been to see Dan and explained Hayley's reaction to why he'd left the police. Lowena had sworn Dan to secrecy because she knew Hayley wouldn't be at all impressed that she'd told him without permission. Luckily, Dan was very understanding. He'd said it all made much more sense now. As Ben pulls her up and they walk to his car she asks, 'So, you think I did the right thing about Hayley and Dan?'

He wrinkles his brow. 'I'm not sure. You've done it now, so you'll have to wait and see.' A worried look from Lowena prompts, 'But you did it because you wanted to help people. You said Dan was grateful you'd explained about the racist abuse her parents suffered and that the police did zilch. The ball's in his court now.'

This makes Lowena feel more justified in her actions. Through the window of Ben's car on the drive back, as she watches the early stars switch themselves on in a navy sky, she thinks of who she's becoming. People have come to Lowena with their problems, something she's never experienced before. Mervyn sought her help about his grandson and the emails, and he's always asking her advice on this or that. Hayley talked to her about Dan, and Jack, the young gardener, had even asked her advice on whether buying his girlfriend a silver bracelet might be seen as going over the top, as they'd only been together three months. Bless him. He comes across so worldly wise, but underneath he's unsure and sensitive. Lowena had told him to go with his gut. She's looking forward to finding out what he did.

Maybe she's changing as a person, becoming more approachable? In the past, while not exactly stand-offish, she had been a bit of a loner, apart from having a few friends like Anna. Actually, if she's honest, Anna was the only real friend she'd had. Now look at her. So many new people in her life, some she can call proper friends too, and they're all so different. Little seeds producing a variety of flowers, but all growing in the same patch. Lowena's certain her wonderful garden has a calming effect, and is a place where people feel they want to be. A place where people can share their love of growing things, while growing closer to each other.

Lowena releases a sigh of contentment and she squeezes Ben's leg. She's so lucky to have found him, new friends, and a feeling that she's in the centre of things with her library barn and a house with a wonderful garden overlooking the ocean... a valued member of her community. What more could a person possibly want? The full moon slips through the long fingers of silver cloud, and a silent and unexpected answer to her question flits through her mind. This answer is swiftly pooh-poohed and banished. It had been a mistake to wish on the magic box for that last thing. The thing she'd not admitted to anyone. The thing she'd kept secret in her heart. Hopefully, the wish about finding 'the one' had started to come true, but the other bit was just pie in the sky. One step beyond. And anyway, wishes on magic boxes were for moonstruck youngsters, weren't they?

'Any more?' Ben asks, nodding at the crumble dish on the side. 'There's custard in the pan too.'

Lowena pushes her chair back and pats her tummy. 'Much as I would love to say yes, my belly says no room at the inn.' She smiles at him across the table. 'It was absolutely gorgeous, the main course too. And the beach walk in the middle. It's been a lovely evening, Ben. I love spending time with you.' Lowena's wondering what his reaction would be if she'd omitted the words 'spending time with'. And would she have meant them? Truly?

'And I you.' Ben gets up from the table and sides their dishes. 'Coffee or a brandy?'

'Oh, a brandy would be nice. Maybe coffee later?' As she watches him take gasses from the cupboard Lowena thinks she might have meant them. Though not rushing things certainly didn't involve allowing those words free range just at the moment.

'Let's take these through to the living room where it's comfier,' Ben says, carrying two generous glasses of brandy to the room where the only light from an open fire is casting dancing shadows up and down the walls. Ben's house is massive, state-of-the-art, the kind you'd find in *Ideal Home* magazine. But the garden is a paved patio. Okay, it has some nice shrubs around it and a pool, but Lowena prefers

Kittiwake Cottage and her garden any day. Ben sets the glasses on the coffee table in front of the big squishy green leather sofa and flops down with a sigh. Lowena flops too, stretching her legs over Ben's.

She reaches for her glass and inhales the spicy, rich tones of the brandy before taking a sip, the liquid warming a path to her stomach. 'Mm, that's a good drop, Ben.'

Ben raises his glass to his lips and then rests it on the arm of the sofa without drinking. Massaging her feet, he says, 'Actually, I had a couple of glasses of wine with dinner... Maybe I should leave this until I've dropped you home. I know it's only five minutes to yours, but I'll be over the limit if I have this.'

Lowena doesn't reply, but her mind has a lot to say. The way that foot massage is making her feel, imagining those capable hands caressing other parts of her body... She swallows hard and says, 'I could get a taxi... or... or I could stay over.' Immediately her heart goes into a crazy frenzy and she watches his face carefully for a reaction.

The firelight turns his eyes to glittering amber and a slow sexy smile sends a tingle through her. 'If you knew how I've longed for you to say those words... I haven't asked you, because I thought you should be the one. I didn't want to pressure you and we said we're taking things slowly... but yes. Yes, please stay.'

'Okay, but separate rooms, yeah?' Lowena can hardly keep her face straight as she takes another sip of brandy, because Ben's face has fallen to his feet.

He takes a big gulp of his drink and says, 'Of course. Whatever you feel comfortable with.'

Ben's forced little smile makes her crack out laughing. 'As if! Come here and kiss me, you gorgeous man.'

He obliges, and then takes his kisses from her mouth to her neck. Quickly he slips her sweater off and his lips find her breasts. 'Shall we go to my room or stay here?' he says huskily as his hands move down her body, his erection pressing into her thigh.

Lowena can hardly think straight but says, 'Your room, or we'll end up in the fire.'

'I'm already on fire,' he murmurs as he leads her upstairs.

'My God, that was bloody amazing!' Ben says into her hair, his body still entwined with hers.

'I've not lost the knack, then,' she says, almost to herself. Lowena's still not got her breath back and is somewhere up in the clouds.

'Ha! That will be a no.'

'And yes, it was incredible. Absolutely fucking incredible!' She laughs and settles back on the pillows.

Ben strokes a finger down her stomach and traces the circle of her navel, before moving lower. 'If you had any idea what you do to me…'

'Keep doing that and you'll find out exactly what you do to me,' she whispers as heat flares in her groin.

Ben's hand stills and he looks so deep into her eyes, she thinks she'll be consumed by them. 'I know we're taking it slowly, but I think I'm falling in love with you, Lowena.' He shakes his head. 'No. *I know* I am.'

Her heart jumps for joy, and the question she'd asked herself downstairs about those three words is answered. 'I'm thinking the same thing.' She takes his face between her hands and kisses his mouth. 'I love you, Ben.' Then his hands do the talking and she's lost.

———

Mervyn is outside the library early on Monday morning. The sun's shining a bright halo directly behind, giving him a look of an aged cherub. A cherub with the collar turned up on his overcoat and a frowny face. Lowena hopes he's not been waiting long; she hadn't been out to check since her arrival fifteen minutes ago. She's been in the back with a cuppa, busy daydreaming about her weekend, reliving every last moment she spent with Ben, mostly in bed.

'Mervyn, you're up and about before the sparrows today.'

He frowns as he stomps past her. 'Hardly. I used to get up at four when I farmed for a living. I've been up since six this morning and here since eight-thirty, which if I'm not mistaken is opening time.' A pointed look at the clock over her desk tells Lowena she's been ticked off. Then he takes a hanky out of his pocket and blows his nose with a trumpet worthy of an elephant.

'Goodness, I didn't realise it was eight-forty-five. I've been in the back… um, sorting a few things out.'

'Never mind, you're here now, and it's not as if it's the

middle of winter.' Mervyn smiles and rubs his hands. 'I need your help with exotic plants. Well, a book on them. I saw a clip on the local news about that Eden Project place the other night, and in the Mediterranean dome thingy they have all manner of strange plants and I just fancied finding out more about them.'

'Yes, of course. I love it there, but I've not been for ages,' Lowena says, leading him to the gardening section.

'Where?'

'The Eden Project.'

'You've been? I've never got round to it.' Mervyn sighs.

Lowena looks at him in surprise. 'But it's only half an hour away from here.

'Yes. I need to make the effort, because I'd love to look in that Mediterranean dome.'

'They're called biomes, though they do look like huge glass domes. The rainforest one is amazing – you can feel the humidity as soon as you walk through the doors. It's so peaceful too. They've got bananas growing and all sorts.'

'Bananas! Good grief.' Mervyn's face lights up. 'I'd like to see those.'

Lowena hands him a book and as they discuss a Bird of Paradise plant, there's an idea brewing in her mind. 'Merv, you know how our little group of people at my party a while back love gardening?'

He gives her a curious look. 'I do.'

'And you know how the Eden Project is the biggest and most incredibly interesting garden in the country and it's right on our doorstep?'

'Ye-es?'

'Do you think they'd all like a day trip there?'

An ear-to-ear grin stretches Mervyn's face, his eyes shining with excitement. 'I'm sure they would. I know I for one would be over the bleddy moon!' He chortles and hugs the book to his chest.

'Then I'll get it organised!' His excitement is infectious and Lowena can't wait to tell Ben. 'A community trip to the Eden Project. What a great day it's going to be!'

―――――――――

Back at Kittiwake Cottage, Lowena pulls her phone out of her bag and sees that Hayley has left an answerphone message. She wants to come over after work for a chat, but she won't keep Lowena long. There was no need to reply, she'd just swing by on her way home. Lowena swills the teapot out in the sink, the great mood she's been in all day disappearing down the plughole, leaving a little lump of anxiety behind. Hayley's voice on the message had been a bit stiff, stilted. What if she's coming to tell Lowena she knows that she told Dan her business? What if she's coming to say she had no right? What if she's coming to end their friendship? The little lump of anxiety grows until it's pushing at the walls of her chest. It's brought a wash of nausea with it too. Then she decides there's no point in thinking like this. She'll just have to wait and see. But what if…?

Lowena's still having an argument with herself when Hayley's car pulls up on the drive. Swallowing down a shedload of trepidation, Lowena opens the door and puts on her best smile. 'Hi there, how's tricks?'

Hayley's expression is neutral, and then manages a tight smile. 'Tricks are fine, thanks. I'd just like to ask you a few questions, if I may.'

Oh dear. Lowena's never heard her sound so formal. 'Yeah, come in. I've just put the kettle on and there's some fruit and walnut loaf I bought from Truscott's at the weekend.'

While Lowena busies herself with the tea and cake, there's an uncomfortable silence. Conrad saves the day, thankfully, as he barrels in through the cat door and leaps onto Hayley's lap. She's soon making a fuss of him and the grumpy face she was wearing is placed back on the hanger. Once Lowena's sitting opposite and sipping their tea, Hayley loses her smile and says, 'Dan called me on Saturday and asked me to come round to his. He said he wanted to discuss how things were between us.'

Lowena swallows a mouthful of cake and nods. 'That's good. Did you go?'

'Yes. And I was very pleasantly surprised at what he had to say. Dan said it was possible that his officers had behaved in a racist manner, perhaps unconsciously, but nevertheless, he should have considered it. He apologised if I thought he'd been suggesting I was naïve, and hadn't fully thought about where I might be coming from. And he hoped we could move on from it and get back to how we were.'

Hayley's still not smiling, despite the positive news and Lowena's waiting for the rest. 'Well, that's good news, isn't it?'

'Yes. Odd though – him just having a complete turnaround.' Hayley pushes a crumb of cake round her plate before fixing Lowena with a hard stare. 'I noticed your dad's fishing basket in his hallway. Don't remember it being there last time I went… Did you take it round?'

There was no way Lowena could do anything else but tell the truth, whatever the consequences. 'Um, yeah. Yeah, I saw it in the shed the other day and thought I'd better take it or it would just rot away—'

'Did you tell Dan about my parents' story?'

To the table, Lowena says, 'Yeah.' She sighs and looks up at her friend's stony face and set jaw. 'Yeah, I did. I couldn't let you two end things. You're perfect for each other. And I know I betrayed a confidence – though you didn't actually tell me not to mention anything – but if you're back on track, I think it was worth it.'

'I knew it.' Hayley shakes her head but Lowena sees a glint of humour in her eyes. 'I thought it was too good to be true that he'd arrived at that conclusion all by himself.'

'But importantly, he did arrive at it. And it didn't take him very long either.' Lowena folds her arms. 'Look, he's a good man, Hayley. A decent man, who's beating himself up for the death of a young lad. Will probably always be. But hopefully now he might be able to see that it wasn't all his fault.'

A slow smile curls Hayley's mouth and she nods. 'Thanks to you. I must admit, at first I was pretty put out by the thought that you'd go behind my back, and so had to come here to find out if you did. But now I know the truth, I'm glad I have a friend prepared to go out on a limb like that. You had my back in the end. That's what matters.'

Relief floods through Lowena and she grins. 'I'll always have your back.'

Hayley leans forward and winks. 'And those three words I thought he'd been wanting to tell me... he said them!'

'When?'

'On Saturday night. And I said them back, so thanks for sticking your big beak in!'

'Oh my goodness, so did me and Ben!'

Hayley's eyes grow round. 'What time on Saturday?'

Lowena has a quick think. 'Must have been about nine' o'clock.'

Hayley thumps the table, her eyes full of mischief. 'I win! He told me at seven, just before I raced him upstairs to bed.'

A giggle in her throat, Lowena says, 'Ben and I slept together for the first time on Saturday too.' She feels like they're teenagers sharing confidences, and she's so happy things have turned out like this. It could have been so different.

'It's about time! Well done!' Hayley laughs and points at a bottle of red wine on the counter. 'I think it's time for something stronger than tea. We need to celebrate. And then you can fill me in on all the details.'

Lowena laughs and grabs two glasses. 'Pin back your ears.'

Chapter Eighteen

Janet sometimes wonders at the logic of picking up plastic and debris from the beach. There's always plenty more the next time she gets her grabby-stick rubbish bag and drags her sorry arse down to the shore. Sometimes, what she's picking up is too small for the stick's pincers, which is most annoying. She feels like some Dickensian crone, scavenging for a dropped penny or two along the Thames' mud flats. Bent double, scrabbling in the sand, her knee is giving her gip, and her back will be shouting at her too, later. Janet thinks she might pack it in, to be honest. She's getting no younger and it's a thankless task. Milly sometimes comes with her, but she was busy with her daughter and grandchildren when Janet asked. Must be nice to have family.

Stopping for a rest, she leans on her grabby-stick, or litter-picker as Milly insists on calling it, and stares at the early-evening beach scene. As if highlighting her aloneness, couples, people with dogs, and a few families dot the sand like chess pieces. Playing each move on the board, they walk arm-in-arm or chase each other, and dogs chase balls while beloved owners look on. And laughter. Laughter slices the air like a generous knife through cake. Happy times. Shared experiences. Maybe Milly might be down here later, or tomorrow with her two granddaughters. Milly adores them. A fleeting image of Janet going too is swiftly kicked into touch. Milly never asks Janet to join her when she has family to stay.

Janet sighs and tells herself she should be grateful Milly is her friend at all, after the way she behaved towards Zelah, Lowena and the others. Even though she apologised, things aren't the same now between Janet and Milly. Something's lost, but Janet can't quite figure out what. It's like the warmth they've always shared has been put in a cool box. A cool box containing leftover sandwiches, that's stuffed in the fridge and forgotten about. Still, she has much to be thankful for. Here she is on a warm evening in early summer, looking out on the peaceful ocean, the blue horizon smudging the edge of the sky, as if it's a chalk drawing that's been folded in half and opened again.

As she turns for home, someone calls her name. Oh God, it's the wonderful Zelah. That's all she needs. Zelah raises her hand in an enthusiastic wave and hurries across the sand towards Janet, the breeze making silver streamers of her hair, a vision in purple and yellow. 'Need some help?' she yells, bounding up next to her like one of the dogs, a big, daft grin on her face, eager to please. Janet imagines if she threw a ball Zelah would chase it.

She forces a smile. 'Hi, Zelah. No, I'm just off home now, thanks.'

'Oh, not to worry. A bloody good job you're doing though.' She points at the grabby-stick. 'I've been meaning to get one of those but keep forgetting.'

'Hmm. They are good for the larger things, but the tiny bits of plastic slip through the pincers. Does my back in bending over to get them.'

'Bet your knee is still giving you gip too.' Zelah's eyes have borrowed bits of blue from the chalk drawing, and regard Janet with a sense of knowing that's uncanny.

'Not so much,' she lies. 'Anyway, I'll be off now... It's getting a bit chilly. I don't like being out when it's dark either.'

Zelah frowns. 'It won't be dark for another few hours.'

Janet's getting ruffled now. Why does she have to explain herself to the woman? She wants to go home and that's that. 'Hmm. Anyway, bye then.' Janet flings a little wave over her shoulder and starts to walk away.

'Why don't you come to mine for a bite to eat? We can have a nice chin-wag.'

There's nothing Janet would like less, especially the wagging of chins. Taking a deep breath, she manages a polite smile and turns back to face Zelah. 'Oh. Thanks for asking, but I've defrosted a bit of salmon.'

'Have it tomorrow.' To Janet's horror, Zelah slips her arm though hers and marches them briskly up the beach, her speech like rapid machine-gun fire so Janet can't get a word in. 'Do you know, I haven't spoken to a soul all day. I said to myself, Zelah, that won't do. Get out and have some fresh air. So I did and there you were, on the beach all by yourself too! I call that serendipitous. And I have a lovely chicken and leek pie I made fresh this afternoon. How about that with new potatoes? Oh, and some elderflower wine I made. It's absolutely gorgeous, if I do say so myself.'

Janet's desperate to get out of it, but short of being blunt, how can she? Zelah might tell Milly she was rude in the face of kindness and the whole problem would start again. 'But I don't have my car... Yours is a bit of a walk from here and—'

'Don't worry about that.' Zelah squeezes Janet's arm. 'I have my old jalopy in the carpark. We'll be home in two shakes!'

As Janet allows Zelah to shunt her into the passenger seat of a VW Beetle covered in psychedelic flowers, she curses under her breath and wonders what on earth she's let herself in for.

Maybe it's the elderflower wine, the cosy atmosphere of Zelah's place, the good food, or all three, but Janet's having the shocking sensation that she's actually enjoying herself. In fact, she can't remember a time when she enjoyed herself so much. The conversation over dinner has been about the people they know, the local news, what's good on TV, and the weather – ordinary stuff, but there's been so much laughter, and a light mood settled inside Janet's chest not long after arriving. Zelah's so easy to talk to, despite her odd ways and appearance. Though now under the lamplight in her living room, Janet has to admit the nose stud looks quite alluring. Alluring? Dear God. What's happening to her? She shifts position on the sofa and sips more wine. Milly would never believe it if she could hear Janet's thoughts. Maybe Zelah's slipped some potion or other into the wine, or baked it in the pie. An image of Zelah in a witch's hat stirring a cauldron pops into her mind, and she has to cover her mouth to stifle a laugh.

'More wine, Janet?' Zelah lifts the bottle and swishes the dregs.

'No thanks. And neither should you, you've got to drive me back.'

'That ship's already sailed, me hearty,' Zelah says with a chortle. 'I'm getting you a taxi back.'

'Really? I don't think—'

'You think too much, that's your trouble.' Zelah divided the last of the wine between their glasses and then plumps the cushion on the easy chair opposite. 'You need to talk more. I said last time that it would help to share stuff. You're too buttoned up and weighed down with your troubles. I can almost see them piled on top of your head like an avalanche waiting to slide.'

Janet snorts with laughter and a dribble of wine shoots down her nose. 'That's a crazy image,' she says blowing her nose, strangely feeling unembarrassed by her snotty antics.

Zelah's eyes twinkle in the lowlights. 'You've a lovely laugh, Janet. It's a pity we don't hear it more.'

'Honestly? I've laughed more tonight than I have for…' Janet pauses. 'Actually, I can't remember. I've really enjoyed myself.' She doesn't mean to say the last bit, but the words are out before she can stop them.

'I'm glad. And I'll bet you're a bit surprised that you've had so much fun, given you didn't want to come here in the first place.'

How on earth did she know that? 'Um… well, I…'

'Right. No more umming. I'm going to get us some cheese and biscuits and then we're going to share our stories.'

'I don't want cheese and biscuits, thanks for asking. I…' But Zelah sticks her fingers in her ears and says, 'la, la, la' to drown out Janet's protestations as she sweeps out into the kitchen. Minutes later, Janet's tucking into crackers and cheese and sipping yet more wine as if this is normal behaviour for her of a Wednesday evening. Milly certainly would never believe it.

'Okay, tell me about your life, Janet. And don't say that you're not ready to spill the beans because your beans have been ready for spilling for many years.' Zelah taps her chest with a long red fingernail. 'And I'm just the woman who's ready to mop them up.'

Janet's held by her intense stare. Zelah seems to be reaching inside her and undoing all the knots, opening the drawers and cupboards in the dark and seldom-used room in her mind and shining a bright torch on all her secrets. No. No, Janet's not ready for that kind of scrutiny. She rarely allows herself in there, so she's damned if she's allowing Zelah free range. No. Zelah can have the version she's told a few close friends and no more. 'Not much to tell…' Janet finishes a mouthful of cheese and cracker, while she wonders how to start.

'I think there's loads to tell. But take it slowly and see where it leads. I'll tell you my story too, so you don't feel under the spotlight.'

Janet sighs. 'Okay, I left school at fifteen and went to work as a bank clerk. I've always been good with numbers and the work was clean, easy and paid quite well. It was a bit boring, but as my parents said, boring is better than uncertainty. Dad always said the same thing if I ever moaned. "It's good, honest work, Janet my girl, and many young women would give anything to be in your shoes."'

'What did your parents do?'

'Dad was a mechanic and Mum was a housewife. My elder brother was the one they favoured. He was an accountant and later had his own business. Seemed he could do no wrong.' Janet noted a trace of bitterness in her tone and coughed to cover it.

'Is he still with us?'

'No. He died of cancer when he was sixty. Poor Brendan…' Though they were never particularly close, Janet still misses him. He was the only family she had left – well, and his wife, Doreen. They never had children, so when she died about three years after her husband, Janet was the only one remaining.

'So how did you meet your husband, and what happened to him? You call yourself Mrs, I noticed.'

Janet considers saying she doesn't want to talk about it, but knows Zelah would keep digging anyway. 'I met

Leonard at the bank. He was my manager and started courting me when I was twenty.'

Zelah raises her eyebrows. 'It sounds like you had no choice in the matter.'

Did it? She supposed it did... because that's how it was. But she says, 'Don't be silly, it wasn't like that. Anyway, we married when I was twenty-two.'

'Your parents liked him because he had a good, honest job and would take care of you. They pressured you into accepting him, am I right?'

Zelah is. Unbelievably so. But her perceptiveness provokes a fiery response. 'They liked him, but the decision was mine. I wasn't some little wimp who people could push around, you know!'

'Really? Back then lots of girls did what their parents told them. Lived the lives that society and their peers expected them to. It's nothing to be ashamed of.'

'Talking about yourself, I expect?' Janet snaps.

Zelah's eyes flash in anger, then her face softens. 'At first yes, I did... but then I went my own way and lost nearly all my friends and family because I did. But I couldn't live a lie any longer.'

Janet's heart flips and a shiver races along her spine like an electric current. Living a lie is exactly what Janet has spent her own life doing, isn't it? This realisation is quickly rejected, given short shrift and banned from her thoughts. Janet struggles to imagine what Zelah has done that is so terrible. Probably got herself pregnant, or started taking drugs and went to live on a hippy commune. She gives a dismissive sniff. 'Hmm. Why's that then?'

'I'll tell you when you've finished your story.' Zelah steeples her fingers and taps them against her lips. 'When did you get divorced, and why?'

Nothing like being direct, eh? Janet considers her answer carefully. The truth is hiding under the table like a dog hoping for scraps, but she can't feed it. Won't. 'We separated after eighteen months. Divorce took longer back then, as you know... He was having affairs.'

'Really? So soon?'

'Yes.' Janet's getting fed up of the twenty questions. She has a feeling that Zelah's not buying what she says and it's making her hot and uncomfortable. She undoes the top button of her blouse and flaps the material.

'And you never married again? Or had another relationship?'

'No.'

'Why?'

Janet swallows a big mouthful of wine. 'Because I was happier by myself.'

Zelah's incredulous. 'You've been alone for what, fifty years?'

'Alone? Of course not! I have friends, you know. Milly and I have been friends since—'

'School. Yeah, you said. Not quite the same though, is it?'

Zelah's wearing an expression of pity. And one thing that Janet hates is the thought of anyone pitying her. 'Oh, for goodness' sake! We don't all have to be paired off two-by-two like animals on the blasted Ark, you know.'

'I know... Please don't get angry, I just want you to get

everything off your chest.' Zelah smiles and leans across to take Janet's hand, but Janet leans back and quickly folds her arms. Zelah shakes her head. 'As I said before, you're carrying so much bitterness and anger around, it has to stem from somewhere.'

'Yes, well I've had enough of getting things off my chest. So, let's carry on with *your* story, eh? After your family abandoned you for whatever you did, I expect you had the best marriage, found the love of your life. Built your perfect little Ark and sailed away, hmm?' Janet can hear the bitter sarcasm in her tone and to her horror, there are hot tears waiting. She doesn't do crying, and certainly not in front of practical strangers. Blinking them away, she takes a bite of cracker, the sound of her crunching incongruous in the uncomfortable silence. Why had Zelah insisted on them sharing stuff? The evening's taken such a dip and they'd been having so much fun.

Zelah sighs and takes a long drink from her glass. 'I'm sorry you got so upset, Janet. But in the long run, you'll feel better for sharing. There's so much you won't or can't say, but I hope you'll trust me enough to tell me the truth, eventually.'

Janet harrumphs. 'Right, quit stalling. I'm all ears.'

'Okay. I left Penzance and moved up here to where my dad's family came from originally. My mum was from Zelah, hence my name. I left Penzance because my partner of forty years died. I couldn't bear to stay in the same town... Everything reminded me. I—'

Janet silently begs Zelah not to cry. She's not good with comforting people. She never knows what to do or say and

The Garden by the Sea

as a consequence, normally gets it wrong. But Zelah *is* crying. Oh God. 'Oh, dear. Don't say any more. It's obviously upsetting you. I'm sorry for being snappy. Here, have a cracker.'

Zelah dabs at her eyes with a tissue. 'I'm fine. Don't worry, it's good to get it out.'

Is it? Janet can't see why it's good to be upset and cry in public. 'Did your partner die recently?' Zelah nods and her bottom lip trembles. Oh dear. That was probably not a good thing to ask. Why does she always say the wrong thing?

'About a year ago. It's still very raw. I miss her so much.'

Janet's puzzled. Who's she talking about now? 'Um...'

'Cancer is such a bastard!' Zelah's eyes flash in fury. 'My poor Catherine battled so hard...' Zelah blows her nose and drinks more wine. 'But there we are. That's life... and death for you, I suppose.'

The puzzle is slowly becoming clear. Janet can hardly believe it. Hang on... Maybe she's put two and two together and come up with six? When Zelah said partner, maybe this Catherine was a business partner and dear friend. 'I'm not totally sure what you're saying...' Janet shuffles on the sofa, hoping she's not said the wrong thing again.

A sad little smile turns one side of Zelah's mouth up. 'Catherine was the love of my life. The one I sailed on the Ark with.'

Janet's heart is racing and the shiver is back like an electric current pulsing through her blood. She opens her mouth to speak, but the words won't come.

'I realised I was gay in my teens, but suppressed it. I didn't know anyone else like me and I had nobody to talk to about the way I felt. Eventually I told Mum, but she told me I was mistaken. She also said that if I carried on with such nonsense, she'd disown me.' Zelah releases a slow breath. 'And in the end, that's what she did. That's what *all* my family did, apart from Dad. He used to meet me in secret... The rest of them said I was a freak, an abomination. A disgrace.'

An ocean of pain and regret rises up in the space between them, sucking the oxygen from the room. Janet's finding it hard to catch her breath. The pain is shared, the regret is all Janet's. And now, now there's empathy snaking through her. And something else. Something that feels as if it's opening up to the sunshine, like the petals of a flower emerging from a winter frost. Relief. The tears well again, and Janet has to get some air. Putting her glass down she heaves herself out of the chair and, ignoring her painful knee, hurries to the back door. Outside, under the stars, in Zelah's lovely little cottage garden amongst the lavender and jasmine, she draws in a huge lungful of cool night air. As she exhales, the tears come in silent rivulets down each cheek, but this time, Janet doesn't bother to check them, not even when she hears Zelah's quiet footsteps behind.

'I expect I shocked you. Maybe you disapprove. Society has come a long way since 1962 when I was a teenager... but we still have a long way to go.'

The flat resignation wrapped around each word breaks Janet's heart. Slowly she turns to face Zelah and wipes her cheeks on the back of a hand. 'Yes, you shocked me. But I don't disapprove. I think you are one of the bravest people

I've ever met, much braver than me. You refused to be someone you weren't, no matter what the consequences.'

Zelah is standing in a square of light from the open door as if she's on a stage. Janet wishes she could shout 'bravo' and toss roses at her. 'Really?' Zelah asks, raising a trembling hand to her lips. 'What a lovely thing to say.'

'It's true. If I'd been as brave, I'm sure my life would have been much happier. And I wouldn't have an avalanche of anger and misery waiting on my head, or whatever you said.' Janet laughs. But then she shrugs and more tears fall. 'Too late now.'

Zelah steps forward, eyes glittering with emotion and gives her a quick hug. 'It's never too late to find some happiness. What is it you should have been brave about?'

Janet clenches her fists and shakes her head, even now fighting the dog of truth under the table. But this time it won't be quiet. This time it snaps, paws and whines. Its demands won't be silenced. So she feeds it.

'Exactly what you were brave about. I'm… I'm gay too.'

Chapter Nineteen

June is certainly living up to her 'flaming' moniker. It's not quite nine o'clock and the sun's yolk is sizzling in the sky. In the endless blue, clouds are too scared to show their faces, and a couple of sparrows start up a half-hearted conversation on the pergola, but soon run out of puff and head for cover in the cool hedges. Lowena slips an arm around the warm wood strut of the pergola, the competing perfumes of honeysuckle and pine resin pungent in the air. Soon the honeysuckle will win the competition. It's growing like, well, like a well-fed climber, and its yellow flowers speckle the roof of the structure like a sun shower. At the other end, delicate white blossoms of jasmine thread themselves through and around, and on breezy days Lowena can smell their fragrance, even by her back door.

The delights of her garden will have to wait today though, because in a few moments Ben will be here in a sixteen-seater mini-bus, and after picking up the others, they'll be on their way to an even grander garden. The long-awaited trip to the Eden Project. Lowena has a giddy feeling in her stomach and has felt slightly nauseous all morning. Yesterday too. At first, she thought it was a bug, but she's not ill enough. It's ridiculous how excited she is about it, but it reminds her of the school trips she had as a kid. Something a bit out of the ordinary to share with your friends, money burning a hole in her pocket for a treat or two and a souvenir. Then, on the way home, they'd sing the latest chart hits at the top of their voices, full of too much junk food and fizzy drinks. Later, the inevitable vomiting child would cause both hilarity and disgust amongst its peers. Lowena frowns. Hopefully there won't be a repeat of that today.

Ben sounds the horn, just as she's locking the door behind her and wondering if she should bring her jacket, just in case. The weatherman said wall-to-wall sunshine, but this is Cornwall after all. Ben says she won't need one and her light-blue fleece will be ample. Yes, he's sure, and no, he doesn't have anything apart from the short-sleeved red shirt he's wearing. Yes, he's reminded everyone of the meeting time, and no, he hasn't forgotten the bottles of water and snacks for everyone.

Lowena climbs up next to him in the front of the bus and gives him a big kiss. 'Have I ever told you how gorgeous you are, Ben Mawgan?' she says, pushing her fingers through the dark hairs at the back of his neck while kissing him again.

'Once or twice, Lowena Rowe,' he murmurs, running his hand along her thigh. 'And if you carry on like this, I shall not be responsible for my actions.' He pulls away. 'Suffice to say, the gang will be waiting in vain for us!'

She laughs as he drives off and counts her blessings, as she does most days. How she landed this wonderful man she has no clue. But landed him she has, and hopefully he won't swim off anywhere. The pain of Rick's betrayal is fading fast. There's no way Ben would ever hurt her like that; he's so different from her ex it's untrue. The fortune in his bank hasn't changed him at all. Lowena's read about winners who are incredibly mean and stingy. He's generous to a fault; the whole trip was paid for by him, even though Lowena didn't ask. Perhaps if they knew about the lottery win, someone like Janet might have said, 'and so he *should* pay, with all his bloody money!' But Ben didn't do it because he was obligated; he did it because they were his friends and he wanted everyone to have a fabulous day out. The gang don't know he paid, of course. They were told the trip came from the 'library funds' set aside for community events.

As they drive to the assembly point of the library, Lowena takes a few deep breaths. Excitement is doing silly things to her stomach now. It's churning fit to make butter and she has to stare straight ahead to quell her light-headedness. Ben swings onto the library drive and there's quite a crowd waiting. A buzz of conversation and laughter greets Lowena as she jumps down from the bus to greet them, making a mental note of who's turned up. Milly, Mervyn, Anna, John, Zelah, Janet, Wendy, Nigel, Hayley, Dan, Jack and his girlfriend Naomi, and Callum has brought a new girlfriend too, but Lowena doesn't know her name. All present and correct.

Mervyn waves and comes over. He looks almost as excited as she is. 'Morning, young Lowena.' Out of his pocket comes a folded bit of A4 and a pen. 'We're all here, and I've taken the liberty of jotting everyone's name down, just to keep check when we're there. We don't want to lose anybody, do we?'

A register. It's feeling more like a school trip by the second, though with only sixteen pupils, it's hardly necessary, but she says, 'Good thinking, Merv.'

Anna hurries over, gives Lowena a hug and for the next few minutes talks non-stop about her daughter Sophie, who's doing so well at uni. As she chats, Lowena watches Janet chatting to Hayley. She's noticed how different Janet is lately. Lowena's not seen her more than twice, but there's been a bit of a change. Janet is pleasant, even warm towards Lowena, her hair's longer, her clothes are casual and colourful, and she smiles. Often. It's as if all her hard edges have been smoothed down. About to share her observations with Anna, she's interrupted by Ben.

'Right. Let's get going, you lot. Make sure you've had a wee, 'cos I'm not stopping on the way. And don't leave any litter on the bus or you'll be in detention.' There are a few salutes and calls of 'Yes, sir!' He laughs and climbs back aboard.

After shepherding everyone onto the bus, Lowena joins him. 'I almost forgot you used to be a teacher. Bet the kids loved you.'

'Oh, undoubtedly, who wouldn't?' Ben gives her a

cheeky wink, and then puts his teacher's voice back on as he turns to the others. 'Make sure you put your seatbelts on and stay in your seats. You got that?'

'Yes, sir!' everyone chimes.

Ben laughs and starts the engine. 'Okay, Eden Project, here we come!'

Milly moves her bag so Mervyn can sit down after checking everyone is aboard. Outside, he'd asked her to save him a seat near the front, as he likes to keep his eyes on the road. She's pleased, because she enjoys his company. He always makes her laugh and they often talk about the old days when Milly's husband Stuart and Mervyn used to go to cattle auctions together. Though it's been seven years, and the Stuart-shaped gap in her life is still very much there, talking about him with Mervyn narrows it for a time.

'I'm looking forward to this, Milly,' Mervyn says, offering her a humbug.

'So am I, Mervyn.' She pops the sweet in her mouth, then wishes she hadn't, as it makes talking very difficult.

'Hope you don't mind me sitting next to you. It just occurred to me that Janet might want to… but she's with Zelah.' Mervyn says in surprise, nodding across the aisle to where Janet and Zelah are laughing together about something.

Milly notices that Mervyn has stuck his sweet into his cheek, so does the same. In a low voice she says, 'She never even mentioned sitting with me. I hardly see her nowadays.

She's always either round at Zelah's or they're off somewhere. I can't believe it, to be honest.' Milly leans in and whispers, 'She's transformed too. Looks ten years younger, with her long curls and dressed all modern like.' As she says 'like' her tongue flicks the humbug out of her mouth and it lands on Mervyn's shoe.

At this, Mervyn guffaws, and his sweet shoots out, skittering along the aisle. 'Oi, sir!' Jack shouts up to Ben. 'Mervyn's spitting sweeties out on the floor!'

Ben lifts a hand. 'Thanks, Jack. I'll have words with Mervyn when we get there.'

After the laughter dies down and everyone settles again, Mervyn leans into Milly. 'Have you asked her why she's thick as thieves with Zelah now, given she couldn't stand her from the off?'

'Yes. But all I got was, "People change." Janet didn't want to explain further, so I didn't push her. Besides, whatever happened I'm very glad. Janet seems happier now than she has for years. She's like the girl I remember from school. Must admit, I do miss her though... Days seem to drag.'

Mervyn frowns. 'But don't you have a lot to do with your daughter and grandchildren?'

'Oh yes. But since our Grace moved up to Devon for her husband's work, I don't see them as much as I used to. Still, I mustn't moan. I see them quite a fair bit and I have the book club, coffee morning and my hobbies to keep me going.' Milly doesn't want Mervyn to think she's a miserable old soul. Because she isn't. Not really. Though not having Janet's company much now does make a difference, even though the woman was always a pain in the bum in the past. 'How's that grandson of yours?' she asks, brightly.

Mervyn's lively grey eyes light up in delight, and he smooths his mop of hair. 'Oh, he's grand. Matthew's staying with me at the moment. He's sorted out his accommodation and everything for his course in Exeter, which starts in September, and he's having a proper holiday. He's made lots of friends already through surfing – that's where he's gone today. He's already a pro, coming from Australia. They can surf before they can walk almost, over there.'

'I bet,' Milly says with a smile. 'It's wonderful to have grandchildren, isn't it? Gives you a new lease of life… It's just a shame that Stuart only saw one of ours born.'

Mervyn gives her hand a squeeze. 'He'd have loved them. Mind you, I've not seen much of mine over the years. But then I wouldn't, would I? Them living on the other side of the world. If my wife and daughter had got on more, it would have been a different story.' Mervyn sighs. 'But my Jennifer wasn't an easy woman to love. And what's done is done. I've got our Matthew here for a while, so I plan to make the most of it.'

Milly had often wondered about Jennifer, Mervyn's wife, who died a good few years before Stuart. Mervyn had never seemed particularly happy with her, Stuart had said – bit of a tyrant by all accounts. But Mervyn wasn't the type to change horses in the middle of a stream, apparently. In other words, divorce was never an option. 'Yes. It must be such a comfort to have him with you. We're both lucky to have family, despite not seeing them all the time.'

'Indeed, we are, Milly.' He goes to offer her another

humbug but thinks better of it and puts the bag in his pocket.

'And when we don't have family round us, we have our friends. Days like this are wonderful for making you feel part of something. Lowena is such a lovely woman. What with the library and her garden, she's building a real community spirit. She organised all of this trip. Well, with a bit of help from you, I hear.' Milly gives Mervyn a warm smile.

'Only a bit. I was saying how much I'd like to go and see this exotic garden we've got on our doorstep, that's all.' Mervyn smooths his hair again, and Milly can tell he's secretly pleased that she said he'd helped Lowena.

Milly points at a road sign through the window. 'Looks like you won't have to wait much longer. Seven miles to go.'

Lowena and Ben lead the group from the carpark and Mervyn and Milly bring up the rear. Mervyn is taking his shepherding role very seriously – maybe because he was a sheep farmer – and has taken the register already. Lowena's glad the sun's decided to allow a few clouds to roll in and they've brought a little breeze with them too. For some of the more elderly members of the group, walking around for hours under a cloudless June sky would have been a bit like an endurance test rather than a day out. Getting all of the group together before entering the ticket area is an endurance test too. People have gone to the loo, wandered off to look at statues and various plants, and some are chatting in little huddles. Ben tells Lowena it's time for him to put his teacher's head on again, and very soon, with Mervyn's help, he's got them in an orderly line to go through the entrance.

The cashier seems a little surprised that there are sixteen adults in one group, but soon they are through and out the other side, all standing at the top of a hill overlooking the zigzag path to the project. Once again, Mervyn brings up the rear, but as soon as he catches sight of the biomes, he hurries ahead yelling, 'Oh my word! Just look at them. They look like giant alien eggs or something. Incredible!' He stops, takes his cap off and shakes his head in bewilderment. 'Absolutely incredible.'

Hayley and Dan are the only other members who are here for the first time and are suitably amazed. 'Wow!' Dan says. 'Can't wait to get inside.'

'This place is fantastic,' Hayley says. 'I feel a painting or two coming on.'

Lowena smiles and gazes at the huge white domes growing from the hillside and greenery like giant mushroom caps. She never fails to marvel at the view, despite having visited at least five times. 'That would be brilliant. I bet they'd sell well.'

'What are they made of? Does anyone know?' Dan asks.

Mervyn nods and says in a good impression of Ben's teacher voice, 'They are constructed of tubular steel, with hexagonal external cladding panels made from thermoplastic. I watched a TV programme about it, and read up the other day.'

'Incredible,' Dan and Hayley say at the same time.

'Incredible,' Mervyn agrees.

'Right, now we've been gobsmackingly amazed, let's get down there, folks, and take a closer look,' Ben says, striding ahead.

Outside the biomes, there's a clash of opinions about what they all want to do first. Some want to see inside the rainforest (the largest indoor one in the world, didn't they know, Mervyn informed them) and others want to see the Mediterranean dome. Others say, because it's such a lovely day, they'd like to look at the outdoor gardens and sculptures. Zelah's already making a beeline for the huge bee sculpture until Mervyn sticks his fingers in the corners of his mouth and whistles her back. Though her expression has been borrowed from a disgruntled child, she trudges back to the group like a faithful sheepdog.

Both Ben and Mervyn speak at once, trying to be the one to sort out the clash. Neither is backing down, so Lowena takes over before the competition gets too fierce. 'Listen up, people, I don't see why we can't go off and do our own thing if we want to. We don't have to stick together in one big group all day, do we?'

Mervyn's bushy eyebrows nearly disappear into the deep V of his frown and he immediately jumps in. 'Is that wise? I made that list of names so we didn't lose people… Then we don't have to be waiting around, wondering where our stragglers are.'

Lowena realises her idea is spoiling his fun and sense of feeling useful, but people want to do different things, and she does have the answer to his concerns. 'We've all got mobile phones, Merv. And we can agree to meet at certain times to share our experiences. Lunch at one in the main café might be the first one?' She looks round as people nod their assent and get ready to depart. Everyone is happy, apart from Mervyn, that is. But then Milly whispers something in his ear and he brightens.

'Okay,' he says with a smile. 'We'll meet up at one. Me and Milly will get there a bit before and get some tables sorted. I dare say we'll need at least three to get us all seated.'

Lowena and Ben wave them all off. Good old Milly; she obviously suggested the table requisitioning to placate him. About to ask Ben what he wants to do first, she notices Jack, Callum and their girlfriends hanging around behind them.

'Before we go off, we thought we should introduce my Naomi and Callum's Lennie to you,' Jack says, shoving a hand through his dark curls and slipping his arm around Naomi's shoulders. She's blonde, slim, small and slightly dwarfed by his burly frame.

'Pleased to meet you,' Naomi says a little shyly, offering her hand. As she does, Lowena notices a lovely silver bracelet on her wrist made from joined hearts.

'You too,' Lowena says. 'And that's a pretty bracelet.' She gives Jack a knowing smile.

Naomi's turquoise eyes shine with pride. 'It was a present from Jack. I love it.'

Callum fiddles with his ponytail and nods at the tall, curvy brunette next to him. 'This is Lennie. Her real name's Leonora but she says it makes her sound like an old lady.'

Lennie laughs and gives him a playful push. 'It does!'

'I think both names are equally lovely,' Lowena says,

shaking her hand. Lennie beams and slips her arm through Callum's.

The six of them decide to go around as a group and set off for the rainforest biome first. Lowena leans in to whisper to Ben as they walk behind the youngsters. 'Oh, to be young and in love, just starting out in life, eh?'

'God, I can't think of anything worse. All the angst and heartache of getting dumped. Then back out to find the next one, hoping that this time it will last – horrifying.'

'You old misery!'

'But you love me.'

'I do.'

Walking into the rainforest biome is like being hugged by a steam bath. Ben points at his shirt. 'And you wondered if I'd be okay in this? Wish you'd put your jacket on?' he laughs, as Lowena strips down to her red strappy vest top.

'Okay, smarty pants. But later it might get chilly.'

'Not sure they have an arctic biome.'

Lowena pokes him in the chest. 'What's that?' she asks aghast.

Ben looks down and she flicks the end of his nose. 'Oi!'

'Ha! Serves you right for being smug.' She squeals as Ben tries to tickle her and runs off up the path towards the banana trees.

Ben gives chase, and as they pass the youngsters, Jack yells, 'Hey, we're supposed to be the kids around here!'

An hour passes in the blink of an eye and in that time,

they have seen so many wonderful plants and birds, walked across a rope bridge through a cloud, seen some amazing African sculptures and waterfalls, and taken part in a quiz. Lowena has also got to know Naomi too. She's a lovely girl and very easy to get along with. She loves plants too, but her main ambition is to be a veterinary nurse. She's doing her training while working at a vet's already, and should have completed it in another year. Lowena mentions that her parents must be thrilled with Naomi's choice of career, and although she said yes, something about the way the girl's smile faltered makes Lowena wonder if things are okay at home.

In the near distance, she notices Milly and Mervyn examining the cacao trees and goes over for a chat. Milly waves and points at the tree. 'Can you believe this is where all our chocolate comes from?'

Over the top of Milly's head, Mervyn winks at Lowena and says deadpan, 'Not just this one tree, Milly.'

Milly says that yes, she does realise this, and whacks him on the arm and they laugh. Lowena wonders if there might be a late romance blossoming there, but obviously keeps her ideas to herself. Ben and the youngsters join them, and Mervyn, finding himself with a small audience, takes the opportunity of telling them all about what they've seen, which is pretty much what they've all seen, but people are too polite to interrupt. 'Did you realise that the shells of cashew nuts have liquor that can be used to treat ringworm and warts?'

There is a collective shaking of heads and Lowena says, 'No. How fascinating.'

'And the wild plantain is pollinated by hummingbirds and sometimes even bats!' Mervyn's eyes grow round as if he's hearing this fact for the first time. His information is received with a few *ohs* and *ahs* and Naomi supplies a 'blimey!'

'And the flowers are marvellous, aren't they?' Milly says. 'That jade plant, well, I've never seen anything so unusual in my life.'

'It's called a jade vine, Milly,' Mervyn says, in his best teacher's voice.

'Ah yes, it's very beautiful,' Lennie says.

'That one's pollinated by bats too, I seem to remember,' Ben says.

'Are you sure?' Mervyn asks, a little frown settling between his brows. 'I think I'd have remembered that.'

'Yes, quite sure,' Ben says with a smile. Lowena wishes she could catch his eye to signal him to leave it. Old Mervyn obviously wants to be right and it's not worth the effort. 'We can go back and check, if you like. It's only five minutes up the path?' Ben makes as if to lead the way until Lowena grabs his arm.

'We don't have time for that. Not if we want to see other stuff before lunch,' she says, slipping her arm through his and turning back towards the exit.

Mervyn looks relieved and says as they move off, 'I can't wait to see what marvels await us at the Mediterranean biome.'

Ben whispers to Lowena, 'Me either. But let's hope we don't see Marvellous Mervyn on the way out of there. Not sure my poor brain could stand more lectures.'

Lowena gives a soft laugh. 'The trouble with you both is you're too similar. You like to pontificate sometimes too. Must be the ex-teacher in you.'

Ben pulls an indignant face. 'How very dare you, young woman.' Then he treats her to a half-moon. 'Now. Did I ever tell you about the banana? One stem can hold up to two hundred bananas, don't you know? And in India, they're used in ancient fertility rituals.'

'Amazing!' Lowena giggles. Then she takes a squint at her phone. 'It's twelve-forty, Merv!' she calls over her shoulder.

'Is it? Blimey! Time flies when you're in a rainforest.' He grabs Milly's arm and sets off at a fair old pace for a man of his years, raising his walking stick as he passes them. 'We've got to sort the tables for lunch. See you later!'

Callum laughs as the two of them disappear round a bend in the path. He says to the group, 'And God help anyone who gets in his way!'

Chapter Twenty

'Mervyn's like a dog with two tails and doesn't know which to wag first,' Wendy says to Lowena as she sits down opposite her in the Canopy Café.

Lowena laughs. 'Why's that?'

'Because he managed to get three tables together. He was just telling me and Nigel that there were only two when he and Milly got here, but then a family left and he pounced on it.'

'Yeah.' Nigel nods. 'Milly cleaned it down with a few wet wipes and then they stood guard until we got here.'

'Dear Mervyn,' Hayley says. 'Gotta love him.'

'You have,' Zelah says from the next table. Then she lowers her voice and cups her hands round her mouth. 'And I think I might know who loves him most.' She tips her head in Milly's direction and does a theatrical wink.

'Really?' Anna asks, surprised.

'No. Zelah does like to jump to conclusions,' Janet says, not unkindly. Then she nudges Zelah's arm. 'You need to keep your big gob shut, madam.' Zelah rolls her eyes, pinches her thumb and forefinger together and draws them across her lips in a zip mime.

Watching Janet and Zelah for a few moments, Lowena suddenly has the strangest feeling that they... No. That's mad. Now who's jumping to conclusions?

The food's delicious and the group talk non-stop about everything they've seen and done. Lowena mops up a bit of mayonnaise with her pizza and Naomi, who's sitting next to her, wonders if she has room for pudding. 'You should have whatever you like, Naomi. You certainly shouldn't worry about putting weight on at your age.'

Naomi's smile falters, and once again, Lowena's aware that she could have inadvertently touched a raw nerve, like earlier when she asked if Naomi's parents were happy with her career choice. 'Maybe not yet at least...'

Naomi takes a sip of juice and then fixes Lowena with an intense stare. 'Lowena, can I have a word with you about something that's been bothering me?'

The grave tone and a lurch in Lowena's stomach tell her this is something quite serious. But she smiles and says, 'Of course. Fire away.'

'In private, I mean.' Naomi fiddles with her hair and looks at her plate. 'You're really easy to talk to and there's nobody else who I can share stuff with. Nobody sensible, I mean. I have friends my own age, but they can't give proper advice about things and…' She wraps the remainder of her words in a shrug.

Lowena wonders where they can go without people noticing they've gone off together. 'We could say we're off to the loo, but go outside on the way, if you like? There are some picnic benches by the door.'

Naomi nods and tells Jack where she's going. Once they're outside and settled on the bench, she says, 'The thing is, Lowena, I have a huge problem and I can't tell my dad. My mum died of cancer when I was twelve, and Dad was hit so hard. We both were, obviously, but he's never recovered, really. Our Harry, my elder brother, is in the army and rarely home. So Dad puts all his hopes into me. I'm the reason he's still with us, I'm convinced of it. When you asked were my folks pleased, well, yeah, Dad is over the moon, keeps telling me how proud he is of me. But this problem I have, well, it might bugger all that up.' Naomi looks at a trail of ants on the table wrestling with an apple core and heaves a sigh. 'There's no might about it. It *will* bugger it up.'

Poor Naomi. This girl is going through hell, and Lowena isn't looking forward to hearing what the problem is, but she knows she must. 'It might not be as bad as you think?' she offers, knowing by Naomi's deflated glance that it probably is.

'Oh, it is.' Unshed tears wait and she brushes them away. 'I couldn't believe it at first when I got the achy boobs, the nausea, the strange smells and tastes. My periods have never been what you call regular, so I did have some hope. But I did a test. I'm pregnant all right. Two months.'

Oh God. Lowena's struck dumb as shock runs the length of her... and not just because of Naomi's news. In place of words, she gives a sympathetic smile, takes Naomi's hand and gives it a squeeze.

'What do I do? Jack doesn't know. I haven't plucked up the courage to tell him. I might not tell him if I...'

After a moment Lowena finds the words Naomi couldn't. 'Terminate, you mean?'

'Yeah. I don't want to, but all my plans to be a veterinary nurse will go out the window. I would probably lose my job at the vet's, and Dad,' Naomi brushes away fresh tears. 'Dad will be so disappointed. He's had so much heartache, suffers from anxiety, and this will finish him off. I know it.'

They sit in silence for a few seconds while Lowena tries to process it all and find a way forward. A way to help seems obvious, but it could go horribly wrong. And there's also a thousand crazy thoughts about her own condition whirling around her mind. Could the nausea and light-headedness she's had for the past few days have nothing to do with a bug or the excitement of coming on this trip at all? Excitement is certainly in the mix now. Both that and shock send her heart rate into the stratosphere, but her sensible side whispers not to count her chickens just yet. Then a roll of nausea kicks into her gut and she has to take a few deep breaths until it passes. Aware that Naomi is waiting for a response, she says, 'If you decide to keep it, you could defer the last part of the course until later. You can even do courses online. And you're so young, there's always time to get back on track.'

One side of Naomi's mouth turns up, in a half-hearted smile. 'Maybe. But my dad—'

'I could come along when you tell him, if you like? You might feel more supported if there's a friend with you.' Lowena thinks this is the bit that could go horribly wrong. Naomi's dad could go ape and blame her for sticking her big nose in.

'Would you?' Naomi's eyes hold a flicker of hope. 'That would make it easier. But even if he was okay about it, how would we manage to afford a baby? Dad only works part-time because of his anxiety, and I wouldn't be able to work as a veterinary nurse until I've qualified, which would be ages. And what if Jack goes nuts? Says he doesn't want anything to do with me or the baby?'

'Let's take one step at a time, love. First of all, you have to decide if you want to keep it. Because if you don't, then I certainly won't be the one to judge you.'

The sweetest smile curls her lips. 'That's easy. I've decided. I love it already.' The intense longing and anguish in the young woman's voice bring tears to Lowena's eyes. 'It's just that everything is so hard. Everything is stacked against keeping it.'

'Not everything.' Lowena's not sure where she's getting this conviction from, but she knows she's doing the right thing. 'There's always a way, and if you already love it, then that's half the battle. I'm not saying it will be easy, but it will be worth it.'

Naomi throws her arms around Lowena and sobs on her shoulder. 'Thanks so much. You've helped more than you'll ever know. I could have discussed it with Lennie and my other friends, but they aren't so wise. And you're older, and have more experience of life.'

Lowena isn't sure about how relevant her experience with babies is, but it's true she's wiser than the average seventeen or eighteen-year-old. 'My pleasure. I'll do what I can. Now dry your tears and we'll go back to the others before they send a search party.'

'When will you come to mine to help me tell Dad?'

'When you've talked to Jack. I think he should know before your dad does. Then we'll arrange a time very soon, okay?'

Naomi smiles and follows Lowena inside. As she walks, Lowena is thinking of her own talk she might be having with the man she loves. One after the other, waves of emotion smash through her, bashing against the rocks of uncertainty, excitement and joy. Mostly joy. Because if she's pregnant too, it would be a dream come true. But before she lets herself run with it, or thinks any more about it, she needs a trip to the chemist.

———————

Zelah and Janet are having the time of their lives in the Mediterranean biome. Zelah, over the last few weeks, has convinced Janet about the power of healing plants and herbs, mainly because her yarrow tea has all but cured Janet's dodgy knee. She's a keen student and a quick learner, and Zelah's in her element, pointing out all the wonders Mother Nature has to offer in the abundance of greenery and colour all around.

'Look!' Zelah shrieks, pointing a glittery purple nail at a delicate red-flowered plant by the path. Janet looks, and, alerted by Zelah's shriek and the whirl of her flamboyant kaftan, so do half a dozen other people. 'Mexican scarlet sage. I read about it the other day, but it's more beautiful in the flesh. It's good for all manner of stomach problems.'

Janet nods and smiles. Although Zelah's enthusiasm is infectious, she thinks she feels an antidote coming on. The shrieking, whirling and pointing at nearly every growing thing is wearing a bit thin. As is all the attention Zelah's gathering. Some people seem genuinely delighted with Zelah and her loud explanations; others shrink from her, give her a wide berth as if she's a deadly nightshade. Since that evening when Janet shared her secret, the two of them have been inseparable and Janet is now fonder of Zelah than she ever thought possible. She's fonder of her than she is of Milly even, and can't imagine life without her these days. They have such fun and silly adventures. But just sometimes, Janet wishes her lovely friend had a mute button.

'Shall we think about making a move for the meeting point? It's almost four, and we're meeting at ten past,' Janet says to Zelah's behind as it wiggles from side to side, having bent double to watch an 'interesting and amazingly beautiful' bird dart through some bushes.

'Already?' Zelah grumbles, straightening up. 'It's all gone so fast.'

'It has, and I've loved every moment of it. But the crowds are thinning out now, and we agreed we'd go before everyone piles into the carpark.'

'Okay, I suppose so.' Zelah turns her bottom lip down which makes Janet giggle.

'We've got the gift shop to go at, don't forget. They might have some *interesting and amazingly beautiful* plants we could buy.'

'Oh yes!' Zelah claps her hands, oblivious to Janet's gentle ribbing. 'I'd clean forgot about that.' Zelah slips her arm through Janet's. 'Come on then, get a wriggle on, we don't want to be late.'

A few moments down the path, Zelah stops. 'Oh hell. I put my bag down near that bush when I was watching the bird. We'll have to go back. I hope nobody's nicked it!'

Luckily the green and red striped bag is where she left it and they're just about to go back down when Zelah grips Janet's arm so tightly she nearly yells out loud. 'Ow. What are you doing?'

'Shh!' Zelah hisses, pulling Janet behind a palm tree. 'Look over there. That woman's stealing some Mexican red sage and what looks like Hummingbird's trumpet!'

As if. There must be some logical explanation to what Zelah thinks she's seen. But, upon closer inspection, oh my goodness, Janet sees she's right. On her hands and knees, partially hidden by a clump of bushes, a middle-aged woman in dark jeans and a T-shirt is busily digging up plants with a trowel and putting them into a large canvas bag. 'I can't believe it,' Janet whispers. 'Oh, wait. Maybe she works here.'

'No chance. If she was moving them, she'd have proper pots to shift them. She wouldn't just stick them in a bag like that. And look at the speed of her, she's obviously nicking them!'

Janet watches the woman a bit longer and has to agree. 'Okay. I'll try and find a member of staff. You keep your eye on her.'

'We don't have time for that! I'm gonna tackle her,' Zelah says, rolling the sleeves of her multi-coloured kaftan up past the elbow.

'Eh?' Janet says, aghast. 'She's younger and fitter than you. God knows what damage she could do.'

'Good job there's two of us then, isn't it? Come on.'

'No, Zelah. This is stupid, I—'

But it's too late. Zelah rushes forward and leaps on the woman's back, sending the two of them sprawling. 'Stop that, you dirty thief!' she yells as the woman gets over her shock and tries to wriggle free of Zelah's grasp.

Janet hesitates for a second until she sees her friend is being overpowered. Oh God. The Janet of old would have stood back in disdain. If Zelah wanted to get herself into scrapes, then she could damned well get herself out of them. But this isn't the old Janet, this is the new Janet, and she has Zelah to thank for it. She rushes over too and grabs the woman's bag. 'I'll take this!'

The woman pushes herself up with a grunt and lunges for the bag, her face covered in dirt and a determined expression, but Janet sidesteps her at the last minute and the woman trips over an olive bush and comes crashing to earth. Zelah gives a blood-curdling yell of triumph and sits on the woman's back, just as two members of staff come rushing over. Seeing the woman might still make a bolt for it, Janet sits on the woman too and they both quickly explain what's been happening. By this time a small crowd has gathered, and one young woman has managed to capture the whole thing on camera.

'I know I should have perhaps lent a hand,' she says with a sheepish smile. 'But I'm a local journalist and those images of you tackling her were just too good to miss.'

At this Zelah's head shoots up in interest. 'Are we going to be in the paper?' she asks, her hair a mad grey cloud, her face aglow with excitement and the effort of restraining the thief.

'That would be brilliant, if you'd agree to it.'

'Whoop!' says, Zelah, as she and Janet clamber off the thief, to allow the two members of staff to make a citizen's arrest and call security.

'My God, what a day it's been,' says, Lowena as they all gather back at the minibus.

'It's been one of the best days I've had in my entire life!' Zelah says, throwing her arms up, and a line of wooden bangles clack together as if her arms are curtain rails.

Janet grins and holds two big bags up. 'And we were given some interesting and amazingly beautiful plants and gifts as a thank you for catching the thief.'

Mervyn pats them both on the back. 'Well done, ladies. Lord knows how many she'd have nicked if you haven't been around. One member of staff said she'd nabbed some rare ones too.'

'Yep. Cheeky mare,' Milly says. 'Why couldn't she buy them in the shop like everyone else?'

'Some shysters like things for free with no thought for anyone else,' Zelah says. 'Imagine what would happen if everyone decided to grab a few plants that took their fancy?'

'Exactly. Very selfish and greedy,' Mervyn agrees. 'But she didn't reckon on having you two to deal with. Well done again.' He leads a round of applause and they move to get on the bus.

Even though Mervyn was genuine in his praise, Lowena can tell he wished he'd been part of the excitement too, so adds, 'And a round of applause for Mervyn, who is brilliant at organising and made sure we were all ticked off the list. And to him and Milly, who made sure that we were able to sit together at lunchtime.'

Another round of applause follows as Milly and Mervyn look suitably pleased with themselves. 'And another round of applause for Lowena, whose brainchild this was and who organised the whole trip, and thanks to Ben for driving us!' says Anna.

After the applause dies down, Lowena says, 'Thanks, everyone. It's been the best day! But right now, we need to get gone before we get stuck in traffic on the A30.'

On the drive home, Ben reaches for Lowena's hand and gives it a quick squeeze. 'It's been a cracking day out, hasn't it, sweetheart?

'It really has. I've loved every minute of it.' She lowers her voice. 'Apart from a chat I had with Naomi. I'll tell you about it later.'

'Oh? Sounds ominous.'

'It might not be. We'll see.'

'Right. You coming back to mine?'

'No. Not tonight, thanks, Ben. I'm pooped and have work tomorrow. In fact, can you drop me at the supermarket? I need to get some food for Conrad and a few bits.' To herself she adds, *and a very important item from the pharmacy section.*

Chapter Twenty-One

The next morning Lowena's still exhausted as she didn't get as much sleep as she needed, and she's been throwing up for the last fifteen minutes. The pregnancy test is waiting on the side of the bath, but she has a sneaky feeling she won't be needing it. She's never been pregnant, but a gut instinct tells her she is. Although she'd been tempted last night to get the result, she'd waited until this morning, because if it was positive, she could ring Ben and tell him to come over quickly. Because she felt so ropey, she'd decided not to open the library today, so they could spend the day quietly together. She's sure they'll have lots to talk about. Besides excitement, this is one of the reasons she didn't sleep well.

Lowena cleans her teeth and goes over the whole scenario again. Ben might well be horrified at becoming a father again at the age of forty-five. His two children are nineteen and twenty-one, after all. And what will they think about having a baby half-brother or sister? They've not even met Lowena yet, so being presented with a pregnant stepmother would be overwhelming, to say the least. She looks at her pallid complexion in the bathroom mirror. Her eyes look like two green leaves in the snow, and her hair's a tangle of brambles. Lowena sighs. Even if Ben is horrified and wants no part of it, she's no doubt he will make sure the baby wants for nothing as he's a decent man. A wonderful man. But, whatever he thinks, this baby is here to stay. *Maybe getting ahead of yourself there, Lowena?* Might be an idea to do the test.

She sits on the loo and pees on the stick, her heart thundering in her chest. The she sits there watching for the lines to show. Two minutes feels like hours, and as she waits, she wonders again how it might have happened, if she is pregnant. Well, she knows exactly how it happened – they can't leave each other alone, but they'd always been careful, hadn't they? Lowena isn't on the pill, as she couldn't see the point in putting unnecessary chemicals in her body when she had no intention of finding a man, so they'd used condoms, though they had talked only last week about her perhaps going on the pill. But... Lowena's inner ramblings are cut short by two pink lines materialising in the little window on the tester. And just to make absolutely certain, in the next window words have appeared. Words that say: *Pregnant 6-7 weeks.*

With trembling fingers Lowena puts the test on the side of the bath and stands up. Then she whoops and yells as joy rockets through every cell and sinew. Racing to her bedroom, she grabs her mobile phone and googles 'foetus size 7 weeks'. It will be as big as a blueberry or a grape!

How amazing. How wonderful! Oh my God, she's feeling dizzy with excitement and has to flop down on the bed. This is all so much to take in. Something she'd always dreamed about, but thought had passed her by, is now a reality. She laughs out loud when she remembers the additional secret wish on the Tintagel box has actually come true. No more pie in the sky, but a bun in the oven!

Eyes closed, Lowena takes deep breaths as she remembers: around six weeks ago, she and Ben had made love for the second time and he said the condom had slipped. They'd both thought it'd be okay. Lowena reckoned her fertility would be much lower now she'd hit forty, and hadn't thought too much of it when her period hadn't appeared. She'd never been that regular, and, to be honest, she'd forgotten to check on the calendar, she'd been so busy lately. The bedside clock says seven forty-five. Is it too early to ring Ben? She can't remember what he said he was up to today. Might be down at the allotment project in Camborne, so she'd better call him before he leaves.

Cross-legged on the bed, Lowena stares at the phone's screen saver, and the screen saver stares back. It's a cow in a field looking over a gate with the backdrop of the ocean behind it. She took the photograph last week and loves the inquisitive expression on the cow's face. Ben says cows don't have the intelligence to be inquisitive, but she disagrees. Anyone could see this one wanted to know all about their lives. Ben had laughed and picked her up, threatened to chuck her over the gate with the cow, until she'd screamed for mercy. The cow had lost interest then and trotted off. Okay, here goes. You can't put it off any longer. Lowena scrolls to Ben's number and calls him. He answers after two rings.

'Hello, my darling. To what do I owe the pleasure?'

Lowena clears her throat and tries to keep a tremor from her voice. 'I wondered if you'd like to come over for breakfast? I have that smoked bacon you like and some field mushrooms Zelah picked for me.'

'Oh, I would love nothing better, but I'm about to leave for Plymouth. That workshop I'm doing is today, remember? And I thought you were working today too?'

The excitement and joy she's just managing to hold back behind a dam wall dry up and wither, but disappointment escapes through a crack and gushes forth. 'Oh yeah. I had completely forgotten! What a shame.'

'Hey, don't worry, the bacon will keep for tomorrow. It's only breakfast, my love. You sound devastated.'

Does she? Yes, she supposes she does. Lowena so wanted the moment she told him to be special. And most of all, she wanted it to be now. This morning. But there's no way she's telling him something so important over the phone. From somewhere she finds a neutral tone. 'No, don't worry. I just miss you, that's all. Even though we've only been apart one night. I didn't sleep well and have a bit of a headache, so that's why I'm not at work. I'll ring Mervyn and ask him to put a note on the library door explaining.'

'Oh, poor you. And what a lovely thing to say about missing me. How about I pop over to you this evening on my way home? I can grab something from a takeaway, or I could cook you something?'

Lowena brightens. Better than leaving it another day at least. 'Okay, but I'll cook, as I'm not working today.'

'You well enough?'

'Yeah. I'll have a nap later.'

'Okay, love you. See you later.'

'You too, bye.'

A few hours later, after a long bath and pampering session, Lowena's in her bedroom getting dry when her phone rings again. Grabbing it from the bed she sees it's an unknown number and expects some scam or someone trying to sell her double glazing.

'Hello?' she says, on her guard.

'Hi, Lowena, it's Naomi.'

'Oh hi! I must have forgot to put your name next to the number when I added you yesterday. How's things?'

'Well, I told Jack last night when we got back and it didn't go as bad as I expected. He was obviously shocked and not what you'd called thrilled. But after it started to sink in, he said he loved me and would love the baby too.'

Naomi's voice cracks and Lowena hears a sniff. 'Aw, I'm so pleased.'

'Yes, me too. I told him I'd been so worried and wondered if he'd think it would be a good idea for me to terminate and he said absolutely no way, bless him. He said it wouldn't be easy, as we're so young and have no real income and nowhere to live, but we'd manage somehow. And by the time the baby arrives, we'll be sorted.' Then she starts to sob.

'Hey, hey. Don't cry, love. It will all work out,' Lowena says, though Jack's scenario is as true as it is bleak. 'Maybe

Ben can find him some more work. He's helping out with talks and workshops to disaffected youth, isn't he?'

'Yeah. And he's got a part-time job in a garden centre. It's not enough for us and the baby to live on though, and certainly not enough to get a flat.'

'But you can get help – benefits and stuff. It will all work out in the end. And the main thing is that Jack is on board. As my mum always used to tell me, you must never give up on your dreams, no matter how hard it might be to achieve them.'

'Yes.' Naomi blows her nose. 'Yes, your mum was right. And I do believe it will be okay. The thing is, I've got the worry of telling my dad hanging over my head right now.'

'Of course. But don't forget I said I can come with you if you—'

'I know. Could you come today? I want to get it off my mind.'

Today? Lowena's mood drops off a cliff. Not only did she not get to tell Ben her news this morning, she's going to help break someone else's to a potentially devastated parent. Maybe she could put it off. But then she pictures Naomi's tearful little face at the end of the line. 'Okay, what time were you thinking?'

———

Lowena parks up outside a row of run-down properties on the outskirts of Wadebridge. The houses are old, but most of the residents have tried to make an effort with their neat little front gardens. Naomi told her they're rented and the landlord lives in London. He does the bare minimum in terms of upkeep, but hikes up the rent whenever he can. Lowena smiles grimly and looks at the little row of houses again. The residents' gardens and their respect for their homes are like putting two fingers up to the landlord, as well they should.

As Lowena walks up the path, Naomi opens the door and ushers her inside. In hushed tones she says, 'Dad's in the living room just finishing his lunch. I made him a bacon sandwich to help his mood.' Her attempt at a chuckle sounds a bit strangled.

Lowena swallows down trepidation and follows Naomi into the living room. There's a thick-set balding man in his forties at the dining table, wiping his mouth on a bit of kitchen roll. He's about to raise a mug to his lips, but stops when he sees Lowena. 'Oh, hello?' he says, looking from Lowena to his daughter, in surprise.

'Hello,' Lowena says with a smile, though her insides are twisting and she hopes she's not going to have another bout of morning sickness.

'Dad, this is Lowena. She's Ben's girlfriend, you know, the guy who looks after Jack?'

'Oh yes.' He nods at Lowena but obviously is wondering why she's here. 'Nice to meet you, Lowena.'

Lowena says, 'You too... er, I can't call you Dad.' In the quiet room, her forced laugh sounds like an assault.

'Sorry,' Naomi says. 'His name's Peter.'

Peter frowns. 'I can speak for myself, you know.'

'Hi, Peter. Naomi and I met yesterday on our trip to the Eden Project. We got on really well. Your daughter is a fine young woman and a credit to you.' Lowena hopes she's not over-egging it.

Peter's grumpy visage irons out at this and a lopsided smile settles on his lips. 'She's a good girl.'

Naomi shoots a panicked glance at Lowena which says, *He won't be thinking that after I tell him.* 'Would you like a cup of tea or coffee, Lowena?'

'No thanks, I had one before I came out.' Lowena isn't keen on being left alone with Peter while Naomi makes it. Too many awkward questions. Naomi sits at the table and indicates a chair at the end for Lowena.

There's an uncomfortable silence punctuated by a slurp or two as Peter drinks his tea. Then all three sit like pigeons on a ledge until Lowena wishes she could fly off over the rooftops. After she sends a meaningful glance to Naomi, the young woman clears her throat. 'Dad. I have something to tell you and Lowena's here to give me a bit of support because it isn't something that you will want to hear. Well, I'm not sure exactly what you'll think really. I know you'll be upset. But it's... well...' Naomi's turquoise eyes become swimming pools and she looks at the table, fat, silent tears plopping onto the butterfly-patterned cloth.

Peter shoots Lowena an anxious glance and then pats his daughter's hand. 'Come on, love. You're worrying me now – just say what it is.'

Naomi blows out a long breath and blows her nose. Then she raises her head, looks directly at her dad and says, 'I'm pregnant and I'm keeping it, Dad. Jack knows and says he'll support us. He loves me and I love him.'

Peter's expression is unreadable, then he blows out an

even longer breath than Naomi. 'Thank God. At first I thought you were going to say you'd got some incurable bloody illness or something.' Then he smiles and it transforms his whole face. He looks ten years younger and his eyes, so much like his daughter's, look like the Atlantic on a sunny day.

Lowena hugs herself in delight and looks at Naomi, who's staring at her father open-mouthed. 'That's a relief for you then, Naomi?' Lowena says. 'She's been so worried, Peter.'

'No need to be. These things happen. Me and her mum, God rest her soul, weren't much older than Naomi when she fell pregnant with our eldest lad, Harry. It was tough, but we managed and we never regretted a single day.' Peter's eyes drift to a photo on the windowsill of two young people in wedding attire on a windswept beach. The bride's laughing and grabbing at her veil as the wind takes it, looking up into the eyes of the groom. He's laughing too, as he looks back adoringly.

When Peter shifts his gaze to his daughter his eyes are mirrors of hers and Lowena swallows a lump of emotion and blinks rapidly. So much pain mixed with joyous memories is plain to see; it thickens the air between them all like another person's come to sit at the table. 'Oh, Dad,' Naomi says, letting her pools spill over unchecked. 'I thought you'd be furious. All I've worked for down the drain – the dreams you had for me at the vet's and stuff. You were so proud. And you've been devastated since Mum went. I didn't want you to be ashamed of me or to bring you more anxiety and grief.'

Peter shakes his head and looks at her in wonder. 'I could never be ashamed of you, my sweetheart. You've always been a joy to both me and your mum. Perhaps we'd have wanted you to have lived your life a bit before settling down, but as I said we weren't much older. And your veterinary nurse training can wait. You've got time on your side.'

Naomi, obviously lost for words, gets up and throws her arms around Peter and they cling together, the love between them as vibrant and strong as a rainbow on the gloomiest day. Lowena thinks what an amazingly wonderful dad Naomi has. In a way, his attitude reminds her of her own dad and by now she's having to squeeze her eyes shut to stop her tears. 'Seems like you didn't need me after all,' she says with a little laugh after a few moments.

Peter looks at her and smiles. 'Nope. Mind you, I'm not sure what you were supposed to say anyway.'

'I was just going to point out that Naomi could defer her course, and there'd be help from the government for housing costs and stuff. I think she just wanted a bit of support really.'

'Yeah,' sniffs Naomi, sitting back down and wiping her eyes with a tissue. 'I was worried you'd be upset and get depressed again. I can't tell you how happy I am now, Dad.'

'I can see you are, maid. And I am too, truth be told. Can't wait to have a little one about the place, into everything. I'll be able to take him or her fishing and to the park, and all sorts. It will be a new lease of life for me. Our Harry's having the time of his life in the army, so I can't see him settling down any time soon, so my first grandchild will be spoilt rotten.'

'There you go,' Lowena says. 'Built-in childcare so you can go back to work. Maybe part-time at first?'

'I'm up for it, no problem,' Peter says. 'I will do all I can to help, apart from the financial bit, 'cos I'm skint as you now. But looking after a little one costs nothing apart from love. And I have bags of that.'

'Thank you so much, Dad.' Naomi looks from one to the other, takes a deep breath and releases it. 'I am totally gobsmacked, over the moon, excited and thrilled all rolled into one.'

Peter stands up. 'Me too. And this calls for a celebration. I made some scones from your mum's recipe earlier. How about one of those and a fresh pot of tea?' He winks at Lowena.

'Thanks. That would be absolutely fab, Peter.'

Naomi and Lowena chat about how wonderfully it's all turned out while Peter busies himself in the kitchen. But all the time she's talking, backstage in Lowena's mind, there's a gaggle of witches stirring the worry cauldron. Will Ben be as happy about their news?

Chapter Twenty-Two

That evening, Lowena tests the chicken casserole on the hob and checks on the roast potatoes and veg in the oven. It all looks delicious. Ben will be here in a few minutes, but her stomach's churning so much she's unlikely to be able to eat a scrap. A good talking-to is what's needed, because all this worrying is slowly deflating the bubble of joy she's been floating on all day. This is the most exciting news she's ever told anyone, and nothing should be allowed to ruin it. Yes, the old argument about Ben not being happy to be an older dad has done the rounds, *again*, and so have all the other negative thoughts. Naomi had the same worries and look what happened there. It will *all* be fine. Then there's a knock at the door and her heart leaps. *Okay, this is it. Let's go and spread some joy!*

'Hello, beautiful!' Ben says as he walks in, enveloping her in a warm hug.

'What a nice greeting,' Lowena says with a smile and kisses him softly on the lips. Outside she's dressed in a persona of calm and peace; inside, there's a tornado of mixed emotion thundering through her. A stiff brandy would do the trick, but she won't be having one of those for many months.

Ben hangs his coat on the peg in the hall and walks through to the kitchen. 'Wow. Something smells delicious. I'm starving. Only had a manky sandwich for lunch at the workshop. Well, if you could call it that. It was more like a curled-up bit of cardboard, and the ham, if it was ham, tasted like nothing at all.' He lifts the lid of the casserole and takes a deep breath. 'Feed me. Feed me now!' he sings.

'*Little Shop of Horrors*?'

'Yeah, loved that film.'

'Me too. Okay, sit down and I'll feed you. Glass of wine?'

'Why, I don't mind if I do.'

Lowena puts the wine on the table and bustles around gathering crockery and transferring the potatoes and veg to serving dishes. Her hands are shaking so much she keeps dropping things and she's only half listening to Ben's conversation. She catches the tail end of it: 'I hope he's okay. But I couldn't stop, as the lights changed.'

'Who?' Lowena asks, putting the dishes on the table and sitting opposite. 'Sorry, I wasn't really listening.'

'Charming.' Ben laughs and sips his wine. 'Jack. I said I saw him in town as I was driving home earlier. He looked like he'd got the troubles of the world on his shoulders. I wanted to see if he was okay, but the lights changed and I had to move on. There was nowhere to pull in, so I'll give him a ring later. Probably nothing.'

Great, thinks Lowena. Hopefully Jack was just lost in thought and not having second ones. She says, 'Yeah. He'll be fine,' and puts a forkful of chicken and carrots into her mouth. As she chews, she wonders whether to break her news now or before pudding. Now. It has to be now, because she can't wait another second.

But before she can even open her mouth, Ben says, 'What was the chat about you had with Naomi? You never got round to telling me. Sounded pretty serious.'

Now what? If she tells him all about Naomi and Jack, their conversation will go off on a different track to the one she wants to be on. But how can she not tell him? Bugger. 'It was serious, but thankfully all's well that ends well.' Then she quickly tells him about the pregnancy and going round to Peter's today.

Ben has been silent throughout and his face looks as if someone had told him he's got a week to live. He's stopped eating, but drained his wine glass in record time. He helps himself to another and heaves a sigh. 'Bloody hell. No wonder Jack looked down. Their lives were just about to take off and now they're stuck. A baby? They're only still babies themselves.'

The tornado of mixed emotion twisting through her from earlier is back, though this time it's not mixed. There is only despair. Raw and cruel, ripping up everything in its path. All her plans, her happiness, her hope torn up and smashed. Broken. She never expected a reaction like this from Ben. If he's so gutted about Jack and Naomi having a baby, there's no doubt how he'll feel about having his own. Ben's staring at her, obviously expecting a response. So she says, 'Ben, the main thing is they love each other. Peter will help them too and they can get benefits. Naomi can still become a veterinary nurse. They'll just have to put things back a little bit.'

'Love won't pay the bills,' Ben snorts. 'Yes, they can get benefits, but it will be really hard for them. Seventeen and eighteen? Bloody hell, it was hard enough for me and Diana and we were in our twenties. And they haven't had time to really enjoy life without worries. That's what being young is all about.'

An anger surge pushes despair aside and she snaps, 'So what's the alternative? Termination?'

Ben's eyes widen and he pulls his neck back. 'Whoa. I never said that.'

'Might as well have.' Lowena shoves her half-full plate across the table and gravy slops over the side.

Ben furrows his brow and reaches his hand across the table. Lowena doesn't take it. 'Hey, what's wrong? Are you anti-abortion?'

'No. I believe it's a woman's right to choose, but I can't believe how negative you are about the whole thing. If they're happy to try and work things out and make a go of it, you should be too. Peter was so understanding, and he's her dad.' Lowena feels tears welling and takes a swig of juice. 'Just disappointed in your attitude, I guess.'

'I'm sorry to upset you, love. I was just a bit shocked, that's all. Jack's a good lad, hardworking. I want the best for him, Naomi too. Course I do. But I remember what a struggle it all was back then when we had the kids. Luckily, nowadays I'm in a position to help Jack and Naomi financially, and I will certainly do that and get them a decent place to live.'

Ben's concerned expression and soft voice bring tears again and she clears the plates so he won't see her cry. 'Good. I'm sure that will be a load off their minds, but let's forget it now,' she says, running water into the sink.

'I'm afraid I've ruined dinner with my insensitivity,' he says coming up behind her and placing his hands on her shoulders. 'Shall I pour you some wine?'

This is where she could tell him the news, try to salvage some joy from the wreckage. But she knows it's futile. There's no way she can tell him now. Yes, their situation is a world away from Naomi and Jack's, but it's not fair to just land a baby on him, is it? Even if by some chance he wanted one. Lowena will manage on her own somehow. She did when Rick turned out to be a waste of space and she'll do it again now. She'll lose Ben, and that will break her heart. But there's a little human growing inside her. A little human that will depend on her for everything. A little human that she already adores with every fibre of her being. 'No. I've had too much lately. I'll stick to juice… In fact, I know it's early, but I'm feeling really tired.'

She feels Ben's hands stiffen on her shoulders then he removes them and walks back to the table. 'Are you asking me to leave, Lowena?' he asks, incredulous.

'If you don't mind.' She takes a deep breath and forces herself to turn round and look at his crestfallen face. 'But you can have a coffee before you go?' Why did she say that? Lowena just wants him gone, so she can stop this pretence and hide under her duvet.

Ben steps forward and traces a gentle finger down her cheek. 'You do look a bit pale. Maybe you're coming down with something.' His eyes search hers. 'You said you were nauseous the other day on the trip, didn't you?' Lowena gives a non-committal grunt. 'No. I won't stay for coffee. I'll just nip to the loo and let you grab an early night, sweetheart.' He does the half-moon and brushes her lips briefly with his before leaving the room.

Lowena stacks the dishwasher and concentrates on not breaking down. A silent scream of despair builds in her chest, but she can't let it out. Not until Ben's gone home. When he reappears, his jaw's set, his eyes are moist and his lips are a thin line. Poor Ben. He's obviously upset and worried about her. In an attempt to send him on his way happier, she says, 'Hey, don't look so worried. It's just a bug. I'll be back to normal very soon.'

He shakes his head in bewilderment and pulls something out of his pocket. 'Found this in the bathroom.' Heat flares in Lowena's cheeks when he holds the pregnancy test up. 'And I'm guessing it's not Naomi's, is it?'

A handful of excuses, evasions and lies fight for position on her tongue, but only the truth wins her voice. 'No. It's mine.'

The next few seconds roll as if she's watching a film. Ben scrapes a dining chair across the tiles and sits down with a thud. He puts the tester on the table and shoves his fingers through his hair so fast it looks like he's been in a strong wind. Lowena wants to laugh, but it isn't funny. Not really. She's at that crossing. Balanced on the edge between hysterical laughter and an ocean of tears. Nothing feels real. A tremble in her legs forces her to sit down too and she wraps her arms around her body, seeking comfort from the warmth of a hug.

His warm hazel eyes sparkle under the spotlights above and a single tear trickles down his cheek, plops onto his shirt. 'The nausea, the short temper, the not drinking. It all makes sense. When were you going to tell me?' His voice is flat. Monotone.

'Tonight.' Lowena's eyes copy his and she wipes them with the back of her hand. 'It was going to be a wonderful surprise.' She holds up a finger as he's about to interrupt. 'Oh, don't get me wrong. I wasn't naïve enough to think it would be all sweetness and light. You're in your mid-forties, you already have grown-up children, and a baby is certainly not in your plan. It wasn't in mine either.' A memory of her additional wish on the Tintagel box surfaces, and her happiness earlier that day. She dismisses it with a shake of her head. 'But it's happened, and you know what? I'm over the moon. It's clear you're horrified, but there's no going back for me. Sorry, Ben.'

Ben flings his arms up. 'How on earth do you come to the conclusion I'm horrified? I haven't had time to say anything yet.'

'You said plenty about Jack and Naomi. I couldn't believe how negative you were, so I decided that I'd better keep quiet about my pregnancy and—'

'For God's sake, Lowena!' Ben smacks the flat of his hand on the table, his face a mask of anguish. 'This is completely different. They're just kids, starting out with nothing and no way of knowing what the future holds for them all. We aren't. Yes, I'm reeling from shock, but I'm far from horrified. Of course I thought my nappy-changing days were long behind me, just like I thought any chance at love again was. But then I met you, my darling, my wonderful, wonderful Lowena, and I fell headlong. I adore you, can't live without you.' His chin wobbles and he blinks back more tears. 'And now we're having a baby,' he says in wonder. 'It's unbelievable.'

Lowena can hardly breathe as a sob swells in her throat. 'Unbelievable is good, right?'

'Yes. Yes, it is, my love.' Ben stands up, throws his arms wide and in two quick steps Lowena is in his embrace. Her face buried into his shirt, she's sobbing and babbling incoherently, while he mutters soothing words and strokes her curls. Thank God, she thinks, as a sense of calm floods through her. At last she can let herself dream about happy ever afters.

After making love a little while later, they cuddle up in Lowena's bed, and talk through what having a baby will mean for them both. Lowena keeps chuckling with joy and squeezing Ben. It's so exciting to plot and plan for the future together. Thank God there is one. As for her irrational overreaction earlier, she's put it down to hormones. She apologised to Ben and he said not to worry. He explained that his wife had been all over the place emotionally as well as physically in the first few months or so, which put things into perspective and made sense, as Lowena normally didn't just go off like a firework at the slightest provocation. She'll have to keep a check on her emotions at work if this is her new normal, or half of St Merryn will get an earful. It might be a good idea to think things through more in future.

As for *her* immediate future, Lowena will continue to work and after the baby is born; she will perhaps take a year off for maternity leave. Someone else will be employed during that time, and then she'll think again. But a nagging voice won't let her get totally swept away, and she voices her concerns about his grown-up children.

'I do worry about Beth and Jacob. I haven't even met them yet and if I were them, I wouldn't be best pleased, to be honest.' Lowena puts on a hi-pitched voice. '*Oh hi, I'm Lowena, your soon to be stepmother, and by the way I'm pregnant.*'

Ben sighs. 'It won't be quite like that. But yes, we need to meet them soon and sort it all.'

Lowena's heart sinks. 'Do you think they'll be upset?'

'I don't know. It will be a bit of a shock, same as it was for us. But they're good kids. Once they see how much I love you, they'll be fine.'

'But what if they aren't?'

'If they aren't at first, then they will be in the end. Promise.' Ben drops a kiss on her forehead.

Conrad leaps on the bed just then and makes them jump. 'Conrad, you little scoundrel. Not sure how you'll feel about playing second fiddle to a baby, either,' Lowena says, rubbing behind the cat's ears.

'He'll be okay as long as he's fed, won't you boy?' Ben leans back against the pillows as Conrad settles on his chest, kneading the duvet with his front paws and purring like a tractor.

One question that's been muscling forward in Lowena's thoughts but she's not sure how to broach won't wait any longer. 'Ben. Where do you see us living when the baby comes?'

'Er, not thought about it. Why?'

'It's just that, I adore it here and even though your place is bigger, I couldn't bear to leave my cottage and wonderful garden. But I would, of course, if you really didn't want to—'

'Suits me. I always said I'd move nearer the sea, and so now I can. And why wait until the baby is born? I could bring my stuff next week. The sooner the better, I reckon.' Ben tips Conrad off his chest and turns to face her, leaning on one elbow. 'I don't want to miss a single second of your company if I don't have to.'

Lowena's love for this man, already as wide as the sky and as fertile as Tintagel seeds, sends out more new shoots in her heart, quickly blossoming into a bouquet of rainbow-coloured flowers. 'I love you so much, Ben.'

'And I you, Lowena. And I you,' he whispers, as he joins his lips with hers.

Chapter Twenty-Three

A ll this eating for two will have to stop. Particularly when the eating involves half a packet of chocolate digestives. Lowena dusts yet more crumbs from her top and continues her stock-take. It's been a quiet morning in the library and the sun outside streaming through the old barn window is calling her to the beach. She'd taken an early stroll around her wonderful garden this morning before work, pulling a weed here, smelling a rose there, and she had to admit, right now, working inside was not at the top of her wish list. By the dahlias she'd got to her knees and stroked the soft, vibrant petals, wondering at the perfection of nature's gifts.

Lowena had a quick conversation with her mum as she often does, her presence being stronger in nature. News that she'll be a grandma before long was offered to the heavens, along with tears and laughter. Oh, how Tamsin would have loved this baby. Lowena promised that even though her mum was no longer here in the flesh, her memory would live on in her child. Lowena would tell them all about their grandma and teach them everything she'd learned from her beautiful, wise mum. Lowena sits behind the desk and closes her eyes for a moment, the sun's rays from the window warming her face.

'Call that working, young Lowena?'

Lowena's eyes snap open to find Zelah stomping across the room, followed as ever these days by Janet. 'Hi there, yeah. Always hard at work, me.'

'Hello, Lowena,' Janet says with a big smile. 'You're looking well.'

Lowena is still amazed at Janet's transformation. That smile is genuine and her eyes are bright and full of life. 'Thank you. And so are you. I was only saying to Ben the other day you look much younger and more carefree lately.'

A blush pinks her cheeks. 'Me? Oh, I don't know about that.'

'Well, I do,' Zelah says slipping her arm through Janet's. 'You look gorgeous, and now you've a personality to match.'

Janet says nothing, just looks admiringly at Zelah. The feeling Lowena had about the two of them on the minibus the other day resurfaces, and she wonders about their new-found 'friendship'. Time will tell, she supposes. 'Now, what can I do for you ladies today?' she asks, standing up.

Zelah whips a newspaper out of her shopping basket and slaps it on the desk. 'We thought we'd stop by and show you this! Just got it from the newsagent's up the road.' Zelah unfolds it and points at the front page. 'We're famous!' She puts her head back and does her trademark cackle. 'But calling us grannies! Cheeky cow! I'm not a granny and never will be one. Besides, I'm far too young, dahlink!' She tosses her grey curls and pouts.

Lowena laughs as she looks at the newspaper headline: *Have-a-go Grannies in the Garden of Eden!* Underneath the headline there's a big picture of Zelah and Janet tackling the plant thief. Zelah's in full yell, pinning the woman to the ground, and Janet's about to sit on her, grimly determined. 'That's a fantastic image!' Lowena says.

'It is. And yeeha! Don't we look magnificent?' Zelah says, laughing again.

'You really do.' Lowena reads on. 'Oh, look, it says you saved one of the rarest plants by tackling her. She had a number of them in her bag that she got from the Amazon biome too!'

'Yes, selfish mare,' Janet says. 'She obviously thinks those flowers were just for her, not the rest of us. And how on earth did she think she'd care for them outside a biome? Silly woman.'

'Well, she'll be thinking again now,' Zelah says, picking up the paper and looking at the photo again. 'You know what, Jan? I reckon we could ask the journalist for a proper copy of this and have it framed. It would look great on my mantelpiece, and be a real talking point.'

Janet pulls a disgruntled face and Lowena's reminded briefly of the old Janet. 'What about having it on my mantelpiece instead?

'Ah, stop moaning. You're at mine more than yours these days anyway. We can get two copies if you want, anyway.'

Is she now? There is so much Lowena wants to ask, but bites her tongue. 'Can I get you two a cuppa?'

'Nah, we need to get a wriggle on. I'm treating Jan to a new dress from my favourite hippy-dippy shop in Padstow. I might even persuade her to get her nose pierced.' Zelah winks at Lowena and smiles at Janet's raised eyebrows.

Janet shakes her head and folds her arms. 'There is no way I'm going that far, madam.'

Another wink. 'Never say never. Come on, let's leave this woman to get some work done.'

The weather turns as Lowena leaves for home, so the idea of going to have a little sit on 'her' bench to watch the ocean and contemplate the universe will have to wait for another day. She's not great at waiting for things, and the idea of keeping her pregnancy secret until the twelve-week mark isn't appealing. After seeing the midwife last week, and having a general check-over, she was pronounced fit and healthy and in her ninth week. So three to go, before it's okay to tell all. Pulling into her driveway, Lowena turns off the engine and ponders this. The twelve-week thing is only a guideline – it isn't set in stone – and she only wants to tell Anna and Hayley, not the whole world. But then again, if she tells them and the unthinkable happens, she'd never forgive herself, would she?

Lowena unlocks the front door and thinks perhaps she'll have a talk to Ben about it when he gets home. Home. Such a small word, but massive to her because of everything it means. Lowena still can't believe how lucky she is, living with Ben and a baby on the way. It's a miracle. Lowena laughs as she scoops a wriggling Conrad up for a kiss. Setting him down by his food dish, she thinks once more about her mum talking about Lowena being her miracle baby, and the wish she made on the magic Tintagel box. Not for the first time, Lowena wonders if the damned thing really is magic, because her mum made exactly the same wish and look what happened. Or it could be the herbs that she's been using that grew from the seeds and soil in the box? It could be a combination of those and the wish? Then she tells herself off and wanders out into the garden.

It's stopped raining and the air has that fresh, dewy smell with a hint of ozone and sea-salt from the ocean. The garden looks like a Van Gogh painting: a whirl of movement and texture, vibrant colours clashing here, blending there; intoxicating perfumes from roses, lavender, honeysuckle, jasmine and lilac all compete for the attention of insects. Under the pergola, Lowena wipes a few raindrops from a garden chair and sits, gazing out at the ocean. The tide's out, revealing a wide expanse of beach, and the navy-blue horizon tucks a blanket of grey cloud in around its belt. Beautiful. Lowena listens to the shush of the waves and feels the tension of the day disappear on the tide. Thankfully, the morning sickness is easing off a little now, but Lowena feels more tired at the end of every day than she used to. It's to be expected though. Pregnant women need their rest. Allowing her eyes to close, she takes a few relaxing breaths and lets her thoughts drift.

Ben's voice whispering her name in her ear wakes her

with a start. 'Ben!' she says as he draws up a chair and kisses her cheek. 'I must have fallen asleep.'

'Yeah. I could hear you snoring miles away. Thought it was roadworks at first,' he replies, a cheeky grin turning the half-moons onto full-beam.

'Yeah, right.' Lowena gives him a playful shove and yawns. 'Early night tonight, I think.'

'You're insatiable.'

'To sleep, Ben. Anything else is beyond me at the moment.'

'Ah, poor baby. Wanna cuppa?'

'Yes, please. But before you go, I've been wondering about telling Anna and Hayley about the baby. I'm bursting to share our news.' Lowena does her best hopeful face.

'Call me old-fashioned, but I think you should wait. It's not long now, is it?'

Though disappointed, her gut tells her he's right. 'No. Probably for the best. But I'll be counting down the days!'

Ben's back in a few minutes and they sit in contemplative silence drinking their tea and watching the scene. Then he turns to her and says, 'I've done a very good deed today. The kind of good deed that makes a person all warm and squishy inside.'

'Ooh, tell me more.'

'I've given my house to Jack and Naomi.'

Lowena's jaw hits the decking. 'Oh, my word. But it must be worth near on a million?'

'Probably.' Ben shrugs. 'I could have sold it, but what's the point? As you know I don't need the money, and Jack and Naomi need somewhere to live. A no-brainer. It will be so much easier for them if they have a house of their own with no mortgage or rent to worry about.'

Lowena didn't think she could love Ben more than she already did but this unbelievable act of kindness pushed those goal posts of her heart a bit wider. 'What an amazingly wonderful thing to do.' She squeezes his hand.

Ben smiles and squeezes her hand back. 'Jack was in tears. He's such a lovely lad and I was so pleased to be able to do this for him. I told him that I'd be putting a lump sum in his bank account when the baby comes too. He was overwhelmed, bless him.'

'I should think he was!' Lowena laughed. Then a thought occurred. 'Won't he be curious as to how you can afford to do all that?'

Ben nods. 'He was really concerned, to be honest. So, I told him I'd inherited the house and a lump sum too. He was still worried I couldn't afford it, but I managed to convince him.'

'Right, good. And will Beth and Jacob be okay with you giving your house away?'

'Yeah. They have no ties to it – it wasn't their family home. And they both have a good few million each from the win.' Ben pauses. 'I was thinking that we'd meet them soon. It's been hard to organise with Beth's training and Jacob's being away at uni, but I know they're both free next month. We could have them to dinner here? But I thought I'd tell them privately beforehand?'

'That's a brilliant idea!' Lowena leans over and kisses him. 'I was only thinking this morning we'd better see them soon. Sounds perfect.'

Three weeks have flown by and Lowena's pacing the kitchen looking at the clock. Anna and Hayley will be here in a few minutes and she can hardly contain herself. She's asked them over for tea on the pretext of discussing the imminent arrival of Beth and Jacob at the weekend. Lowena's told them she's worried about what to cook and how to approach the whole situation. In reality, she's not worried at all, but a bit of advice wouldn't go amiss either. In the full-length hallway mirror, Lowena turns to the side and strokes her tummy. While she wasn't exactly a skinny woman to start with, there's much more of a defined bump there now. Today, she's accentuated it with a clingy lilac T-shirt over floral floaty trousers. Zelah would definitely approve.

Anna's car pulls up in the drive with Hayley in the passenger seat. Though Hayley lives just a spit away, Anna said she might as well collect her on the way. Lowena's so pleased that they're getting on well. They've even been to the garden centre for lunch together, when Lowena cried off at the last minute due to morning sickness. She told them it was a bug, of course. Needs must.

Lowena opens the door and goes out to greet them. Spookily, they have chosen variations on lilac today too. Hayley's in a linen shift dress, and Anna's wearing almost the same shade shirt and dark purple shorts. Anna remarks that all three of them would disappear if they stood next to the lilac bushes. After the hugs and 'how are you?'s, Lowena stands slightly to the side to give them the best chance of noticing her bump. 'Wanna have tea and cake inside or in the garden?' she asks in what she hopes is a nonchalant manner.

Anna frowns. 'What are you standing so awkward for? Have you cricked your neck?'

Lowena rolls her eyes and turns to face her. 'No. So, inside or out?'

'Outside, I think,' Hayley says. 'It's such a lovely day and I've brought a bottle of something for later. It's one of Zelah's lilac wines. Blows your socks off!'

Anna pouts. 'I'm driving. So I can only have enough to roll one sock down.'

They all laugh and Lowena goes in to get the tea – smiling at the thought of her socks remaining on – while the other two go off to set the table up under the pergola. As she carries the laden tray down the garden, she decides to come straight out with her news as soon as they've put the first forkful of her gooey, creamy chocolate cake in their mouths. It will be so funny to watch them trying to swallow it fast, so they can say something.

Hayley helps Lowena put the things on the table, and Anna turns in her seat and says, 'We reckon you should cook your trademark lasagne at the weekend for Ben's kids. Garlic bread and salad too. You can't go wrong with that.'

'Unless they're vegetarian,' Hayley says, handing Anna a mug of tea.

'Oh! I hadn't thought of that,' Lowena says, starting to worry a little.

'If they are, then do a veggie lasagne. Just as easy... If they're vegan, mind, that will be a bit trickier,' Anna says, already shoving her fork through a slab of cake. So much for telling them her news immediately.

'I think you're supposed to be here to put my mind at ease about this weekend, Anna, not to fill me with anxiety.'

'Who's filling you with anxiety? I'm just trying to be practical!' Anna says through a mouthful of cake and a few crumbs drop onto her top. 'Oh my God, this cake is to die for!' More crumbs.

'I never get that saying.' Hayley ponders, a forkful of cake poised mid-air. 'If you died for something, then you couldn't enjoy it, could you?'

''Cos you'd be dead.' Anna nods vigorously and slurps her tea. 'It's a stupid saying, but it gets across in a dramatic way how wonderful something is. Like this cake.' She sticks her fork in again and transfers it to her mouth like she hasn't eaten for days.

'Oh my God!' Hayley says. 'This cake is to stay alive for!'

Anna shakes her head. 'Not the same impact. In fact, it's rubbish.'

'Yeah. It's total crap,' Hayley agrees.

Lowena takes a sip of tea and says quietly, 'When you've quite finished your double act, I have something—'

Her attempt at sharing the news is thwarted again as Hayley says, 'Oh, guess what, I'm moving in with Dan!'

Anna throws her hands up. 'Yay! That's what the lilac wine's for – to celebrate!'

'Wow! Congratulations, Hayley,' Lowena says and they do an awkward group hug, trying to avoid plates of cake and spilling tea.

'Tell us what happened,' Anna says to Hayley.

'We were just walking on the beach the other day and he said how much he loved spending time with me and that he was so pleased we managed to iron out that blip a few months back.' Hayley gives Lowena a warm smile. 'The ironing was done expertly by you, Lo, and I can't thank you enough.'

While the comment is gratefully received, Lowena replies, 'It was a pleasure, but I only helped. You'd have got back together because you're made for each other.'

Hayley sighs with contentment. 'You know, I really believe we are. He said he'd never felt so close to anyone before and he would be devastated if he ever lost me.' Her eyes fill and she flaps her hand in front of them. 'Look at me getting all weepy.'

'I think it's lovely,' Anna says. 'And I'm getting a bit jealous, what with you and Lowena here all loved up in new relationships. Me and John have been together five trillion years, so might seem a bit dull in comparison.' She holds her hand up as the others protest. 'But I would never swap him. Love the bones of him.' Anna blinks a few times and laughs. 'Now who's getting weepy?'

'That's lovely. We all are so lucky, aren't we?' Lowena gets ready to follow on with her baby news, but Hayley starts up again.

'So I'm moving my stuff in this weekend. It will be great to have a proper big house after my little flat above the shop. And it's got a garden, so you'll have to give me some tips, Lowena.'

'This calls for that wine!' Anna says, jumping up. 'I'll grab it from the fridge.'

'What happened to your sock roll?' Lowena says, wondering if she'd ever get to tell them about her baby.

'One won't hurt. Back in a tick!'

Hayley and Lowena chat for a few moments about how wonderfully everything's turning out for them both, and then Anna's back with the bottle of wine and three glasses. Though the chocolate cake has been consumed without incident, Lowena eyes the wine and makes one last plan to make this a bit of news to remember. When the wine is poured, Lowena raises her glass and says, 'Right. On your feet, ladies. Let's have a toast to happy days and Hayley and Dan!'

'To happy days and Hayley and Dan!' they all say. Well, Hayley says, *Me and Dan*, and Anna and Hayley take a big gulp of wine.

As they do, Lowena shouts, 'And I'm bloody pregnant!' Immediately, Anna's wine snorts out of both nostrils in pink rivulets and Hayley's eyes bulge as she tries to keep the wine in and then has a coughing fit. Lowena punches the air. 'Result!'

She puts her untouched wine glass on the table and collapses on a garden chair in fits of laughter. This was worth the wait. Priceless. 'Jesus, Mary and Joseph and all the saints an' all!' Anna says after she's wiped her nose. 'I can't believe it!'

Hayley shakes her head and flops into a chair. 'That is incredible news! How far on are you?'

302

'Just a day over twelve weeks. I have been absolutely dying to tell you both.'

Anna points an accusatory finger. 'You've kept it secret? You? The most impatient person on the planet?'

'I know! But it's been worth it to get that reaction. I had planned to do it while you were eating the cake so I could see you struggling to swallow it as the shock hit.'

'Nice,' Hayley says, with a withering look.

'The truth is, I had expected you to guess when I turned sideways when you got here. But Anna thought I had a bad neck!' Lowena laughs.

'I did notice, but I thought you'd just put weight on!' Anna howls.

'Me too!' Hayley giggles.

'Well, I have, but because I have a little person on board.'

They chat about whether it will be a boy or a girl, and what Ben's reaction was and what his kids will think. Then Hayley says, 'Seems like your wish on the old box about finding "the one" came true.'

Anna frowns. 'What old box?'

'Oh, it's just a silly idea really. I found an old box in Mum's attic the day you helped me clear the house.' Lowena tells Anna all about the legend and the wish. She also reveals to both of them that she added another wish that one day she might have a child too. Just like her mum did, all those years ago. 'It's probably the healthy eating and the herbs I've been growing too.'

'The herbs that came from the seeds in the box,' Hayley says pointedly. To Anna she adds, 'I made a wish on the box too about me and Dan and now look at us.'

'Ooh, I want to wish on the old box too!' Anna says.

'What would you wish for?' Lowena asks.

'I don't know... but I'll think of something.'

'Best to wait when until you have something really important,' Hayley says.

'Hmm. I'll have a think.'

'What's all this then?' comes Ben's voice as he walks down the garden towards them. 'Wine and gossip in the afternoon. Can anyone join?'

Lowena stands and gives him a big hug. 'You're home early.'

'Couldn't bear to be away from you a minute longer, my darling.'

'Oh please!' Anna makes pretend retching sounds.

'Congratulations, daddy-to-be!' Hayley says, hugging him too.

'And from me!' Anna flings her arms around him and kisses his cheek. 'Wait until I tell John. He will be in shock.'

'We both were for a while,' Lowena says with a chuckle.

'Right, time we went and left you two lovebirds to do whatever lovebirds like to do at four in the afternoon,' Anna says with a wink.

'This lovebird could do with a nap,' Lowena says, resting her head on Ben's shoulder.

'Then you should have one,' Hayley says giving Lowena a hug. 'Pregnant women need their rest.'

'Particularly those who aren't spring chickens,' Anna teases, and receives a slap on the bum from Lowena as she skips past.

After dinner, Ben comes into the kitchen with her jacket and suggests they go to 'their' bench to watch the sun go down. Lowena hadn't managed a nap earlier and just wants to snuggle up in front of the TV, but she doesn't want to disappoint him, as he seems eager to go. As it turns out, a walk by the sea boosts her energy and she's glad she didn't give in to being a couch potato. She should never get blasé about walking by the sea on a glorious July evening. Or any other evening, unless it's in the middle of a winter storm.

'Penny for them?' Ben says, as they reach the bench and sit down.

'Just thinking how lucky we are living right next to all this.' Lowena sweeps her arm at the tangerine sky and sleepy blue ocean. A few oystercatchers dot the shoreline and three fat herring gulls sit on the rocks nearby. Only one or two walkers remain, watching the orange ball of the sun flatten itself along the horizon, and the beauty and peace of the scene fill her soul.

'We are very lucky.' Ben stands and looks down at her, his wavy dark hair falling over his brow, his face serious. The glitter in his hazel and spring-grass eyes sets Lowena's heart thumping, and her gut tells her something wonderful is about to happen. Ben takes a deep breath and says, 'And I would be the luckiest man in the entire world if you would do me the honour of being my wife.' Dropping to one knee he presents an open ring box on his palm.

'Oh my...' Lowena's remaining words stick in her throat

because her heart's beating fit to burst as she looks at the beautiful diamond and emerald ring.

'Hope you like it. The emeralds reminded me of the colour of your eyes when it's sunny.'

'Oh, Ben. It's stunning.'

'Like its owner. You will *be* its owner, won't you?' His gaze is as intense as it's hopeful.

'Of course. Of course I'll marry you, Ben! I adore you and you make me happier than I could ever have imagined possible.'

'Phew! And ditto.' Then he kisses away tears of joy from her cheeks and pulls her into his arms.

Chapter Twenty-Four

A week later, the three friends are back in their favourite spot at the end of Lowena's garden. They've had lemon drizzle cake and a pot of tea, but they have so much to talk about and organise that Lowena's just about to go back inside for cherry scones and coffee to fortify them. They've moved on to weddings, now they've exhausted the discussion about last week's dinner for Beth and Jacob, which went so much better than Lowena expected. Ben's children were both lovely and the spit of their dad. They were shocked but also delighted by news of the baby. She and Beth especially had hit it off and Beth told her privately that she'd been worried about her dad being lonely after her mum died. And because of the lottery win, she knew he could fall prey to some unscrupulous woman; therefore, she was over the moon Ben had met someone as wonderful as Lowena.

'Yes, but even if it's a summer wedding on the beach, we have to be prepared for every eventuality,' Anna is saying now. 'This is Cornwall, not the tropical Maldives. It could be scorching at lunchtime and snowing by three.'

'Yes. So maybe a covered area too?' Hayley ponders. 'A canopy of some sort. Or a marquee?'

Lowena's doubtful. 'Would a marquee be allowed? It is a public beach after all. Some people might not like it.'

'Eh? Who wouldn't like to see a wedding on the beach?' Anna starts to pace up and down by the pergola shaking her head. 'Bloody miserable sods.'

Lowena laughs. 'I only said some *might* not like it. It will probably all be perfectly fine.'

'If you get permission from the council or whoever owns the beach first,' Hayley says, 'I can't see there'd be a problem.'

'Now,' Anna says, stops pacing, hands on hips, and looks at Lowena. There's a determined expression on her face and, as she's dressed in a tie-dye red and white top, she's got a look of Zelah. 'The most important discussion your two maids of honour, or handmaidens as I prefer to call us, should be having with the bride-to-be is The Dress.'

Lowena's stomach lurches with excitement. This wedding is really happening. Since Ben proposed a week ago, and she told the 'handmaidens', she's been living in a surreal world of wedding venues, guest lists, catering companies and service ideas. Ideas for the dress have floated through her mind now and then, but nothing concrete has settled. She smirks at that. A concrete dress would be most uncomfortable.

'Didn't you say you wanted something simple?' Hayley asks.

'Yes, but I have no idea what it looks like in my head,' Lowena replies, picking up the tray of cups and plates. She nods at her stomach. 'And I have to allow for Little Bumpy, as Mervyn calls it.' Lowena had told Mervyn about the baby the other day when he'd popped into the library to return a book. She imagined everyone in St Merryn and Treyarnon would know about her pregnancy by now.

Anna spreads her arms wide. 'That's easily solved. Hayley's our resident artist. Grab some paper and a pencil while you're inside and she'll design one!'

Hayley raises her eyebrows in surprise, and then says, 'Well, yes. I'm not a dress designer but I could have a go, if you like?'

Lowena's just about to answer when Janet and Zelah come round the corner of the house.

'You invited more handmaidens?' Anna says, with a smirk.

'I most certainly have not,' Lowena murmurs as she walks down the path to greet them.

Zelah takes the tray from Lowena, sets it on the ground and flings her arms around her. 'Congratulations! Mervyn told us about your baby and your forthcoming nuptials. We decided we had to come and wish you well, didn't we, Janet?'

Janet wants to say that isn't quite true. Zelah had insisted they came. Janet thought it might be better to ask, before showing up unannounced. It looks like Lowena and her friends are having a get-together and Janet feels like they're gatecrashers. Marvellous. But she answers, 'Yes. It's such delightful news.' She hands Lowena a bunch of wildflowers, hand-picked from Zelah's garden.

'Thanks so much.' Lowena smiles and gives Janet a hug. 'I'm just about to make coffee, and I baked cherry scones earlier. We're talking wedding plans. Would you like to join us?'

Janet can tell Lowena's just being polite, and would rather just get on with her planning, but Zelah has no inbuilt subtext-detector. 'Yes, that would be wonderful! And tea for me, if you don't mind.' Zelah beams and slips her arm through Janet's. 'We'll come and help you carry things. Pregnant women need lots of help.'

In the kitchen, Zelah grills Lowena until she's overcooked, about the wedding. Where would it be, who was coming and had she got the dress? While Janet just quietly follows direction from Lowena as to where the extra cups are and finds another tea tray. Zelah is definitely an acquired taste, but Janet is addicted. She's been so happy since the night she told Zelah her secret, and began to live the truth instead of a lie. The lie is still on show to Milly and everyone else, but when she's with Zelah, she can be herself totally. Janet had even told her the truth about her husband, that she'd married him because her parents had pressured her into it. That's what you did then. You married a good man with prospects who would look after you. She'd only slept with him twice. It repulsed her. And as a consequence, he'd started an affair. This gave her an excuse to suggest they divorced, and he'd readily agreed.

They had never loved each other; Leonard had married Janet because he too had been pressured – imagined it was the right thing to do. He'd got to a certain age and decided it was time he married a respectable girl and had a family. He was fond of her and she him (as a friend), but she should have had the courage of her convictions to refuse the poor man. The courage Zelah had had. But Janet hadn't, and that was that. No good wishing away the past. She might as well wish an incoming tide stopped rolling to shore. Then there was the feeling that she'd never been wanted in the way her brother had. She was always made to feel second best. Zelah had understood all that completely, and they had grown ever closer. Their friendship had been balanced precariously on the end of a diving board over a pool of something more, but they were unsure and too afraid to dive in. Then, last week, they'd taken the plunge.

Janet's heart flips when she remembers the first kiss they shared. Despite their advancing years, they'd agreed to take things slowly. Janet especially said she was the one needing time. But it's hopeless. Janet knows she's already falling for the crazy, outrageously eccentric, incredibly wonderful old bat. Can you fall in love for the first time at seventy-four? Seems like it.

'What are you doing standing there smiling like a dope?' Zelah says, handing Janet a plate of scones. 'Put those on the tray and get a wriggle on.'

'Yes, ma'am.' Janet does a mock salute. 'Whatever you say, ma'am.'

As the sun grows hazy and the ocean's fist bashes the rocks below, a party atmosphere settles over the five women as they eat far too many scones and drink gallons of tea and coffee. The introduction of Zelah to any proceedings is like adding a special ingredient in a signature dish, thinks Janet. Something quite ordinary before the addition zings on the palate afterwards. That's what Zelah does to life. Makes it zing. Anna had popped Hayley back to her house to grab some pastel crayons and A3 paper and she's done a few stunning dress designs. They are all arguing over which is best. Well, Janet isn't. She not that interested, and is quite sure that whatever Lowena decides upon, she'll look stunning.

'The dark green one with the crossover back straps. It's so simple but effective,' Anna says.

'I like the colour of that one, but the halter neck is my favourite,' Hayley says.

'And I like the olive green best with the slash neck. It will bring out the colour of her eyes,' Zelah says with a winning smile.

'Oh, I don't know. I think green is good for bringing out the colour of my eyes, but I do love this turquoise one. It will look lovely against the ocean backdrop,' Lowena says with a sigh. 'And I do have bits of greeny-blue in my eyes in certain lights.'

Zelah looks at Janet. 'What do you think, oh silent one?'

'I don't know.' Then, because the other four are all staring at her, she says, 'The turquoise one. I agree with

Lowena about the ocean. And I suppose your eyes could be described as aquamarine.'

'Thanks, Janet. This one it is!' Lowena replies with a big smile.

Excitement electrifies the air and they all start talking at once. Then Zelah says, 'Right, the dress is sorted, or will be. But what about the food? And where are you having the reception?'

'We've not decided yet. There are a few options.' Lowena tells her what they are.

'Hmm.' Zelah taps her fingers against her lip, a thoughtful look in her eye. She flips her long curls over her shoulder and says, 'I think it would be absolutely wonderful if you had the reception here. It was a lovely day when you had the garden party. And any venue would be hard pushed to have a view like this one.' She flings her arm towards the ocean and her metal bangles jingle together.

This idea goes down well, but then Anna scratches her head and frowns. 'Might be too many people this time though?'

'How many?' Zelah asks.

Hayley checks the notes. 'Probably twenty-five to thirty.'

'A bit tight, but we could put a gazebo at the side here.' Zelah flings an arm. 'And with extra seats dotted around the pond and through the roses with their heavenly perfume, it will be absolutely delightful.'

Janet worries Zelah's taking over, but nobody seems to mind, and Janet's tuned in her subtext radar to make sure.

'Wedding cake,' Anna says tapping her pen on the pad. 'Thoughts?'

'Probably should have one,' Janet says dryly, just to get a reaction. Sometimes she can't help her old self popping in.

Anna gives her a disparaging look. 'I meant what kind, and who should make it.'

'The same catering company we have for the rest of the food? Not sure if they do cakes though,' Hayley muses.

'I can make cakes!' Zelah says, crashing her mug down on the stone wall, making everyone flinch. 'And I could make fairy cakes to go with it. Lots of them. I used to be a baker at one time and people came from miles around to taste my wares.' Zelah adds a cheeky wink. 'That was not a euphemism, by the way.'

Doubt spreads from one expression to another like fire through kindling. Just as the silence is on the verge of deafening them all, Lowena says, 'Oh, we wouldn't want to put you to any trouble. It would be a big job to do all that…'

Janet's subtext-detector is bleeping and flashing in her head. Will Zelah take the hint?

'What you're really saying is you don't want some crazy old lady making a pig's ear of your wedding cake and ruining the reception.' Zelah raises an eyebrow, then grins to show she's not hurt.

Janet's impressed. That's exactly what her detector was bleeping about.

Lowena flushes and opens her mouth to protest, but is rescued by Anna. 'Yes, basically. I reckon you've hit the nail on the head there, Zelah. But not because you're crazy, which you undoubtedly are, and I for one wouldn't want you any other way.' She pauses to do a big smile. 'But because a proper professional cake person will have reviews and stuff. So, because of that, we know that it's unlikely to all go tits up.'

Zelah ponders for a moment, then says, 'Thanks for your honesty, Anna. I find it so refreshing. Right. How about I make you a few samples for you to… sample?' She howls at her own joke. 'Then you can decide yay or nay.'

Anna shoots a questioning look at Lowena and Hayley. They answer with shrugs and smiles. 'You're on. But can you do it fairly soon? Because if we decide against using you, we need to crack on and find a professional.'

'Of course. I'll get them to you next week.' Zelah stands and dusts a few crumbs from her multi-coloured dungarees. 'And now, I think it's time Jan and I took our leave.' She leans down and kisses Lowena on the cheek. 'Congratulations, once more, sweetheart. I'm thrilled for you, and so excited about this wedding!' Then her hand flies to her mouth. 'Oh. Just realised I'm assuming we're invited. Don't feel obliged!' Janet can't believe she's actually witnessing a flush of embarrassment on Zelah's cheeks. Such an occurrence is rarer than snow in July.

Lowena flaps her hand dismissively. 'Of course you're both invited! It wouldn't be the same without you.'

As the two of them get into Zelah's car, Janet says, 'I never knew you were a baker?'

'I've been lots of things. But yes, I won prizes for my cakes in my heyday.'

'Lovely. Mind you, it's a lot of work.'

Zelah laughs and starts the engine. 'Not at all. I can't wait, because the fairy cakes are going to have a few magic ingredients.'

Janet's heart thuds to basement level. 'Oh my God, Zelah. You can't do that!'

'Do what?'

'Put pot in the cakes!'

Zelah throws back her head and cackles so much that Janet fears she'll lose control of the car. 'Pot! Who calls it pot nowadays? And of course I'm not going to do that. I'm putting something *far* better in them. A love potion.'

'A love potion?' Janet is beginning to fear for Zelah's sanity.

'Yep. Handed down through generations. It's always worked like a treat too.'

'From your herbs, you mean?'

'Yep. And the best thing is that if the person eating the cake doesn't really love someone, it has no effect. It's not as if I'm going to turn the wedding reception into a random love fest!' Then she hoots with laughter again until Janet tells her to keep her eyes on the road.

'But what happens if they do really love someone?' Janet asks, making a mental note to steer well clear of the fairy cakes.

'They tell the person they love how they feel. Sometimes people need a little push. It will be the perfect thing to do on a wedding day.' She winks at Janet. 'Maybe old Mervyn might surprise Milly.'

'Hmm. I don't like the sound of this. It smacks of meddling to me.'

'Pah! Meddling, shmeddling! As I said, if the person eating the cake isn't in love with someone, it has no effect. No declarations of love will happen.' Janet blows down her nose and shakes her head. 'Oh, lighten up, you old killjoy. It will all be absolutely fabulous!'

Chapter Twenty-Five

Little Bumpy is restless this morning. Maybe he or she knows it's a very special day for Mum. Lowena smiles as she strokes her tummy and gazes out of her bedroom window and down the sweep of her garden in bloom, set up ready for the reception. A little marquee to the side, chairs and tables with bows on them thread through and around, and coloured streamers and wisps of gauze twist about the pergola like captured clouds. As always, beyond the garden lies the sleepy blue ocean, an August sun casting a sparkling line of diamonds along the horizon.

Ben stayed the night at Anna and John's, just to keep tradition, but Lowena's missing him already. Still, in two hours she'll be Mrs Mawgan and they'll never be apart again. Anna and Hayley are downstairs doing last-minute stuff and organising this, that and the other. They have both been fantastic. Lowena's not had to do a thing, which at first was a bit daunting as she's not used to letting others take over. But she has to admit, in the end she's enjoyed it. It's made a refreshing change to sit back and not worry about anything.

Suddenly, a few nerves join Little Bumpy in kicking at her insides and Lowena turns from the window to look in the mirror. Gloria, the local hairdresser/beautician, has made a wonderful job of her hair and make-up. Lowena was going to do it all herself, but Hayley and Anna wouldn't hear of it, and she's glad she listened. Her long tousled mane has been tamed into more orderly curls, though not regimented, and Gloria secured a few side twists with pink rosebuds from the garden. The pink of the rose matches her lipstick exactly, and subtle shades of aquamarine line her eyes which accentuate their colour perfectly, and that of her dress.

Lowena steps over to the dress, which is in its cover hanging on the back of the door. Zipping it open she marvels again at how close it is to Hayley's original design. Anna's cousin Karen made it. Though she's just a local dressmaker, as far as Lowena's concerned, it's good enough to grace any catwalk. She strokes her hand across the silky fabric and loves the way it ripples like an ocean wave on a sunny day. Such a stunning colour. The design is simple. A sweetheart neckline, cap sleeves and high waist from which soft folds of material sweep to a handkerchief hem at her calves. Lowena's opted for bare feet as it's a beach wedding, but around each ankle she's wearing little daisy chains made by Zelah. Another one of the dear lady's fab ideas. The heart-shaped wedding cake she made is stunning, as were the little cakes she made as samples.

The bouquet was one thing Lowena insisted on making herself. Of all the flowers in the world, it had to be made from her mum's dahlias, didn't it? Beautiful whites, yellows and pinks all tied together with some artist wire and dark-teal ribbon provided by Hayley. When she'd finished it last night and put them in water, the simple beauty of them had taken her breath away, and the presence of her mum was there in every petal. *Oh, Mum. I wish you were here.* Images of her mum pottering in the garden by the sea and cradling her new grandchild in her arms spring unbidden, as does the lump swelling in Lowena's throat.

Thankfully, right then, Hayley shouts up the stairs, cutting into her thoughts and stopping tears from ruining her make-up. 'Hey, it's about time you were thinking of having a quick snack. Then we'll get you dressed!'

Lowena feels too nervous to eat, but then if she doesn't, she might feel a bit faint later. 'Okay, coming down now!'

'This is it then,' Anna says, a wobble in her voice, as Lowena walks in. 'You look absolutely stunning.'

'You do. Absolutely perfect.' Hayley nods and dabs at her eyes.

'God, we'll need to carry a box of tissues with us at this rate,' Lowena says, a laugh struggling past a knot of emotion. 'You two look stunning too. Handmaidens, a vision in green.'

'We'll all blend in so well with the ocean we'll disappear,' Hayley says.

'Ben should have worn a gold suit to blend with the sand.' Anna laughs.

'As if,' Lowena says. 'He's in sober charcoal, but I did

persuade him to go for an aquamarine-ish shirt. He hates dressing up, so he'll be back in shorts for the reception.'

'Okay. Enough chatter, Mervyn's looking worried out there.' Hayley checks they have everything and ushers Lowena from the kitchen.

'He's so thrilled about giving you away, Lo,' Anna says. 'Hope he doesn't get too giddy and drive us over a cliff on the road down.'

'Thanks for that image, Anna.' Lowena sighs and heads for the door.

Apart from the wedding guests seated in front of the beautiful turquoise-gauze-draped wedding arch, erected near the protection of the rocks, there's a gaggle of ever-growing onlookers. Some are pretending not to be onlookers, just nonchalantly drifting back and forth past the wedding party like bits of flotsam, but most of them are blatantly staring about and waiting for something to happen. The something is Lowena. She's out of the car at the top of the sandy slope leading down to the beach and wishing she'd opted for a little indoor do somewhere. She's never been a showy-offy person, and now she feels like she's about to go on stage.

'You ready, my dear?' Mervyn asks, offering an arm. He looks so smart in his navy suit with his eyebrows trimmed and usual mop of grey hair slicked back. Behind his eyes, Lowena sees a wild child who's been tamed, scrubbed and forced into his Sunday best for church. Like Ben, she knows he'll be out of that suit and into civvies as soon as the ceremony's over.

'I'm ready, but wish there wasn't such a big audience.' Lowena shakes her head. 'Never crossed my mind there'd be so many here on our little beach.'

'People love a good wedding, maid. Don't let a few nosy parkers upset you. Come on, best foot forward.'

'Ooh! Wait up!' Anna says, stopping them all in their tracks. 'Talking of feet, we haven't put your daisy chains round your ankles. Zelah gave me them not ten minutes ago too.'

Once the chains are on, Lowena takes a deep breath and they set off again. Mervyn walks her along the makeshift aisle of beribboned chairs to where Ben waits in front of the celebrant. As they walk, Mervyn squeezes her arm to his side and whispers, 'You okay, Lowena?'

'Yeah. Feeling less nervous now.'

'Good. And I'm incredibly honoured that you asked me to give you away, my friend. It's a day I'll always remember.'

Mervyn's voice wobbles on the last three words and Lowena swallows hard as he kisses her cheek and stands her next to Ben. This should have been her lovely dad's job, but as that's impossible, she couldn't have asked for a better stand-in. They broke the mould when they made Merv.

Ben turns to her, and with eyes full of love takes her trembling hand. 'Wow. You look amazing,' he whispers.

Lowena goes to reply but her words are lost in a tumult of emotion. This man before her is the moon, stars and sun. Her entire world. She gives him a big smile and a silent promise that she will love him with all her heart, and try to make him happy every single day of her life.

The whole ceremony passes in a blur. Lowena's so full of happiness, all she sees is Ben's beautiful flecks of green-as-spring-grass eyes, and half-moons dazzling her as she says her vows. If this is a stage, then the backdrop is achingly beautiful. The ocean shushes and sighs along with the other guests as she and Ben pledge their love, and a few seagulls chip in now and then as if cheering them on. 'The First Time Ever I Saw Your Face' plays them out along the beach as they're showered with rose-petal confetti, and the gaggle of onlookers join in the clapping and whooping.

'Have I ever told you how much I love you, Mrs Mawgan?' Ben says, as they pose for photographs by the shoreline.

'You have, but you've never called me Mrs Mawgan before.' Lowena giggles and kisses her husband's lips.

'It was a lovely ceremony, wasn't it?'

'The best. I had a bit of stage fright to start with, but once I looked into your eyes all the nerves went. And this is such a beautiful setting.'

'A beautiful setting for a beautiful bride.'

'Look this way, Lowena!' the photographer calls, perched on some boulders nearby.

'She's too busy looking at her husband at the moment!' Ben shouts. Then he pulls Lowena in for a kiss while the seagulls yell their approval and the crowd clap.

Lowena shrieks as the incoming tide catches them unawares and swirls around her ankles. 'Oh no, my daisy chains are all wet now!'

Zelah, a vision in floaty yellow and red, shouts, 'Let them free. They'll float across the ocean and a little girl in America will find them and marvel.'

This is doubtful, but Lowena tosses them over her shoulder. 'You've got to chuck your bouquet over your shoulder in a minute too, haven't you?' Ben says, leading her up the beach away from the waves. 'Can't wait to get home, to be honest, and get out of this monkey suit.'

Smiling at how well she knows her husband, she stands at the beginning of the slope to the carpark and announces she's going to throw the bouquet. In her peripheral vision she sees a few guests jostling for position amid shrieks of laughter.

'Okay. You ready? One. Two. Three!' Up and over her shoulder goes the bouquet and spinning round she sees Hayley is the winner. Then she notices a few dahlias have come loose, and Zelah's waving them in triumph, laughing like a hyena.

'Me and Hayley next then!' she yells, doing a crazy dance on the sand, while Janet looks on, shaking her head.

Hayley laughs and shoots Dan a shy glance. He smiles, puts his arm around her and leads the way up the beach.

Chapter Twenty-Six

'If I were any happier, I'd pop,' Lowena says to Naomi as they stand side by side in the rose garden. The whole garden and house are buzzing with guests and the reception is in full swing. Lowena's so glad she allowed Ben to get a swish catering company in, complete with waiter service. There's no way she and her friends could have made sure everyone had food and drink while still enjoying the day. Ben and John have just delivered their groom and best man speeches, and there's a lovely relaxed, buoyant feel to proceedings, as if everyone there has collectively undone a few buttons on their clothing.

'Me too. In fact...' Naomi nods at both their baby bumps. 'Looks like we might just do that!'

'We've a way to go yet.' Lowena sips her sparkling elderflower water and takes a bite of salmon en croute.

'Yeah. And if it weren't for your fantastic husband, we'd be in a fine old pickle when he or she makes an appearance.' Naomi's eyes fill and she gives her head a little shake. 'I still can't believe he's gifted us his wonderful home. I adore it. And it is beyond our wildest dreams. We're moving in next week – can't wait.'

'You'll get no argument from me. My husband is fantastic, and I'm so lucky to have him. What does your dad think about it all?'

'He's over the moon for us. And he's like a dog with two tails over the baby. Planning what he'll do with it, where they'll go, and he's already bought two outfits.'

Lowena puts her hand on Naomi's arm. 'So thrilled it's all working out, Naomi.'

'And I want to thank you for all your support too. You made it all seem so possible that day at Eden. Until then everything had seemed just the opposite. You and Ben are the most wonderful couple and deserve every happiness.' A tear trickles down her cheek and she sniffs. 'I'm doing this all the damned time lately. Waterworks on and off like a tap.'

'Snap. It'll be the hormones.'

Naomi nods. 'Seriously, thanks for everything you and Ben have done for us. Means so much.'

They share a hug. Then Lowena feels a light touch on her shoulder. 'Do you have a spare one of those for me?'

'Beth. Of course, any time.' Lowena puts her arms around Ben's daughter and kisses her on the cheek.

They step back and Beth tosses her dark curls over her shoulder and puts her head on one side, her eyes exactly like Ben's, twinkling with emotion. 'You have made Dad so happy. Thank you.'

'Yeah. Not seen the old man so happy in years,' Jacob

says, wandering up behind his sister. Apart from being a few inches shorter, he's a carbon copy of his dad. 'And I can't wait to see my baby half-sister or brother too.'

'I know. Who'd have thought it?' Beth says. 'Life can bury you under a heap of shit sometimes, like when we lost Mum. But it can also chuck in a few diamonds occasionally, too. I reckon you're one of life's diamonds, Lowena.'

Lowena's eyes copy Naomi's and a sob catches in her throat. She presses a forefinger under each eye. 'Oh my. What a lovely thing to say.'

'True though,' Ben says, strolling up and slipping his arm across Jacob's shoulders. He says to Jacob. 'And less of the "old man" comment. I'm in my prime, you know.'

They share some banter and then Zelah clambers on a chair near the pergola and taps on a wine glass. 'Can I have your attention, everyone?' The buzz of conversation simmers down and they all look at her expectantly. 'Charge your glasses, because the bride and groom will be cutting the cake in ten minutes!'

Ben raises his brows at Lowena. 'We will?'

'Yes. And woe betide anyone who doesn't follow our Zelah's instruction.' Lowena laughs and slips her arm through Ben's as they walk towards the pergola.

Waiting for people to get drinks and make their way over, Lowena and Ben mingle with a few guests already standing at the cake table. Wendy and Nigel chat with them for a while and seem very comfortable in each other's company. It seems that since the garden party they have rarely spent time apart, and they seem very cosy. Lowena's convinced that day was the start of many good things for the people attending. And not for the first time she wonders how much the magic box had to do with things and the bounty growing all around them that sprang from it.

Milly and Mervyn come over and Mervyn tells them how overjoyed he is that his grandson Matthew is thinking of making Cornwall his permanent home in the future. 'Apparently, he's met a girl from the surfing crowd he's friends with, and adores her and the area so much. He says he feels at home here – can feel the strength of his roots. And once he's finished his degree, he can't see himself returning to Australia.' Mervyn's not sure his daughter will be thrilled about it, but he sure as hell is. 'It will be a miracle having flesh and blood nearby again after all these years.' He shakes his head and sniffs. 'Never thought I'd see the day.'

Milly nods. 'Family is everything, I reckon.' Then she pats Mervyn's arm and says with a wink, 'Friends are pretty good too.'

Zelah arrives as Milly's saying this and nudges Mervyn. 'Friends can become family sometimes if you let them.' She gives them a pointed look and sweeps past to the cake table. 'Okay, are we ready?' There's a mumbled assent from those gathered. 'Then the bride and groom will cut the cake. And don't forget the cupcakes.' She points a sparkly nail at the long line of pastel-coloured cakes. 'They are a special recipe handed down the generations. Stunning creations, though I say so myself.'

Ben and Lowena step up to the table and poise a knife over the huge heart-shaped wedding cake. It's white, lemon and turquoise with little icing-sugar sea shells crafted around the edges and sides. 'It's so pretty – a shame to cut it,' Lowena says.

'But it will be worth it when you taste it!' Zelah says. 'Come on, get on with it.'

'Okay. Here goes,' Ben says and clasps his hand to Lowena's as they press the knife through the icing to a round of applause.

The guests have thinned considerably, and it's much quieter now. That's how Janet likes it. Her extravagant side is contemplating another glass of champagne, but her sensible side is asking if that's wise, given she's already feeling a bit sleepy. Besides, how's she going to haul herself out of this deckchair? Her knees are better since she's been taking all the herbal stuff Zelah's been making for her, but Janet thinks she's been a bit ambitious slumping down so low. Like an old dog, the late afternoon sun has lost its ferocity, preferring instead to bathe her face in a lovely, warm glow. Perhaps she might close her eyes for a second and then decide whether to have another drink or not. Janet's drifting when she feels something sticky pushed under her nose. 'Ugh? What the hell…?' She swats at it with her hand and is treated to one of Zelah's hoots.

'Careful, you nearly sent one of my precious cupcakes flying.'

Janet eyes the little plate with the cake on it and wipes the cream off the end of her nose. There's no way she's eating one of those bloody love potion things. 'No thanks. I can't eat another thing.'

'Ah, go on.'

'No, thanks.'

A deep sigh. 'Well, loads of other people have had them and thankfully I haven't lost my touch. Look over there at Milly and Mervyn.' Zelah nods at their two friends sitting close together hand in hand, deep in conversation.

Janet raises an eyebrow. Wow. That is quite a turn-up, but she's not going to say so. 'Hmm.'

'And Hayley and Dan.' Zelah flings an arm towards a group of guests dancing. Hayley and Dan are gazing into each other's eyes lovingly.

'Yeah, well, that's no surprise, is it? They were already an item.'

'Spoilsport.' Zelah pulls up a deckchair and flops down next to Janet. 'Oh, and Wendy and Nigel too, look.' She nods over to where the couple are dancing cheek to cheek to a slow song.

'Yeah. Well, that's not a surprise either, is it? You and your silly potions.' Janet shakes her head but gives her a smile too.

'The thing is, Jan…' Zelah gives her an intense stare, her eyes reflecting the sky, the sunlight setting a sparkle on her diamond nose stud. 'The thing is, I ate one too.'

Janet's stomach flips over. She can tell whatever's on Zelah's mind is pretty important. Janet's insides feel wiggly and she can't drag her eyes away. 'Was it nice?' she asks, in a high voice.

'It was delicious. It was the most delicious cake I've ever

eaten because afterwards I realised something which I've known deep down for ages. Since the time you were first rude to me, I think? There've been so many times you were rude, I can't remember, to be honest.' Zelah winks and takes Janet's hand.

She's taken her hand in full view of everyone, Janet thinks. But she doesn't remove it. They're past all that. 'What have you known?' her voice trembles and she has to swallow. Hard.

'I realised that I love you. Simple as that.' Unshed tears sparkle like the diamond stud and a wobbly smile curves Zelah's lips.

There's a pause as Janet makes a decision. Janet's truth that they have shared for some time has always been hidden from the others. But right here, right now, this is where she could choose to tell the world. The lie she's pushed into the shadows, hidden in dark places for all of her life, will die, be subsumed into the night sky, and tomorrow a bright new day will dawn and it will drench her in sunlight. 'Well, that's funny.' Her smile mirrors Zelah's.

'What is?' Zelah's face is full of hope.

'Well, I haven't had a cake, but it's funny because I love you too.' Janet wipes a tear from Zelah's cheek and regardless of who might be watching, kisses her on the lips.

Chapter Twenty-Seven

Ten Months Later

Spring is creeping along the hedgerows, her fine needle threading them through with white hawthorn flowers, and dotting nodding daffodils along the verges like splashes of sunshine. In Lowena and Ben's garden, buds are emerging, shoots are forming and the days are growing ever milder. Lowena spends as much time as the weather will allow outside with baby Tristan. Being outside calms him. Even though he's only a few months old, as soon as Lowena carries him into the garden his cries stop, his little fists unclench and he rests his head on her shoulder. Pure contentment. Through the kitchen window Lowena can see the sun is out and the wind has stopped bashing the camellia and rose bushes about, so she decides to take her son out for a breath of fresh air. Tristan woke a few times in the night and a walk around the garden will blow away the mugginess that sleepless nights have made a permanent resident in her head.

The wind is in the west, and as soon as they step out, a lungful of sea air mixed with dampness and the scent of growing things sets her spirits soaring. How lucky is she? Lowena thinks this every day. It's only two years since she lost her mum and so much has happened in that time. She has a new home and a paradise garden, a wonderful husband and baby son. Her little miracle. Conrad too, he can't be missed off the list. She has lots of new friends. A great job, which Callum's girlfriend Lennie has taken over while Lowena's on maternity leave. Lennie had lost her job and Lowena was happy to offer her a place at the Library Barn and train her up. Lennie's loving it and is doing a grand job, so Lowena's thinking that now the library is so popular, it might be an idea to open full-time. That way, Lennie can go in most days, and Lowena will be very part-time until Tristan is older.

Under the pergola, Lowena tucks a rainbow blanket, knitted by Janet, tight under Tristan's chin and pulls his hood up. He looks up at her with his spring-grass eyes and gurgles with pleasure. 'You love it out here, don't you, my darling?'

Tristan gurgles again and pulls a hand free of his mother's tucking in, and grabs a strand of her hair.

'Hey, you. Your hands will get chilly.' Lowena tucks them under the blanket again. Tristan immediately pushes both hands back out. Lowena laughs and gives up. Stubborn as they come. She turns Tristan to face the ocean and beach. 'See that bench over there?' She points. 'When it's a bit warmer we'll sit there and have a snack. I'll tell you all about your grandparents and how wonderful they were. They would be totally smitten with you, my boy.' Lowena stops because her words stick in her throat. Instead, she imagines her parents sitting by her side cooing at their grandson.

With Ben's parents gone also, Mervyn and Milly are his surrogate grandparents and spoil Tristan rotten at every given opportunity. Though they haven't spelled it out, Lowena thinks they might be more than friends these days too. But who is she to poke her nose in? Not so reticent about spreading the word are Zelah and Janet. Well, Zelah's not reticent about anything, to be honest. Lowena had an idea, the day they went to Eden, that something was going on between them, but didn't want to jump to conclusions. She's thrilled that they have found each other so late in life. So are the rest of the gang. Milly said she was pleased Janet had found someone to make her happy, and 'thank God she's stopped being a cantankerous and miserable old trout'. Janet had taken it in good part and pulled a trout face at Milly. Just shows it's never too late to follow your heart and dreams.

Hayley and Dan are living in bliss at Dan's, living their best life, as Hayley puts it. Hayley often pops over to see Tristan and says she's going to do a family portrait of them all soon. Dan's coming on well as a fledgeling painter under his partner's tutelage, but he's yet to persuade her to go with him on a fishing trip. She has no trouble eating the fresh mackerel Dan catches though, which are many. Dan says it's Lowena's dad's fishing basket that brings him good luck. Like Hayley had last year, he told Lowena the other day that he would be ever grateful for her intervention in the misunderstanding he and Hayley had in those early days of their relationship. Lowena had smoothed the waters and allowed him to take stock. Lowena said the same as she had to Hayley. They'd have got there anyway as they were made for each other, but it was nice to be appreciated.

Being appreciated is a big part of her life now. Lowena feels a true part of the community, because of the library and the garden. People gravitate to both like homing pigeons. In the end, it's mostly the garden that draws them, because in Lowena's opinion it's magical. This garden. Their garden. So many people from different backgrounds met here and are now lifelong friends because of it. Lowena is truly *blessed with a beautiful garden, bountiful crops and love of her fellow man.* And this love has grown and spread and bloomed in all of them. It won't be long before one or another of the gang will pop by. Though, she has to admit, a visit here now has the added attraction of little Tristan. Turning her baby round to face her, she's greeted with a huge yawn and he flails a hand at her nose. 'Hmm. I think it's time for a little nap, don't you? I'll pop you in the pram outside the shed. I've a little job to do for Aunty Anna.'

After just a few pushes of the pram up and down the patio, Tristan's fast asleep. Good. Lowena opens the shed door, parks the pram next to it, and steps inside the chilly, damp interior. There are a few gigantic spiders overwintering in the corners of the windows, and they've cast thick, sticky webs between seed trays and plant pots. Luckily, what she's after lives on the middle shelf in the driest spot in the shed. The other day, Anna was over for a visit and asked Lowena if she remembered the conversation they'd had about wishing on the Tintagel box, the day Lowena had revealed her pregnancy. Lowena kind of did, but not the detail, so Anna had elaborated.

'Yeah. I said I wanted to wish on it too, but I couldn't think of anything right then I really wanted. But now I can.' Anna had fluffed her short auburn hair and flushed. 'Thing is, me and John love each other, there's no worries there. But we've lost that spark. You know, the loved-up feeling people have in the early days? I know that fades for everyone, and after twenty-odd years I don't know if that ever comes back, but I'd like to try.' Anna had wiped a tear. 'We don't talk or laugh together much, and seem to do our own thing nowadays. I couldn't bear it if we drifted apart... but I feel like we might. We've talked things through, and we're gonna work at it. But maybe a wish on that box would help? I know it sounds desperate and a bit daft, but I'll try anything.'

Lowena had given her friend a big hug and told her they'd do it next time, because she had to do something with the box first. And that something was to give it a dust down and put some of the soil in it from the original patch in the garden where Lowena had sprinkled the seeds. Wishes certainly wouldn't take root in an empty box, that was for sure.

Taking the box from the shelf, she runs a sleeve over it and traces the beautiful carved tree with her fingertips, remembering the time she'd first wished upon it. All her good fortune since could be logically explained, without flights of fancy and Tintagel legends. But something inside wouldn't let the idea go that this box was indeed magical. Accepting this properly at last, she drops a kiss on the lid and whispers, 'Thank you for everything you've given me, old box. I'll be forever grateful.'

About to take it outside to fill it with soil, Lowena carefully opens the lid and stops dead in her tracks. There's no need to put soil inside because it's already full. Carefully disturbing the dry, crumbly earth with her fingertip, she sees there's something hidden underneath. Her stomach twists in anticipation and her heart thumps like a jackhammer in her chest. *Oh my God.* A yellowing square of faded paper is revealed. Its edges have been folded over two or three times to form a packet, and with trembling fingers she carefully lifts it to the light. Something shifts inside it. Something shifts inside her too, as, incredulous, she forces her fingers to tease the folds open. *Seeds! Exactly the same as before!* Tears of wonder and joy fill her eyes as she carefully refolds the packet and tucks it under the soil, then puts the box back in its place. Goosebumps prickle her skin and every hair stands up on her forearms. Lowena knows now without doubt that Anna's wish will be successful, and her wonderful friend will find love and happiness with John once more.

Lowena closes her eyes and takes a moment to steady herself, and to be thankful for her life, her beautiful garden and the love of her fellow man. Then Tristan sends up a plaintive wail into the fresh spring air, and she hurries out to attend to her miracle baby.

Acknowledgments

A big thank you to the team at One More Chapter for all their hard work getting this book ready to launch into the world. An extra enormous shout out to my editor, Charlotte Ledger, who has been a total legend throughout, as always. Thank you too, to Rachel Goldburn, who is the lovely librarian at St Agnes Library. She explained the day-to-day duties of a librarian for me, which are many and varied! And a big cheer to my lovely writer friends who have lent their ears to me for various moans and grumbles during the writing process. You know who you are. To all the wonderful readers and bloggers, thanks for the continued support of me and my books! And last but not least, to my husband, family and friends. Without you all, I'd be sunk!

AMANDA JAMES

A

Secret

Gift

'A charming and
original concept'
Sunday Times bestseller
KATIE FFORDE

It will change her life forever...

**Escape to Cornwall for another enchanting, heartwarming
novel about friendship, hope and second chances…**

Three years ago, Joy Pentire lost her firefighter husband and
she still hasn't returned to the woman she once was. But
then she meets Hope, one of the residents at the nursing
home where she's a carer.

Hope has a secret gift that she wants to pass on.
And Joy's life is forever changed.

Surrounded by the community in her Cornish hometown,
Joy's unexpected inheritance soon leads to new
opportunities, new friends, new love, and the part of herself
she'd thought forever lost … her joy.

ONE MORE CHAPTER

One More Chapter is an
award-winning global
division of HarperCollins.

Sign up to our newsletter to get our
latest eBook deals and stay up to date
with our weekly Book Club!
<u>Subscribe here.</u>

Meet the team at
<u>www.onemorechapter.com</u>

Follow us!
@<u>OneMoreChapter_</u>
@<u>OneMoreChapter</u>
@<u>onemorechapterhc</u>

Do you write unputdownable fiction?
We love to hear from new voices.
Find out how to submit your novel at
<u>www.onemorechapter.com/submissions</u>